Grave Concerns

SAVING THE WORLD AND OTHER BAD IDEAS

JAYCE CARTER

Saving the World and Other Bad Ideas
ISBN # 978-1-83943-743-4
©Copyright Jayce Carter 2021
Cover Art by Louisa Maggio ©Copyright September 2021
Interior text design by Claire Siemaszkiewicz
Totally Bound Publishing

Published in 2021 by Totally Bound Publishing, United Kingdom.

The Omega's Alphas
Owned by the Alphas
Shared by the Alphas
Saved by the Alphas
Protected by Her Alphas
Caught by Her Alphas
Tamed by the Alphas
Claimed by the Alphas
Exposed by Her Alphas
Trained by the Alphas

Ready or Not
Fake It 'til You Make It
Opposites Attract
Third Time Lucky
Enemies Closer

Grave Concerns
Grave Robbing and Other Hobbies
Hell Raising and Other Pastimes
Saving the World and Other Bad Ideas

Collections
Sun, Sea and Sinful Delights

SAVING THE WORLD AND OTHER BAD IDEAS

Dedication

To Havoc, the best writing buddy I could have
ever asked for.
You will be forever missed.

Chapter One

"I could tear your soul right out of your stupid, entitled body!"

The man I'd yelled at stared at me as if I were crazy, but that didn't even slow my tirade. He might think I was a nutjob — and maybe I was — but that didn't mean I wasn't fully capable of doing exactly what I'd threatened.

"You're insane," the man said.

"You're the one who's attacking that poor woman who works here."

"She made my drink wrong."

"So?" I set my hands on my hips, giving him my best *melt him into the ground right where he stands* look. "You think you're entitled to everything you want? You think the world revolves around you?"

There beside us stood the barista we were arguing over, her dark eyes wide. In fact, she looked far more concerned about our interaction than about him acting like a spoiled brat. When I had been standing by the bar, waiting for mine, he'd brought his back to tell them they'd made it wrong.

"It really is okay," the barista told me. "It's not a big deal. I can just remake it."

"No," I responded. "It's *not* okay. People can't just expect others to be perfect, to have it all together all the time. He needs to be understanding."

"I don't expect perfect," the man said. "I asked for iced and she made a hot drink. That's it."

"So? She's trying, damn it. She's the one working, so you should just say thank you and move on. What makes you so special that you think you'll get whatever you want?"

His mouth hung open, like he'd never dealt with someone telling him off before. "I wasn't even rude," he argued. "All I did was ask her to remake it."

"She's doing her best," I repeated for what had to be the tenth time, that same thing that stuck in my head. "She's just human, and maybe she's having a bad day. Maybe she recently lost someone she cares about. Maybe she went to hell and is now in some sort of existential crisis because she doesn't know how to bring the person responsible to justice. Did you ever think about *that*, or did you just decide to criticize her?"

The chime above the door rang, and when I turned, I realized *maybe* I'd gone just a little overboard.

Troy walked in, and I doubted he was there as my friendly neighborhood werewolf just making the rounds.

Which meant someone had called the police on me.

For what? A little disagreement?

Or maybe because I told him I'd rip his soul out of his body...

"Finally," the man said as if Troy were his saving grace.

"You called the police?" I muttered *pussy* under my breath, low enough that Troy wouldn't catch it.

The sharp look in his silver eyes said he had. *Stupid werewolf hearing.*

"You are going to get arrested," the man said in the mocking, self-assured voice of a kid who had tattled to Mom on his sibling.

"I doubt that." I leaned in and kept my voice low. "Because I'm fucking the detective."

Then, just when I was pretty sure my childish behavior couldn't sink anymore, I stuck out my tongue at him.

At least he looked shocked.

My high horse didn't last long, however, not when Troy wrapped his large hand around my upper arm. In a different, sexier moment, I might have even liked his macho bullshit. "I'm very sorry," he said to the man as he pulled me toward the door. "I'll handle her."

Handle me?

I would have told Troy exactly what I thought about that, but he lowered his voice to all but snarl into my ear, "You should probably keep quiet."

The rumbled reprimand shocked me into silence. Troy *never* used that tone of voice with me. He was typically soft-spoken and the most likely of the men in my life to let me get away with…well…everything.

So his commanding tone kept me quiet until he opened the passenger-side door of his car and tossed me in. By the time he came around and got into the driver's side, my brain had started working again and I realized—I didn't let *anyone* talk to me like that, not even my sort of boyfriend who turned into some sort of wolf creature and had plenty of weird emotional hang-ups.

"Don't you manhandle me," I snapped.

"What was that?"

"What was what? I was protecting the staff against a male Karen. That's called being a good person. Not my fault you don't recognize it."

"You were arguing with a stranger so aggressively that the staff called us about *you*."

I crossed my arms and sat back. "He was getting mad at her over one little mistake and she was trying her best."

He let out a long sigh, as if my words had been more telling than I'd meant them to be. The damn man was far too observant. "I know it's frustrating to have no leads."

Frustrating didn't even *start* to explain it. After Lilith had killed Gran, after I'd sworn she would pay for it, everything had stalled out. Swearing revenge like that was supposed to be some sort of catapult to action, to lead almost immediately to a big showdown where things got resolved. People didn't swear to make someone pay then spend six weeks doing absolutely nothing about it.

It was said revenge was a dish best served cold, but it turned out I lacked the patience to let it cool.

It didn't matter how much I wanted to rain hell down on Lilith—I had no idea where she even was, and neither did anyone else.

The only thing I'd been able to do was help out the werewolves and vampires by removing Lilith's influence from infected immortals. Doing that felt like a tiny jab back at her, a way to give her the middle finger, but it just wasn't enough. I could only do it so often, and many of the afflicted had to be killed before anyone could capture them, so it didn't feel like much of a win.

"I thought we'd have *something* by now," I admitted, letting my head fall back against the seat.

Troy set his hand on my thigh, the weight of it reassuring even when I didn't want it to be. Something about him having my back never failed to make me feel a bit more optimistic. "Ava, you survived hell. You faced off against Lucifer. You destroyed a reaper. You'll get through this, too. It just may not be as fast as you'd like."

"Hell was easy. We knew which way we had to go. This, though? I've got no idea where to even start."

He squeezed my leg. "You look exhausted. Are you not sleeping well?"

"I've got enough horrible things going on in my life when I'm awake. Why should I sleep? Just so I can dream about the mist there?" Just saying it made me shudder.

I'd had those nightmares all my life, but since going to hell, they'd gotten worse. I woke up choking, coughing, gagging as I clawed at my throat with the memory of that damn mist. Even after I could breathe, I couldn't shake the horrible drowning feeling.

"You can always sleep at my house," he offered, his voice having lost its sharp edge, having quieted as if coaxing me to agree. This was the sweet man I was used to.

"You might be able to scare away most things, but I'm afraid you aren't the best dream catcher." Despite what I said, he had a point. Even if he couldn't keep the damn dreams away, no doubt it would be better to wake up next to him than alone.

But I wasn't that girl, the one who threw away everything for a man—or four of them. I'd survived those dreams my whole life, so I could deal with them alone now.

"What if Grant gets some ambrosia? You slept and didn't dream when you took it before," Troy pointed out.

"I'm not ever touching that stuff again. I saw it grown in body parts — I almost was the body some was grown in — and that made it lose its magic. No thanks."

I kept to myself the fact that I hadn't actually seen Grant. He and Hunter had both all but disappeared upon our return.

It stung.

After everything, they had just dropped off the face of the earth — or hell, whatever — without a word.

Was it because of what I was? Maybe the reality of sleeping with a reaper was a turn-off they couldn't ignore anymore. Fucking the cute, eccentric girl who talked to ghosts was one thing — getting naked with a reaper must have been a hard limit.

Cowards.

"What's wrong?" Troy asked, probably having caught my expression.

"Nothing."

He sighed, the sound telling me he knew I was lying. "Ava..."

I turned to face him. "It's just more of not knowing where to go, of not having a plan, of being totally and completely stuck. You know, same old, same old."

He pressed his lips together, as if he knew there was more I wouldn't say, but he shook his head. "Why don't I drive you home?"

"What, no handcuffs?"

That glow in his eyes started, the one that said he really wanted to do just that.

Not that I'd gone without...

In the six weeks since we'd returned from hell, I'd ended up in bed with Troy countless times. Always at his place, and usually because I went there, because I craved his scent, his taste, the feeling of his strong hands on me.

It made me wonder if there wasn't something to this whole mate thing, some bond that drew me to him, that made me need him like I hadn't before.

Or maybe I was just addicted to his stupid knot.

That was *very* possible.

He inhaled, slowly, the glow of his eyes brightening. *Right.* He could smell me, always knew when I was thinking such things. There weren't a lot of secrets in a relationship with a werewolf.

He leaned forward, as if drawn by the smell of my desire, driven by the need to satisfy me.

I put my hand up and over his face, stopping him before he could kiss me. "No time."

His groan was muffled by my palm. "I can be quick."

"No, you can't."

Normally, that would have been a wonderful compliment, because the reality was that I never left Troy's bed unsatisfied. In fact, I usually fell asleep there because I couldn't stay awake another moment, not after he'd had his way with me, some wild part of his wolf needing to turn me boneless, as if laying a claim.

He nipped my palm before sitting back. "Will you at least promise to stop harassing strangers? I don't want to get called out on you again."

"I wasn't harassing anyone." At his lifted eyebrow, I blew out a long breath. "Okay, so I may have threatened to rip his soul out of his body."

Disapproval flooded his expression.

Which I guess was fair.

Maybe that wasn't the smartest thing I'd done recently. Or maybe it was. It hadn't been a very good six weeks.

"I know you're frustrated, Ava. I know you want to find Lilith, that you want to handle this, but going off the rails isn't going to make it happen any faster. If you end up in jail or rushing into trouble, it isn't going to help. You need to relax."

"How am I supposed to do that? Yoga? Meditation? *Tea*?"

"I have tomorrow night off. What if we go out?"

I paused at the offer, which had taken me off track. "Like…a date?"

He nodded. "We're involved, aren't we? Let me take my mate out, have dinner, act like any normal couple."

"I don't think you get to use the word 'normal', not when we went to hell, had a threesome with a vampire and your penis gets stuck inside me when we have sex."

He let out a rough laugh. "You're impossible, you know that?"

"I've heard that before, yeah. So, you're not going to arrest me?"

"Not today." He caught my arm as if calling me on how I hadn't actually agreed to the date. "Dinner tomorrow?"

Maybe trying to date like some happy couple wasn't the best idea in the middle of everything else, or maybe that was exactly why I needed it right then.

"Okay," I said, inexplicably nervous. Then again, when was the last time I'd had a *real* date planned?

Maybe never? Certainly never with someone I actually loved.

I went to get out of the car, but he didn't let me go. Troy shifted his hand to the front of my shirt, then tugged me in until he could take my lips in a possessive kiss, one that screamed *mine* in a way that melted me.

Whether it was him or his wolf leaving a mark on me, I didn't know, and honestly, I didn't really care.

Being claimed by both of them was fine by me, and one of the few things going exactly right in my life.

Chapter Two

It had been three days since Kase had bothered to answer my calls. Worse, he'd sounded different each time I'd talked to him, his voice more strained.

I'd chalked it up to stress at first. We had been through a lot, after all.

Now, though, I couldn't shake the worry that it was something more. I'd had this creeping fear since returning from hell that Lilith would try to get to me through one of the men, that she'd do something horrible to them. She'd proven herself capable and vicious, and the fear plagued me that I'd show up to find someone I cared for gone.

So when Kase decided to ignore me, I figured it was time for a more *in his face* method of confrontation. It was easy to ignore my calls, but I could make the job a lot tougher in person.

Thus, I knocked on his door at nine in the morning. Where else would he be? Taking a nice sunny stroll somewhere?

There was no answer at first, leaving me standing on his porch like a spurned one-night stand who just wouldn't take the hint.

"Let me in," I said, sure he was on the other side, listening to me. "Because I can be very loud and disruptive."

"You should go home," he answered through the door, his voice low. "I will call you later."

"Sorry, but you don't seem to know how to use your phone. Not a chance."

"I am not opening this door. If you wish to wait on the porch all day, you're more than welcome to. It is your time you will waste, not mine."

My mouth dropped open at the smug bastard's words. He was so sure he had me there, that I'd listen and go home like a good girl, that I'd wait until he decided to call me.

Has he even met me?

"Oh, I'll show you waiting," I said, knowing damn well he could hear me through the door, before I pulled my shoulders back and raised my voice. "It doesn't matter if you want to claim it or not—it's your baby! I swear, Kase, I'll take your ass to court if I have to. You're not going to walk just out on us—"

The door opened and I found myself yanked inside the poorly lit house. "I've killed mortals for less," Kase muttered, along with other insults and threats I didn't catch.

He shut the door behind me, locking it.

It was funny how different it felt from the last time I'd been there, back when I'd shown up to get information about Olin, when him twisting that lock had made me want to bolt. Then, I'd been nervous. The thought of being alone in Kase's house—in any vampire's house—had made me wonder if I'd end up as a cautionary tale to stupid women who made horrible choices.

Woman goes into vampire lair and gets killed – nobody is surprised.

Now he was cursing and not-at-all-subtly threatening my life, and I wasn't afraid in the least. Everything had changed. I recalled the press of his lips to mine, the touch of his hands over my body. He was difficult and stubborn and *mine*.

I *knew* him, and while he might growl and bare his fangs when he wanted to, I didn't believe he'd really hurt me.

"Why are you avoiding me?" I asked as he walked past me, farther into his place, into the dim rooms. "And why aren't you turning on the lights? Are you having a midlife crisis? Is this some sort of vampire moping?"

He went to the kitchen before turning, the counter between us, his face bathed in shadows. "I haven't been hiding from you, and if I am only at midlife now, well, I'm not sure I can fathom another few thousand years of life."

I paused, his words not registering because of something else that struck me. As I so often had heard from teachers as a kid, it wasn't what I said but how I said it.

"What do you want?" His question shook me free, let me push off my worries. I was just being paranoid. It was nothing more than Lilith, and the stress of our investigation stalling out.

"I've been calling you for days."

"I've been busy. We were in hell for what turned out to be nearly a month's time here. In case you have forgotten, I have responsibilities to the coven that needed tending."

I narrowed my eyes. "Well, your coven problems aren't going to matter much if, you know, the world basically ends because we can't find and stop Lilith in time."

"Does that mean you have discovered where she is?"

The question was harsh, and it made me pull back. Kase could be difficult, but he wasn't usually like that with me, at least not since we'd bartered some sort of understanding. In fact, what I'd come to find was that his sharp tongue was usually nothing more than a *keep away* sign he used when he wanted me to be cautious, when he wanted space.

Which again pricked my senses.

"Are you okay?" I asked instead of focusing on his question.

He froze, that unnatural stillness no human could imitate. "Of course," he said after a long moment. "Now, if we're done." He took a step around the counter, as if to show me out, but I pulled back.

"What's wrong?"

"Nothing."

This time I was sure of it—he wasn't right. He was trying to rush me out before I saw it, before I realized it.

I went for the light switch on the wall. A cold hand set on top of mine, and he stood behind me, not touching anywhere else but so close I could feel him.

His skin was far cooler than usual, which couldn't be a good sign.

"Don't." His voice had dropped to nearly a whisper.

"If you won't tell me what's wrong, what choice do I have?"

He sighed, his breath sliding across my neck. "You won't let this go, will you?"

"You should have forced a less annoying girl to work for you if you wanted privacy."

He released a disgruntled sigh before releasing me.

I flipped on the light, then turned.

I didn't bother to hide my gasp. What was the point? He'd hidden from me, then made the house dark. He obviously knew how he looked.

His eyes had a much thicker rim of red around them, and his veins had grown dark, almost black, giving him the appearance of someone diseased.

I reached out, then froze when I remembered the last time I'd touched him when he hadn't expected it, when I'd come to understand his boundary.

Right, he isn't a touchy-feely sort of man...

No reason to further complicate this.

"What's the matter?"

"Nothing to concern yourself about."

"Are you hungry? Can't the coven get you someone? I'm not really good bait—I don't think I give off the sexiest of vibes—but I can help find someone to eat."

He shook his head and pulled away, turning his back as if he didn't like me seeing him. "I have fed."

"So what is it? Some vampire STD?"

He didn't even chuckle at that, but I guess that wasn't all that uncommon. He didn't appreciate my jokes nearly as much as he should.

"It really isn't anything for you to worry yourself about."

I slid around him, careful not to grab him. He was already on edge, and even though I wasn't afraid of him, I knew better than to push my luck. "Talk to me, Kase."

He took a deep breath before lowering his gaze to mine. "You recall I fed from Troy."

My cheeks heated at the memory, at how I'd ended up sleeping with both of them afterward. "Yeah, I remember." I hoped the words didn't show just how much I thought about that.

"I believe I explained to you the risks."

That made me pause. "Addiction? But you fed from a human afterward. In fact, I remember the far-too-pretty woman Lucifer provided for you."

He nodded. "I tried to, but the blood didn't settle. The more time that passed, the more obvious it became that my body was no longer processing human blood."

"You said it usually takes a few times."

"We both know usually doesn't mean much when it comes to reality. I am exceedingly old, as you like to say, and Troy is surprisingly powerful for a werewolf who isn't so old. It seems the one feeding was enough."

Fear clawed at me as I realized that maybe I should have asked more questions. I'd been the one to push for Kase to feed from Troy.

Of course, it wasn't as if we'd had a lot of other options. Kase had been hurt and needed blood to heal, and as it turned out, humans were hard to come by in hell. It had felt like the options were him feeding from Troy or him dying. What had it gotten us, though? Just a bit of time?

"Breathe," he said.

I gave him an annoyed look. "You don't breathe, so maybe don't coach me on it."

He set a hand on my back and all but pushed me — not toward the couch, but through the doorway to an area I'd never been.

His bedroom.

Not that he looked ready to put that room to any good use in his state.

It was dark in there, even more so than the rest of the house, and when he tugged me into the bed, when he settled and pulled me against his side, it felt too normal, too casual.

Still, I gave in and set my head on his chest, having finally gotten used to how it didn't rise and fall unless he was speaking.

"Why haven't you called Troy?" I asked.

"He was put in that position once because we had no other choices. That is no longer the case."

"Are you saying there are other werewolves you can feed from?"

"No. Feeding from werewolves is forbidden, and given the tense lines between our factions right now, there won't be werewolves lining up to offer. I refuse to forcefully feed from one, either."

"So what does that mean? What are your options?"

"The addiction sometimes resolves. Given I only fed from him once, there is a chance that after a period of withdrawal, my body will reaccustom to human blood."

"That sounds like you don't believe it."

He tightened his arm around me, pulling me closer. "I don't. I have seen this before, have strapped down vampires taken by this addiction to keep them from attacking werewolves and causing wars."

I twisted so I could glance up at his face, but he wasn't looking at me. He stared off at the ceiling.

"It isn't pretty, Ava, the way they go. It is like a vampire starving to death, but worse. They lose everything about themselves, waste away, until a stake or a fire is a mercy."

"I'm not going to let that happen," I swore to him.

He looked down at me, and the crease in his cheek said he had almost smiled. "You always surprise me.

Even after all these years, you can almost make me believe that if anyone could find another option, it would be you, my little reaper."

Reaper.

The first real mention of what I was. So far, all the men had stepped around that fact, ignoring it like they knew but no one wanted to be the one to bring it up. It was the horribly cut bangs in the relationship.

"You're not afraid of me because of that?"

He snorted, as if that were the dumbest thing he'd heard recently. "I once ran across a god killer."

"What's a god killer?"

That crease deepened, and he settled in as if he planned to tell a long story. "They're old creatures, some say older than the Elder Ones. I have found that the universe requires balance. In the event anything takes too much, something else is created to counter it. God killers are the answer to supernatural beings, as if mortals needed something to balance the scales. They are strong, powerful, able to steal the power of supernaturals, but they still age and die like mortals."

"Why haven't I heard of them?"

"There aren't many. Perhaps one every hundred years, if that. So when, a very long time ago, I heard of one in a nearby country, I decided to face it."

"Why would you do that? If something's called a god killer, I'd stay away from it."

"I was tired. It felt as though it was worth it to face the god killer, that one of us would die."

"And you didn't care that it might be you who died?"

"Not really, no. I found it in a cavern, a boy no older than eighteen, despite the fact that he had killed so many of my kind."

"What happened? You killed it?"

He shook his head. "No. That is a story for another time, though. My point is, if I wasn't afraid of him, a thing made specifically to kill me, I'm not going to fear you."

It wasn't that he trusted me, that I wasn't different, but rather that he'd dealt with far scarier things than me.

Still, I chose to take it as a win. I'd even feared when he'd refused to talk to me that it had been because of that, that he'd decided a reaper was a complication he didn't need in his life.

"Besides," he said, before he ran his fingers through my hair, "I don't have any reason to be afraid of you."

"Why's that? Because you know I wouldn't ever hurt you?"

"No. Because reapers snatch souls from bodies and, as you like to point out, I don't have one."

I let out a soft laugh against his chest as I settled in. Sure, I had a lot to do, a lot to worry about, but it all seemed a little easier to handle there, against him.

Chapter Three

I tugged at the hem of my dress, suddenly missing hell.

Not the fire or brimstone or constantly being almost killed thing. Those had sucked, to be honest.

The wardrobe, though?

To die for.

Which was an unfortunate saying in a lot of ways. When something finally killed me, if I ended up there — did reapers have souls? I was pretty sure I hadn't seen any reaper dead in hell — I doubted Lucifer would be quite so willing to share the sick threads.

Leaving Kase alone hadn't been something I'd wanted to do, but after a few hours of cuddling, I'd suspected he could use the rest. Besides, I'd needed to get home so I could have a meltdown about my date.

Troy sat in my living room, patient as ever, as I put on my third outfit of the night in my bedroom.

Why was I so nervous? It made no sense!

I'd had sex with Troy numerous times, I'd trekked through hell with him, so what was the point of worrying about how a dress looked on me?

In fact, we were *mates*.

Finally, I gave up. The reality was that Troy had seen me at my worst. I doubted a little black dress that was a tad shorter than it had been when I'd bought it five years and a good fifteen pounds ago would make him throw in the towel.

He twisted when I walked in, the sort of automatic turn that always made my heart speed. It was like he had an extra sense when it came to me, as if he were drawn to me no matter what else happened around us.

And that never failed to excite me. Something about his almost predatory edge turned me on, especially because of how much in control of himself he always was.

He inhaled slowly as his gaze drifted over me, his silver-fox look making the suit he wore even more regal.

He'd never been a guy to dress up, but when he did? *Damn.*

He gave Kase a run for his money.

"You know, I don't sleep with men on the first date," I blurted out, the joke stupid but all I could think of to break the tense moment.

Troy let out a deep sound full of something between affection and annoyance — my sweet spot. "Well, that would be the only time you don't, then."

I paused. "Did you just make a sex joke?" The idea that Troy could do such a thing felt like Hunter being serious or Grant obeying any sort of law — it was just wrong.

Troy rose, towering over me as he always did, yet it was somehow more obvious in his suit. "I can make jokes."

"Yeah, but you're a dumb-joke sort of guy," I pointed out. "You do the whole, 'Hi, hungry, I'm Dad', thing."

He reached out and caught my hand, then tugged me forward. I melted against his front, surprised as ever at how effortless things seemed with him.

It had been *so* hard to crack through all his layers of *stay away*. He'd spent so long worried that he might hurt me, that I'd get killed either by him or due to his own inaction, that now, when we moved past it, it was hard to believe.

Even my own fear, that he'd never really let go of his old mate, that he'd always long for her, had mostly gone away. Something about the way he kissed me managed to reassure me each time.

He leaned down, not enough to reach my lips but enough to make an offer—one he knew damn well I'd take him up on. Troy's lips were addictive—wild and soft and tasting of thunderstorms and full moons.

The kiss didn't linger, but not because I had the good sense to pull away. Instead, he did, an unhappy grumble escaping him about dinner.

"We could miss dinner," I said. "I don't have anything edible here, but I'm sure you do at your house."

"We're supposed to go out," he said.

"So? Why go to a noisy restaurant when we could eat egg rolls naked and cuddle?"

A deep growl rumbled from his chest, his fingers clenching and releasing as if he were fighting himself.

When our eyes met, I realized it wasn't just him there.

It was his wolf. The bright eyes shone, flickering as if both he and his beast wanted a say.

"I don't mind him," I said, my voice low, the discussion of his other side always a tricky one.

"I know," Troy answered, his voice harsher than usual.

Which drew a flinch from me.

He blew out a slow breath, the kind he did when trying to regain his control. After a moment, when his eyes had returned to their normal silver, he spoke again. "Please, can we go to dinner? I want to take my mate out, to be..." He paused, as if searching for the word. "I want to do this right."

I would much rather have spent the night stripping him of out his sexy suit and enjoying the benefits of having a mate, but I nodded.

The things I do for those I love...

* * * *

The restaurant was fancy. Not like, 'I should have covered my cleavage a bit more' fancy, but 'they might not let me in because my boobs are real' fancy. It sat in an out-of-the-way area of town, in a lot filled with pine trees and with no sign at the street.

It seemed like poor planning for a place that served the public, at least until I walked in and realized why.

The place was full of supernaturals.

It felt like when I went into the party in hell, that moment of realization that things weren't as simple as they appeared on the outside. Wasn't that what I'd kept learning? That life refused to be as straightforward, that it hated being nicely fit into boxes? Life was a kid with ADHD who got bored easily.

I didn't mention it when the hostess seated us, when she left me with a menu and more than a few questions.

Troy *hated* the supernatural. He hated what he was, hated tangling himself up with anything that wasn't human. When he'd mentioned a date, I'd expected the Italian place in town that did the unlimited breadsticks — nice enough to be a date destination but down-home enough that all the food was listed in English and neither of us would have to search on our phones for what the entrées were.

So a supernatural restaurant with linen napkins and a few hulking security guards with horns hadn't appeared on my list of expectations.

Worse? As I glanced over the menu, it became obvious they didn't serve mortals.

I spotted the delicacy on page six — roasted Swedish virgin — and had to amend that statement.

They did serve mortals, just not the way I wanted.

I lifted my gaze, ready to ask Troy what the hell he'd been thinking, when I found his eyebrows furrowed.

He looked no happier than I was.

After a moment, he put the menu down with an exasperated huff and met my gaze.

I didn't even need to say it. I didn't need to ask what he'd been thinking, why he'd picked it, because it was *obvious*.

"Kase?" I asked.

He snorted. "And Grant."

"Hunter didn't have a hand in this?"

"Of course not. If Hunter knew about a date, he wouldn't be suggesting restaurants and adding security — he'd simply make a joke about eating in that would make me want to wring his neck."

I chuckled at the truth of that until the rest hit me. I'd assumed the security was there for the restaurant, but after a closer look, I realized their attention was solely placed on *our* table.

"Kase hired them? Why?"

"Because he didn't like the idea of you coming out in public like this without more protection."

"I'm out in public all the time."

Troy shifted, a sure-fire giveaway.

"Please tell me I didn't have people following me."

Again, no answer.

I dropped my head to the table, and the position muffled my voice. "I was doing private things. Who was following me when I went to buy tampons?"

Troy cleared his throat. "I believe Grant had someone on you, then. You got whiskey, too."

"And chocolate. I made a milkshake."

"Wouldn't that be a whiskey-shake?"

"Let's not play semantics." I lifted my head. "Last I checked, I took out a reaper for you guys. In fact, I *am* a reaper. Why do you think I need protection?"

He shrugged. "I'm not hiring people to follow you."

"But you're taking me to places they tell you to go."

"Because I knew we'd have a shadow anyway, and it seemed like less work to go somewhere they wouldn't stick out."

"This is crazy." I took out my phone and called Kase.

The bastard didn't answer. He *knew* what I was calling about, I'd bet. At least, that was what I told myself.

I refused to think anything might have happened to him, no matter how bad he'd looked the last time.

I pressed Grant's contact next, and to my amazement, he *did* answer, in a far-too-cheerful tone. "I know what you're going to say, and no, I won't call off the guards. Also, have the salmon—it's fantastic. The lemon salmon, not the ambrosia one, though. The last time you had ambrosia, you stole Lucifer's underwear."

So much for giving him the benefit of the doubt, for thinking he hadn't really been involved in this plan.

"You can't hire people to stalk me."

"Of course I can, and from what I gather, they're pretty good at it." His voice wavered as if he were holding the phone between his shoulder and his ear and had moved around while speaking. "Why are you on the phone with me, though? I was pretty sure Troy would manage to keep you busy enough that you'd stay out of my hair."

Ouch.

"Well, fuck you," I muttered and hung up before he could say anything else. *Weeks of nothing and that's what he has to say to me?*

When my phone rang, I set it on the table. It vibrated against the wood, and the glares of other patrons said it was the height of rudeness.

It was, but they could go to hell.

Literally. I'd been—they might enjoy it.

The ringing stopped, then picked up from Troy's phone. He reached for it, and I pointed across the table. "I am closer to your balls than he is—I suggest you let it ring."

Troy shook his head, that same old annoyance in his features, the one I'd seen for years before we'd known the truth about one another. "You shouldn't be mad at him."

"Oh, *you're* defending Grant? You, who are the most jealous man I know, are actually going to sit here and tell me I shouldn't be mad at him?"

"I'm not *that* jealous."

I offered him an *are you shitting me?* look. "You basically rumble out *mine* every time you look at me."

"Well, you are mine. I've just come to the conclusion that you're also far too much trouble for me to keep you out of it all on my own. Besides, Grant has been busy."

"I'm busy, too."

Which wasn't true, at all.

In fact, I'd been exceedingly bored since returning from hell. I'd come back and needed to figure out exactly how I fit into a world I hadn't fit into before. At least before I'd been able to pretend.

Now that I had my feet under me, now that I knew and couldn't keep the fantasy that I was mortal, the men who had filled so much of my last few months had scattered to the wind.

So excuse me for not giving a damn how busy they all suddenly were. They'd stepped into my life, tossed around all my perfectly laid pieces then just disappeared?

Assholes.

Yet, no matter how much I tried to cling to that anger, it was hurt that really held me.

Troy reached across the table, ignoring his phone as it rang again. "You aren't alone, Ava."

I lifted my gaze, a sense of shame inside me. Troy was there, so *why* was I so hurt by the actions of three other men? I'd never expected to have four men in my life, yet the rejection from the others felt personal, as if I'd lost pieces of myself along with them. "So where are they?"

Well, Kase I knew…

Troy ran his fingers over my arm. "Hunter has been researching ways to track Lilith. Grant is working with the guild for the same thing."

"And they can't even contact me? Can't stop by? Seems more like ghosting." *Or purposely avoiding me…*

"You need to have some faith."

"Faith in what? Because I have to say, after meeting the devil himself, my faith isn't there much."

"How about in the men who you thought were worth risking your life for?"

Easier said than done.

* * * *

When I finally got out of Troy's bed the next morning, it was empty, since Troy always woke and left early for work.

By the time I showered and changed—at his place, because the idea of going to my empty house was too depressing—it was nearing eleven in the morning.

"You should answer your phone," came a familiar voice from Troy's living room.

"You shouldn't break into homes that aren't yours," I told Grant as I passed him and headed for the kitchen.

"If it were my house, it wouldn't be breaking in."

"Do you even *have* a house? I feel like you're probably a vagrant who just crashes on people's couches."

He didn't rise from the couch, his sneaker-covered feet on the coffee table as he twisted to stare at me. "I do have a house."

"So why were you always staying at a hotel?"

"Because I don't go to my house when on jobs. I prefer when people don't know where it is."

Guess that makes me just people.

He sighed and let his head drop back. "You know, conversations with you are like skipping across a minefield."

Even as he said it, though, he didn't offer to take me there, to change it as if it had been some big oversight.

I slammed items while I made coffee, figuring that if I broke something of Troy's, I could replace it. The banging of items against his granite counters made me feel better, like each one was a curse word I didn't have to say out loud.

Grant strolled into the kitchen, the first time I'd actually seen him since returning from hell. His hair wasn't as neat as it had been, the sides having grown out.

He also looked a lot less well-rested than he had the first time we'd met, when he'd walked into my house to set up wards, as though he'd aged years in the months since then.

"The truth is that I'm always on jobs," Grant said as if trying to make up for his statement. "I haven't been to my house in two years."

"How do you know it's even there anymore?"

"Well, I'm sure as hell paying every month, so it had better still be there."

"You're paying on a house you never go to?"

He shrugged. "I got the house because it was the huge place that everyone is supposed to want. I just never have time to go there."

I was nearly ready to let him off the hook until I remembered the whole 'person following me when I bought tampons' thing, and my annoyance came back front and center.

"Why are you here?" I asked and forced myself to only put enough coffee into the machine for one cup.

Was it petty?

Sure, but I felt like being petty right then.

"You didn't pick up when I called you back last night."

"Well, you've done that to me for weeks. I figured turnabout was fair play. Besides, I'm surprised you didn't show up last night."

"I thought a night with Troy might just wear you out enough to turn you docile. Judging by the way you're slamming things around, though, it didn't work. Might need to send him diagrams and directions if he's this bad."

I jammed my finger against the power button of the machine, then turned toward him, my arms crossed. "So get on with it. If whatever you had to say was so important, get it out."

He narrowed his eyes, and for a moment, I remembered how much of a lie his youthful face was. I recalled the piles of ashes left behind when he incinerated a person, the suspicion the acting Magistrate had given him, the fact that he'd murdered the old guild council—including his own father.

Grant might look like a frat-boy rebel, but the reality was that he was so much *more* than that.

"I didn't mean to upset you last night," he finally said, though his tone screamed it was a conversation he didn't care to have.

"It's fine."

"It's not. Look, Ava, being back hasn't been easy on any of us." He sighed, then pinched the bridge of his nose. "It's been years since I've been around guild mages, since I've interacted with them in any real way. It isn't exactly a leisurely stroll."

His words made me take pause and take notice things I hadn't before—darkness under his eyes, a bandage on his arm, spots of red soaking into the left leg of his pants.

"What happened?" I asked, starting to realize that perhaps it hadn't been as simple as just ignoring me.

"I'm finding everything I can on Lilith, and when it comes to information, the rule is that *someone* at the guild knows. That means I've got to play games with people I haven't in a long time, and let's just say mages don't play nice."

"You could have told me. I could have helped."

"I didn't want to risk it, to give anyone any ideas about using you. Word's spread about what you are, but a lot of people don't believe it's possible, or think you're weaker than they say. I didn't want to bring trouble to your door just because I couldn't stay away." He stared down at his hands, opening and closing them as if the motion meant something. "Haven't had anything to risk except my own skin in a long time. Maybe ever."

I let out a soft sigh while some of my hurt faded away. I was forced to remember that despite my recent issues, my life had always been less complicated than his.

I didn't have a guild to deal with, a coven, a pack. My life had sat, as if on hold, while I'd been gone. Sure, I'd lost my job, but Kase had put someone in charge of my finances, making sure my bills got paid so I could come back to my house, at least.

The same wasn't true of the others. Fredrick had smoothed things over with Troy's boss, claiming a family emergency, though that had indebted Troy to the pack. Kase always had coven issues going on, and the crazed supernaturals hadn't slowed, meaning there was more than enough work. Hunter was...well, I had no idea, but I had to assume it was important.

All in all, they'd returned to a mess that had required work to clean up.

Not that it fixed the part of me that just wanted to feel like I belonged again.

Grant held his arms open, an offer I took him up on. The speed at which I returned the hug told me that my anger only had to do with my own hurt. The second I had the chance to breathe him in, to feel the lines of Grant's slim form against mine, I jumped on it.

In fact, I was pretty sure that if he gave me the option, I'd strip him down in that kitchen just to reacquaint myself with his body, to remember each tattoo on his skin, to trace them with my lips.

Except, he pulled away too fast, as if he knew where my mind was going and couldn't let it travel that way. Still, he seemed less tense. Maybe he'd needed the hug as much as I had.

Grant placed his hands on the edge of the counter and hopped up, but the motion wasn't as smooth as usual. It was more proof that Grant hadn't been relaxing somewhere over the past few weeks.

A chime behind me announced that my coffee was done, and guilt gnawed at me until I poured the coffee between two smaller cups instead of the huge one I had planned for myself. I poured a good heft of creamer from Troy's fridge into both cups and stirred before handing Grant's to him.

He took it with a quick thanks before downing two large gulps. It had to have burned his throat, but if he noticed, he showed no sign.

Talk about someone needing the caffeine.

"Are you really okay?" I asked, voice lowered because we didn't talk about such things. It took me back to when we'd lain in bed together after the banshee, after Grant had nearly been killed and I'd been forced to bargain with Lucifer to save them all.

No matter how strong they seemed, Gran had taught me that strength and power didn't always save people.

If it did, she'd still be here.

Grant stared at me, quiet for a moment as if he could read my thoughts. Then again, maybe he had. It didn't bother me as much as it had before. The idea of him slipping into my thoughts wasn't such an invasion as everything we'd been through.

"I'm okay," he said finally.

"You've got blood on your pant leg."

He glanced down and frowned. "Damn it. I liked these pants."

"Can't you magic it away?"

He shook his head. "Surprisingly enough, blood and chocolate cake just don't come out of fabric, even with my skills."

I pressed my lips together, his answer entirely unsatisfying.

He quirked his lips, as though my annoyance spurred him to life.

And that made me feel a little better, when some of the color returned to his cheeks and he looked a bit more like his old self.

"So what got your arm?"

He lifted it to show me. "My wards needed some beefing up."

"You didn't do that much damage to me when you set up mine."

"You never listen. Magic requires sacrifice for things like wards. The bigger the sacrifice, the better the protection. What was after you wasn't as dangerous as what's on my ass."

"What is after you?" I had assumed we were talking about Lilith, but maybe Grant had a lot more problems than I knew about.

Grant shrugged. "Mages are worse than some of the other factions when it comes to gathering power. See, werewolves and vampires get more powerful as they age, but mages only gain political power. They're sort of stuck where they are in terms of base power. That means we're much quicker to take out potential enemies."

"But you're not even part of the guild…"

"Depends on who you ask. Besides, whether I am or not doesn't change that I've got to interact, now. Well, that means I'm back on their radar. It isn't the nicest ones who know anything about Lilith, either."

"Did you find anything?"

"Nothing that tells me where she is. It's a lot of stories, a lot of legends, a lot of seeing her from a distance a time or two. For someone as well-known as she is, no one seems to actually know shit."

Ah, there was that guilt again.

He was getting involved because I hadn't figured out what we needed to know, because I had no idea what to do next.

Damn, that was depressing. Somehow, even my night with Troy hadn't quite washed that away.

Grant reached a foot out and pressed it against my shoulder. "Knock it off."

"Knock what off?"

"Pouting."

I sighed. "If I hadn't—"

"If you hadn't nothing. Lilith is fucking shit up, not you."

"But you wouldn't be involved if it wasn't for me."

"Sure I would. It would just be when the whole world was torn apart, and I have to say, I prefer being proactive here." He curled his lips into a smile, then crooked his finger.

I would have followed his demand happily, but he didn't give me the chance. Something tugged me forward the few steps between us, until I stood between his knees and he caught my chin. "You've got to stop blaming yourself for shit that you can't control."

I opened my mouth, ready to tell him I was supposed to be able to control it. That was basically what Gran had said, wasn't it? That I was the only person who could do anything about this.

Except, as usual, Grant knew what I was going to say before I could get it out. He leaned in and danced his lips across mine in a sweet kiss, one that made it impossible to think about anything else.

I reached out and grasped his side, clutching him, wanting to get even closer, to use his heat to distract myself from everything.

Except he pulled in a sharp, pained breath that broke the kiss.

A frown touched my expression before I took the bottom of his shirt and lifted it.

There, on his side, was a black-and-blue bruise spanning from hip to ribs.

Again, I was reminded just how dangerous the things we were dealing with were, and worse? I couldn't seem to help. No matter how much I learned about myself, how much power I showed, I couldn't use it in any real way that would help the men I cared for.

Frustration chipped away at me, the same one that had had me yelling at a stranger in the coffee shop, the same one that had me up at night instead of asleep.

I stared at the bruise, fear gripping my chest, unable to look away.

"It's fine," Grant said. "Just a bruise."

"A bruise this big? Are you sure you don't some sort of serious internal bleeding?"

He took my hands in his, letting his shirt fall back down. "I'm sure. It looks worse than it is."

But…that wasn't true. It was obvious, each time I saw the men, that this was wearing on them.

Troy didn't smile enough, Kase was wasting away from addiction, Grant had injuries all over him, and Hunter?

Maybe he wasn't even alive. Maybe he'd chased leads until one had ended him, and all because I couldn't do anything.

Which was when I decided I'd damn well do *something*, no matter how dangerous it was.

Chapter Four

Gran's shop felt empty, like a husk of the place that had meant so much to me before. After getting back, I'd received the paperwork to show that she'd left her occult shop to me.

I hadn't gone in, though. The keys had sat on my kitchen counter for weeks, and eventually, I'd realized I couldn't ignore it anymore.

Still, nothing could have prepared me for the crushing feeling of loss when I walked into the shop.

Everything was exactly the same and yet different. The shelves hadn't changed, and the products lining them remained the same, yet I couldn't seem to feel whatever had been there in the past — that sense of home.

Instead, it was empty. It seemed as hollow as the place inside my chest, the warm feeling I used to get when I thought about Gran.

Maybe I should have called Troy to come with me. Having someone else would have been nice, would have given a sense of back-up.

However, I'd opted out of it, not wanting anyone to witness just how deep this hurt was. They'd seen me at less than my best—such as when I had turned into a reaper to save them—but this was different. Each time the men had tried to help shoulder the burden, I'd turned them down.

Besides, Kase was busy going through some sort of werewolf withdrawal, Grant was dealing with guild complications and I had no idea where Hunter was.

I'd gone from having four men who were always on my heels to just the one, and I couldn't believe I would ever have said this, but I missed having my boys around…

There had been a family then, a feeling that I belonged. Now, only Troy remained, which made me laugh since he'd been the one to constantly pull away.

Maybe he'd overcome the nonsense in his head.

My foot caught the corner of a shelf, and I ended up sprawled out on the hard tile floor.

I sent a hard glare at the inanimate object, because how many times had I walked this shop? I knew every inch of it, so what the hell?

A discoloration on the floor caught my attention, as did the scrapes in the linoleum behind it. It showed someone had pushed that shelf from its normal place. Not far, only about six inches, but just enough that I didn't notice and fell flat on my face.

As I lay there, my chest aching from the fall, face to face with the dust sitting beneath the shelving, I couldn't stop the laugh that started inside me.

Gran did this.

There was no real question of it—she was the only one who worked in the shop, the only one who could have moved that, and it was *so* on brand for Gran to have done it.

I remembered when I'd come in one day, years before, frustrated by the constant spirits who refused to leave me be. I'd had one following me for days, a man who'd liked to cat-call me while also making sure to point out every woman who looked better than I did.

Gran had made me a cup of tea and had me sit at the counter with her. She'd said that frustration happened when we fought the inevitable, when we focused on what should be and not what was. It caught us and made us land on our face.

And that was what she'd done. She'd *known* she wouldn't be coming back, that the shop would end up going to me, and she'd moved that one shelf to put me flat on my face.

She was telling me that I had to stop fighting, that I had to stop expecting things to be like they'd always been and to open my eyes.

Even now, even after she was gone, Gran was still giving me the lessons I needed in the most obscure and painful way.

And it helped me not feel quite so alone.

* * * *

I sipped my tea while I sat on the floor of the back office, folders spread out around me and papers piled up. Somehow, the tea tasted better, like it always had when Gran made it.

Or maybe I just felt more grown up? Like I was finally the sort of person who drank tea? Or it was possible I was exactly the same but more determined than ever to fake it, as if that would suddenly make Gran proud of the adult I'd become?

Still, drinking that didn't make sense of *anything* I'd found. The more I pulled out of the desk and cabinets, the less sense any of it made.

She had invoices for things like a barrel of sheep testicles — suddenly, I thought back to and worried about the times she'd made me snacks — one for ley line rerouting and yet another for a trunk of nightmares.

Was that a usual unit of measurement? How did one buy nightmares, and even if they could, how would they fit into a trunk?

I leaned back against the desk, shaking my head. Clearly, I wouldn't be running this shop. Even if I wanted to, even if I thought I had the time, there was no way I had the expertise. I didn't even understand what most of the things in that shop did, let alone being able to sell them.

So why exactly had Gran left it to me? I was the least-qualified person for this job.

Maybe coming here had been a mistake. I should have put it off for another month. I wouldn't know what to do with it any more than I did now, but I'd probably at least hurt a little less.

Or I'd be dead because I failed to stop Lilith, but if that happened, at least I wouldn't have to make any choices.

I'd even been foolish enough to think I'd find something at Gran's that would give me the answers I needed. I'd open the right drawer, and the special anti-Lilith weapon would be sitting there, complete with a manual of how-tos for me.

I hadn't found that, of course. Instead, it was just stuff, and most of it things that confused me all the more.

The shop doorbell rang, but before I had to worry that it was some other big disaster just waiting to throw what was left of my life into chaos, a familiar voice called.

"Hello, shadow-girl!" Hunter walked in through the doorway of the office, his hair looking even wilder than before, as if the weeks apart had changed it. It also had a more reddish tint. "A sight for sore eyes," he said before he took a seat across a pile of papers from me.

"I'm sure you have lots of sore things since you decided to disappear for weeks."

Wow, was it my voice that had come out like a scorned lover? Like some housewife annoyed that her husband had stayed out all night without calling?

Hunter laughed before picking up a file and opening it. "I had things to do."

"Things more important than—" *Me?* I cringed at my own neediness. "Lilith," I went with instead.

"It was for that." He frowned and turned a page. "Gran was either involved with massive tax fraud or she had people raised from the dead to claim as dependents. Or possibly both. You might want to just burn this place down before the IRS comes after you."

I laughed, slightly at ease talking about Gran, at the ability to laugh about her even with her gone.

I lifted my gaze to Hunter. "So, what were you really up to?"

"I was following up on a lead."

"And?"

"And I've got an idea."

I blew out a slow breath. "As I remember from your last idea, they aren't always good. In fact, last time you and Grant took me to another dimension to meet some Elder One."

"We traded her a cat for information. Yeah, I recall."

"So you're saying this will be a better idea?"

At that, he paused, as if even *he* couldn't really claim such a thing. "Not exactly," he hedged.

"It can get worse than a woman you used to sleep with for favors?"

"Yeah, it can."

"Out with it," I said. I'd found that the waiting, the nervousness, was worse than anything else.

He sighed before giving me a tired look, proof that the past months had been harder on us all than we were letting on. "How do you feel about calling in that favor from the devil you have?"

* * * *

I frowned and looked around the tattoo shop Grant has asked me to meet him at. A woman with half her head shaved stared at me, her gaze as sharp as the wings on her eyeliner. She had tattoos over her arms, a snake twisting around her neck and a huge rose with bloody petals on her chest.

This was *so* not a place I belonged.

I wanted to. I saw the way she'd snapped at a man who walked in, one who had a good hundred pounds on her, when he'd made a comment about wanting to see just how far down her tattoos went. Something about her, about the confidence she had, drew me in.

I was smart enough to know my limitations, though. It seemed I might be able to destroy a reaper, but hanging out in rough tattoo shops was a step too far. Still, I sat in a chair, trying to not look so out of place as I waited for Grant.

As usual, he'd given me no real information. An address and a time — that was it. In fact, I wasn't even entirely sure it was the right *day*.

Isn't like I've got anything better to do.

The hinges on the door squeaked, and relief hit me at the sight of Grant walking in. He fit in far better than I did, and he'd even worn a short-sleeve shirt so the expanse of the ink on his arms was on display.

"Grant," the woman said, her smile honest but not flirtatious. "Unless you want me to touch that pretty face of yours, I'm afraid you've run out of room."

He chuckled, then held his hand out to me. "Not for me, today, Hayleen."

Damn it. She even has a cool name…

Hayleen looked at me again, a different expression on her face, as if she had to reevaluate me. "Wait a minute, is this *the* one?"

I didn't get the chance to ask what exactly that meant before Grant nodded. "Yeah."

"Will she even take spell ink?"

Spell ink?

"She has before. That's actually why I'm here — we need to look at removing some."

I turned toward Grant. "Excuse me?"

He frowned. "You said you wanted the spells gone."

"Yeah, I said that in passing. You don't think we should have discussed this?"

"We're discussing it now."

Why he could continue to surprise me when he acted as he always did, I had no idea. I rubbed the bridge of my nose. "You're supposed to talk to me about it before we show up at a place to do it. If I decided you needed a circumcision, do you think the exam room is the right place for us to talk about it?"

Hayleen laughed, a deep one that said she wasn't the sort of woman to giggle demurely. "I like her. Come on back—I'll take a look and we'll talk options."

Grant moved his gaze between the two of us, as if he wasn't sure he approved of us being friendly. It wasn't jealousy, but more like it was a bad idea or he was already seeing all the ways we'd end up in trouble.

Still, it gave me the courage to follow Hayleen back into a smaller room, one with a few chairs against the wall, a stool and a padded table. Artwork rested on the walls—page after page of tattoo ideas—along with photos of actual tattoos. On a worktable sat something that looked like a toolbox with pull-out drawers, and on the shelves were old leather books and jars of ingredients that didn't seem like they fit. Flowers, plants, crystals…all sorts of things.

Grant took a seat in one of the chairs while Hayleen nodded at a more comfortable-looking padded chair. She sat on the stool and rolled over after I took my spot.

I held my arms out, twisting them to show the marks on my forearms—or what was left of them—while being careful not to accidently send her flying across the room. I was pretty sure she wouldn't be inclined to help if I did that.

She made a soft sound as she traced the scars with her fingers. "These were put on when you were young."

"Before I was three," I explained.

"Whoever tried to remove them was a hack." She turned her gaze to Grant. "You kill the idiot?"

"It was a human doctor," Grant explained. "All he could do was try to pull the color."

She shook her head, narrowing her gaze to study the marks. "This is good work. A spell like this, *especially* on someone who doesn't take to magic well, isn't easy."

"Do you know whose work it is?" I asked, then immediately regretted it. Every time I thought I was beyond wanting a connection to my past, to my parents, a breadcrumb was all it took to set me right down that path again.

"There's a pretty short list of mages who deal in ink magic like this, and the number who could handle a job like this is even smaller. My bet? Only three or four in the world. I can make a list for you in a few days. You want that?"

Yes. Except, the word wouldn't come out, because did I? I had so many other things on my plate, so much uncertainty — did I really want to drag up any additional problems?

"Why don't you make the list and send it to me," Grant said. "If she wants it later, I'll have it."

Hayleen nodded, a spark of pity on her features, as if she realized it was a tricky situation. "Okay, so first things first. You've actually got two spells here. There's a protection spell and a defensive spell."

"The defensive is the whole blasting people across the room thing?"

"That's it. The two are tangled together and weakened — the protection spell especially. It's like they've been scrubbed raw recently."

"She went to hell," Grant explained. "She also sort of turned into a reaper."

Hayleen didn't seem shocked by either point, only nodding again as if that made perfect sense. "I'd guess it was the form change. Magic like this rests in the skin, so for beings who alter their very nature, it's like loosening a tooth. The magic doesn't hold so well."

"Does that mean you can remove them?" Grant asked.

She tilted her head, leaning close enough that her warm breath moved over my skin. "Yeah. I can take both off, or I can just take the protection off. I could bolster the defensive so it wouldn't fade so much from the whole changing-forms thing."

Grant turned a look on me, a question there.

Did I want the spells gone? One or both? I'd lived so long being unseen that there was a part of me terrified of the idea of removing that. What if people still didn't notice me, but I couldn't blame it on magic anymore?

Except…the girl I'd been before, the one who hadn't known how strong she was, she loved the shadows. She'd wanted to belong but had still found solace in being ignored. I'd grown so much since then, come into my own, recognized that I didn't need to hide.

"Take the protection one off," I said. "Leave the defensive. I sort of like being able to throw people when I need to."

Hayleen grinned. "Let 'em see you coming, huh? That's my policy, too. Yeah, let's get this shit done."

* * * *

Getting a tattoo probably sucked, and getting one removed *definitely* sucked. As it turned out, getting magical ones removed and bolstered was far worse.

By the time we were done — it had to be three hours later — my forearms felt like they'd been stung by a million pissed-off wasps that I had personally insulted, which was saying something, because it didn't take much for a wasp to sting in the first place.

She'd rubbed some sort of ointment on me first, chanted, then held her hand above the scarring. It had felt like knives wiggling their way out, as if each speck of ink that had had been placed – along with the magic behind it – had pulled free, slicing through my flesh along the way.

Grant had stood beside me, his hand on my shoulder, telling me to breathe. It was sweet, even if entirely unhelpful.

Why was it that people thought breathing fixed everything? As though taking a breath would suddenly make the pain go away?

I had a feeling that if I ever tried to have a baby, I'd punch the first nurse who told me to breathe.

After removing that spell, however, she'd had to bolster the other. It turned out that that required tattooing in the lines again. She used white ink, so they wouldn't stand out any more that they already did.

Her voice was strong and controlled as she chanted in a language I didn't recognize. Even though I could read languages, it seemed I couldn't understand them when they were spoken.

Hayleen wiped a wet cloth over my forearms, clearing off the blood from the tattoo. "There we go."

"Please tell me that's it."

She closed her eyes and held her hand above, as if sensing the magic. Finally, she nodded and tossed the cloth onto the workbench. "Yep. That's it. The protection spell is gone, so you won't go unnoticed so easily. I increased the defensive spell, so it packs *quite* the punch. I also connected it better to your will, meaning you shouldn't accidently throw too many people."

"Can you make it so she can't use it against me?" Grant asked.

"I could, but I won't. I happen to think you usually deserve whatever happens to you."

Grant offered a glare that implied he wasn't actually all that mad. "Well, short of that, I think we're good."

"Awesome. I'll put it on the tab."

I went to argue about that, to say I'd pay for it myself, but then I recalled how we'd paid for the Elder One's help. The reality was that payment in the supernatural world could be anything, and I didn't want to get stuck with a bill I didn't understand.

Haylee reached for a jar with a dark substance inside it, nearly black. She opened it, then drew some out with her fingers. "This will speed the healing and numb the pain. It'll be fine by nightfall." She dragged her fingers over the marks, but as she'd promised, the pain faded.

In fact...the drag of her fingers was sort of nice. I looked at her, the bright red of her lipstick, the way her eyeliner and tattoos gave her a dangerous edge. She was beautiful.

Her lips quirked on one side. "I've got no idea what's going on between you and Grant, but I'm not a jealous woman."

I swallowed at the blatant offer, unable to deny a temptation there.

"We're leaving," Grant said, voice hard and leaving no room for refusal. He took my hand, careful to avoid the healing tattoos, and pulled me to my feet.

Once we were outside, he turned back to offer a glare to the tattoo place. "Good thing she's the best, or I'd never come back."

I lifted an eyebrow. "Are you jealous or something?" It seemed odd, since Grant had never shown the least bit of jealousy with the other men. Was this different somehow?

He crossed his arms before returning his gaze to mine. "Looks like I am."

"Why her? Because she's a woman?"

He snorted. "Hardly. Once you become immortal, things like that don't mean a whole lot. Gender doesn't matter the way it does to humans, and you get old enough to recognize that sexuality is a lot more fluid when you have such a long lifespan."

"So what is it?"

He caught my chin, lifting my gaze to his, capturing my attention with those deep green eyes of his. "I've been through a lot with you, with Kase, Troy and Hunter. We've got..." He paused, as if searching for the right words. "A comfort. An understanding. A history."

"And what does that mean?"

"It means I dislike the idea of that changing. Also, I know Hayleen. She enjoys the chase, the taste of someone with power, but little more than that. Besides, if she hurt you, I'd have to kill her, then I'd need to find a new tattoo artist. It doesn't seem worth it."

"Well, maybe I was going to get a few orgasms out of it, and those are worth a rather lot."

That got his attention. His pupils expanded as he took in a deep breath, a reminder of exactly how much I missed him. Just as quickly, he offered a smirk full of promise. "Well, if orgasms are your only concern, I'm pretty sure I can help with that..."

And while I didn't always believe Grant was telling me truth, that was one statement I trusted fully.

* * * *

Hunter smiled, that charming grin disarming me as it always did. Funny that a man *that* dangerous could look so damned tempting.

He wasn't like a snake, like Kase, with sharp lines that screamed danger. He wasn't like Troy or Grant, either, who looked innocent enough to hide their vicious nature.

Instead, Hunter looked every bit as dangerous as he was, but in a way that was oddly endearing, like a lion with huge teeth but a fluffy mane.

Not that I hadn't seen his other side, the dragon beast he changed into, but it didn't bother me. How could it, after seeing what *I* changed into?

I was petty, but I wasn't a hypocrite.

"Hey there, shadow-girl," he said as I entered the room he'd given me an address for. It seemed that a lot of my life consisted of being sent to random addresses without explanation.

Worse?

I usually followed them. This time, it was an empty house, one without furniture or personal effects beyond a blanket tossed on the floor in a corner.

"Did you sleep here?"

Hunter peered over at the blanket. "I sleep wherever I can for the night."

"I have a house...there's no reason to crash in random, vacant places."

He lifted an eyebrow. "Little early to go moving in together, isn't it?"

"Fine. Sleep on the street for all I care."

He caught me by a hand behind my neck and tugged me toward him, as if my little snapped comment meant nothing. "You're pretty when you snarl."

"You do realize that isn't an endearing thing to say to a woman, right? It's pretty patronizing."

"Would you rather I say you're not pretty? Or I could be honest, and tell you exactly how hard I get when you show off your teeth. Because I have an amazing vocabulary when it comes to talking about how badly I'd like to fuck you."

I shuddered at the way he spoke, and at how he pulled me against him so I could feel exactly what my harsh words did to him.

"You are beyond tempting," he all but purred, and brushed his lips to my ear before nipping the lobe. "I've missed you, my shadow-girl. Do you have any idea how much I've thought about you? My own hand is a piss-poor substitute for your sweet cunt."

I moaned. It was a pathetic sound, but who could blame me for it? He'd shown me again and again just how talented he was with his…well…everything.

A clearing throat forced me to lower my head to his chest in frustration.

Being cockblocked by the devil had to be the *worst* timing.

I turned to find Lucifer standing there, though his image shimmered, making me suspect it wasn't actually *him* there. Then again, I recalled the vague mentions of him having less access to earth than he used to.

"Could you please not fornicate in front of me?"

"I thought the devil was all about the orgies. Didn't figure you for a prude."

"It seems reapers are a personal hard limit for me, because you dry up any sort of lust."

His use of what I was made my stomach roll, especially with the derisive tone, as though he could think of nothing more objectionable.

When my shoulders curled in, Hunter pressed a hand to my lower back, forcing my spine straighter.

It was a subtle reminder that I hadn't bowed to Lucifer before—I shouldn't now.

"I called you for my favor," I said.

He tilted his head, a sign of interest. Then again, he seemed to love a good bargain. "And what is it you want?"

"I need something of Lilith's that Hunter can use to track her."

Lucifer lifted one of his dark eyebrows, his horns catching the light from the bare bulb above him. "You believe the hellhound can follow that trail to her?"

Hunter answered, despite Lucifer not directly addressing him. "I've followed plenty of other things. I'm a damn good tracker."

"You aren't following escaped souls or hell beasts. You're talking about my daughter, about the first and only of her kind. Your party tricks will do you little good."

"Well, it isn't like you've managed it," Hunter responded. "So maybe I'm better at it than you are."

Lucifer didn't show any anger in his expression, no tightening of his jaw or lines in his forehead, but his eyes darkened. "You test my patience, dog."

I could have focused on Hunter and Lucifer's little tiff, but it didn't seem all that important. Sure, Lucifer was probably someone I should be worried about, but he hadn't done anything to me yet. Instead, I considered his words, his history.

"Do you want us to even find her?" I asked, frowning.

"Of course I do." Lucifer lacked some of the heft to his voice. "She betrayed me, and I do not take kindly to that."

"Yeah, but that doesn't mean you want her to be found. You might be pissed, but she's still your daughter."

Lucifer lifted his gaze to Hunter, and I let out a sigh.

Men liked to claim women were complicated and difficult, that women were the emotional ones, but I felt like all I did in life was dance around the egos of men.

"Hunter, can you give us a minute?"

He hesitated.

"He could have killed me in hell," I reminded Hunter. "I don't think there's really much risk right now."

"Even if there was," Lucifer tagged on, "you wouldn't be able to stop me."

Hunter snorted, an entirely disrespectful and dismissive sound.

Lucifer's gaze hardened. "You doubt me?"

"Doesn't really matter if I could do anything to you," Hunter pointed out. "Pretty sure shadow-girl here could put you on your ass herself."

Lucifer narrowed his eyes, but Hunter turned his back on him as though he mattered little. Hunter pressed his lips to mine — and boy, his kiss was a hell of a claim — before he strolled out of the house.

Lucifer's gaze followed Hunter. "I'm going to need to put that thing down at some point. He doesn't seem to understand his place in the world. I once had a wolf creature I found when it was just a pup. I brought it into the palace, expected it to be a faithful guard dog. It worked fine when it was a pup, but it grew larger, bolder and eventually stopped listening, stopped respecting my authority. It thought it could take me."

"What happened?"

"It couldn't," Lucifer said simply. "I believe your hellhound will follow the same suit. They both have the same hardheaded nature."

I pointed my finger at Lucifer. "I thought we discussed not threatening them."

Lucifer crossed his arms. "I don't think I will ever understand your obsession with those four. They'll be the end of you."

"Maybe it's like how you're still trying to protect Lilith?"

Fire sparked in his eyes, the deep red so similar to what had danced across the landscape in hell. "Careful, Ms. Harlin. I've granted you leniency because you are likely to be useful, but do not make the mistake of overstepping my patience."

The look in his eyes made me want to pull back out of instinct, the same reaction as when a person heard a rattlesnake.

I swallowed it down, though, because I hadn't called Lucifer to walk away empty-handed. "I can't blame you for being torn. She's your daughter—anyone in your place would want to protect her."

Lucifer's shoulders lowered a hair, the only outward sign that I'd landed a point. He let out a slow breath. "She must be stopped."

Talk about an understatement.

"So help me stop her."

"She was my first, the only thing I made with purpose. My other children are only half mine and created by random chance. They are a mixture of genes, just accidents. Lilith, though? I made her in my own image, gave her all I could."

I stared at him, even as his gaze was locked on a far wall. It was easy to think of Lucifer as unfeeling, but that wasn't true, was it? It was written in his expression, and even if it wasn't obvious, even though he didn't wear it on his sleeve, that he was hurting.

I'd never had children, didn't know if it was even possible—certainly not with the men of my life at the moment. Parental love was a foreign concept to me, something I'd never understood or really seen up close.

At least, other than Gran, and that hadn't turned out all that well for her.

Still, in that moment, I saw it from Lucifer. Lilith might be horrible, might have betrayed him, might be trying to destroy the world, but she was still his child.

And how depressing was it that the devil made a better parent than my own had been?

"I need to stop her," I said, softening my voice. "You can't ignore this just because it's her, because you don't want to deal with it."

"She didn't used to be like this," he whispered back. "She was never a child, but when she was new, she was different—lighter, happier. After Adam rejected her, she hardened. It is never easy when one's children suffer, when there is no way to fix what is wrong. I have so much power, yet I have no recourse. I have tried for so many centuries to help her. Perhaps…" He let out a sigh. "Perhaps I failed her."

"I can't give you parenting advice. There's a reason I haven't popped out any kids…" I let that statement hang, unwilling to go into my Daddy and Mommy issues with the devil. "But this isn't about just your child. This is about everyone's kids. If we don't stop Lilith, she's going to tear everything apart."

"And? What do I care about mortals? Maybe tearing apart the status quo could be worth it?"

"So you don't care about us mortals, but isn't there anyone you would want to save? Anyone worth it to you?"

He paused, shadows in his eyes. He didn't need to answer, though. It was clear as day there, a memory of someone he felt worth saving. He didn't answer right away, as if the scene played before him, as if he were reliving whatever it was in his past that I'd brought forward.

Which made me wonder—exactly who would the devil value? What sort of person would he find important enough to save the world for? Important enough to risk his daughter for?

Lucifer nodded, then brought his gaze back to me. He hadn't needed to say anything, to admit I was right, because the set of his shoulders said it for him. He held a hand out and a small box appeared in his shimmering palm.

"I took a box from you before, and it didn't go well."

"If I'd known what trouble you would be, I wouldn't have summoned you. I can assure you, the last thing I want is for you to return to hell."

How much it seemed he didn't want me around him placated me, so I took what he offered. My fingers passed through his as I took the box, reiterating that he wasn't actually there.

I opened it, and a ring sat inside.

It was silver with a beautiful red gem, the band like twisting vines. "What is this?"

"Lilith's ring from her marriage to Adam."

My lips tipped down. "I'd figure she'd hate this thing. How does it give us a link to her?"

"That is not just a gem. When Adam and Lilith were paired, we bound them in a ceremony no longer used, one that took a tiny piece of each's life force and trapped it in their ring, as a sign of their oath to the other. This is that ring, and it holds a spark of Lilith's life force. Should Hunter possess any tracking skills at all, he can follow it to Lilith, wherever she may be."

I looked down at the ring, at the link we needed, the break in the case.

"Promise me something," he said, stopping me.

I turned, the old adage about never making deals with the devil running in my head. "What do you want?"

"I know my daughter very well, because she is so much like me. I have no illusions about how this must go. Only one of you will walk away from it. So, I ask that you remember she was not always what she has become. It is easy to see her only as she is now. Things have not been fair to her, and while that doesn't excuse her, it does, perhaps, explain her. If anyone could understand the truth, could look beyond what is easy to see…I hope you can."

That drove it home, reminded me that as much as I wanted to see this one way, things were never so simple. No one could do anything without waves, and just as Gran had told me before, others would have to live with the choices I made.

I would make my decisions, and everyone else would end up paying the price for it.

Whether that was Gran losing her life, Kase losing his freedom or the pain of a grieving father...

There was so much pain left to come, and I was afraid of how heavy it would be on my shoulders.

Chapter Five

I had wanted nothing more than to see my men all together again, yet now that it had happened…

It felt odd.

Grant — along with a new bruise spanning his left cheek — stood near the window of the large warehouse Kase had secured for our use. He walked the perimeter, adding marks on the floor and walls.

Kase sat near the corner, shadowed and keeping his distance. I had to assume it was because he'd rather people not see his condition, though that seemed foolish right then. With the excellent sight Troy and Hunter had, they could no doubt see right through the dimness.

Still, he'd shown, and that alone warmed me.

Troy paced, moving his gaze between Hunter, Grant and me, as unsettled as he always was by magic. Funny that a man who turned into a wolf would so hate anything out of the normal, but he did.

No doubt it came down to him not liking the idea that creatures who seemed so fragile could kick his ass with magic.

"You ready for this?" Hunter asked when he walked up beside me.

"I'm not the one doing it," I reminded him.

"Yeah, but you look the most nervous."

I crossed my arms and gave him a withering glare. "How sure are you that this will work?"

"Assuming Lucifer isn't lying? That it is her essence in that ring? It'll work."

"What do you mean by assuming?"

"Well, if I really wanted to fuck someone over, I'd put the essence of something really nasty into a ring like this. Imagine if I thought I was tracking something fluffy and cute, but someone sticks in the essence of a warden in it. I show up expecting a bunny and end up face to face with something that will kick my ass."

I swallowed down sickness at the risk I hadn't even known existed.

Hunter bumped my shoulder with his. "Stop worrying. If Lucifer wanted to screw me over, there are several easier ways to do it. I'd bet it really is Lilith's trail."

I nodded, trying to trust his opinion. "How long will it take?"

"Not long, I think. This isn't the tracking I usually do, which occurs in the null space between the afterworld and here. This time, I have to start this hunt here, because she isn't in the afterworld, so it'll be…different."

"I don't like different."

"I don't either, but that's where we are."

I took a deep breath, then caught his arm. "What can I do?"

He peered down at where I held him, a curious expression on his face, as if my question confused him. He shook his head. "Nothing much. I'm going to track her in my smoke form because it'll let me move faster and travel between the null and here. My regular body will stay here."

"You're just going to leave it here like luggage?" That unsettled me, reminding me of the dead bodies I'd seen far too often. I didn't like the idea of Hunter looking like that.

"Yes, but if you want to take advantage of me, I'd prefer you wait until I'm back in my body so I can enjoy it."

I cut him a sharp look, and he promptly wiped it away with a kiss. He slipped his fingers into the front of my jeans, just behind the button, to tease the skin there.

I bit down on his bottom lip harder than I needed to before pulling away, the threat clear. "Don't be reckless, and hurry back."

He smiled, despite the mark on his lip from my bite, as if he enjoyed the hell out of that claim. "Sure thing, shadow-girl. I'll be back just as soon as I can."

He moved away, going to speak with Grant, who had finished placing marks near the door.

Kase rose and walked closer, his steps slow. He remained near the edge, where shadows kept him in the dark. I took pity on him and approached.

"I don't like this," Kase admitted, his voice rougher than usual. His gait was off, too. It wasn't as smooth as usual, as if just moving caused discomfort.

"You don't like anything," I reminded him.

"I've got to agree," Troy added, having walked up behind me. "But at least it's Hunter taking the risk."

That earned Troy a disapproving glare as well.

"What? You said he threatened Lucifer. That's like taunting a bear—if you do that, you don't get to hope for a long life."

Even as Troy spoke, however, he lacked the anger he used to have. It seemed he really had settled into the idea of me having multiple lovers.

"I'm surprised you all came." I tucked my hands into my pockets.

"You never know what can be drawn back," Kase said. "When doing things like this, when dealing with Lilith, it's best to have the numbers." At the last word, Kase's voice cracked, something so quick that I nearly missed it.

Troy, however, didn't. His gaze narrowed. "Are we going to talk about this?" He gestured at Kase.

Kase offered one quick shake of his head. "No."

That one word left no room for misunderstanding or argument. Kase had made it pretty clear it was a 'not happening in a million years' sort of conversation.

"So we just ignore it?" Troy pressed.

"Yes."

I sighed, the talk not going as I'd hoped it would. Troy had to know what was wrong, and some stupid part of me had expected them to talk, to come to some understanding.

It was a double-edged sword.

Drinking from Troy would alleviate the symptoms but increase the chance that Kase would never be able to get off werewolf blood. Still, if he didn't, it was possible that withdrawal would end up killing him.

Yet, despite the looming issue, the huge *look at me* sign in the room in the form of the black veins that stood out stark against Kase's skin, neither man seemed willing to actually deal with it.

Which again made me want to kick each of them in the shin, then lock them in a room until they figured it out.

Instead, Hunter's voice from behind me called all our attention. "It's time."

I wanted to say that we had more important issues to deal with, but the more I said that, the more I realized it wasn't a hierarchy of problems. I couldn't say which was first, and which was last.

It was just a big clusterfuck of issues that I was somehow expected to untangle and solve.

In the center of the warehouse, Hunter took a seat on the floor, Lilith's ring clutched in his hand. Around him, on the ground, sat marks seemingly scorched into the concrete. They glowed red, as if still smoldering.

Grant approached, his gaze focused, telling me he was no more a fan of this than the rest of us.

In fact, only Hunter seemed entirely comfortable with it. Then again, it always felt easier to accept risk for the person taking said risk.

"Let's get this done. Should only take a few minutes." Hunter peered up at me, his lip curled into a half smile. "Only time you should expect me to be quick."

Troy snorted but said nothing about the comment. Kase had left the shadows, his skin looking even worse, appearing more corpse-like than he ever had before.

Still, I tore my gaze from him because I couldn't think about it right then.

I took a step forward, wanting to sit right beside Hunter, but Grant put a hand up to stop me. "Not so fast there, Ava. Haven't you ever seen protection lines?" He pointed at the symbols on the ground. "When Hunter does this, he'll leave his body here. That will create a bridge between this place and wherever Lilith is, and who knows what nasty stuff she's hanging out with? The lines will keep whatever can follow Hunter back contained."

"This is a bad idea." I couldn't ignore anymore that he was taking a risk I didn't want him to. "What if it doesn't work? What if she's expecting it?"

"Hush, shadow-girl." Hunter's smile spread, as if my being nervous helped him somehow. "It's fine. Quick jaunt to find Lilith, figure out where she is, then I'll be back. Nothing to it."

I went to respond, but he offered me a wink before closing his eyes and slumping forward. The tattoos on him moved as they had in hell, like living things creeping along his skin before they dissipated.

Seeing him there not moving, not laughing, with no marks on his skin, felt beyond wrong. It wasn't Hunter, not the man I knew, the one who never missed a chance to make a stupid joke or innuendo.

After almost a minute, I started to fidget. I couldn't stay still, couldn't stop my brain from spinning, from thinking about all the things that could go wrong.

What was taking so long?

Why wasn't he back yet?

When I went to complain, a sickening, gasping, choking sound came from inside the protective lines.

Hunter fell backward, arching up, eyes open but empty, as if he still weren't there but was reacting all the same.

"What's happening?" I asked, my eyes wide, needing someone to explain.

"I don't know." Grant moved his hands, then whispered words to himself. Instead of anything happening with Hunter, however, the symbols on the ground brightened as if he'd just strengthened the protections instead of doing anything for Hunter.

I walked over to Grant and shoved him, breaking his concentration. "Do something!"

"Like what? Hunter is the only one who can travel like this. I can't pull him back, can't do anything but make sure whatever is attacking him doesn't break through and get *us* next. He's smart, though, and if there's a way he can fight this, we have to trust he will."

I turned back toward Hunter, to where mist escaped his open mouth, seeping from him and into the protected circle.

Mist?

I went forward, but the line stopped me.

I couldn't cross it, but I was pretty sure I knew something it wouldn't stop...

"Don't you dare," Grant said, warning in his tone that I one hundred percent ignored as I shifted into my reaper form and passed the barrier.

"Damn it, Ava," he cursed as I turned corporeal again on the other side.

Mist filled most of the circle now, cold and threatening. I crouched beside Hunter and set my hands on him. His skin was freezing, and still he twisted, his chest heaving as if he couldn't draw air.

I closed my eyes, trying to do what I'd done with Troy, with the other immortals, when I'd reached inside and removed Lilith's influence. I found *nothing* inside Hunter, though. I couldn't find his soul—or whatever he had — couldn't find the shard of something else, the piece of Lilith she'd left behind before. Instead, a leash sat, like a dead body tethered to a soul that was elsewhere.

Which struck a terror inside me I had no idea could exist. Was Hunter dead? He couldn't be if he were still moving, right? Despite all the things I'd seen so far, zombies weren't real.

Please don't let zombies be real.

Instead of worrying about that — I wasn't ready to consider zombie hellhounds — I followed the leash, just as I had before when searching for souls, like I'd done to start this whole thing with Rachel's body.

At the end of that trail, I fell head-first into the void. The first time it had happened, it had knocked me out.

That had been so long ago, though, like a different person. That had been an Ava running from who she was, someone who hadn't accepted herself.

I *wasn't* that woman anymore.

And I had things that mattered to me more than my own fears, now.

So when I fell into that abyss, into the freezing, endless darkness, the silence and the ocean Gran had described, I didn't let it strip me of my wits.

I screamed into it, following the trail Hunter had left, no matter how deep it took me, no matter the crushing darkness, or the way I couldn't breathe. None of that mattered.

There, at the point I wasn't sure I could push through, I found him — nothing but twisting, writhing smoke. The world took shape, dim but forming around him as if darkness cleared away.

A stone floor sat beneath us, mist rolling across it like thick fog, and just beyond Hunter's smoke dragon, a woman with dark hair stared at us.

Lilith.

She did as she'd done before, when she couldn't see me but sensed my presence. She came forward, her steps slow but sure. "You're here, aren't you? I can *feel* you."

I didn't answer, standing above Hunter, my eyes locked on Lilith.

What if I could end her right now? What if I use my reaper form and kill her? A tingling inside me, a chill, made me want to reach for that power and use it against her. Could it be enough? Could I get revenge for Gran right here? End it all here?

"Try it," she whispered as if she *knew* what I wanted to do, egging me on.

A choking sound left Hunter, weaker than before, and I dropped my gaze from Lilith.

Right. She didn't matter right now. I needed to help Hunter. We could deal with Lilith later, now that I knew where she was.

I leaned down and grabbed Hunter, my fingers moving through the smoke until I touched scales, the truth of his real form.

I met Lilith's gaze once more before yanking backward, holding tight to Hunter, bringing him with me, following the trail through that abyss again, and slamming back into my body.

Hunter rolled, hacking as if he could cough up his lungs themselves. His fingers dug into ground, the concrete cracking beneath his strength, his tattoos returning to his skin and swirling over him as if panicked.

I collapsed backward, breathing hard, the mist thinning around us until it disappeared as though it had never been there in the first place.

I knew exactly where Lilith was, but getting there was another issue.

Purgatory wasn't the sort of place I ever wanted to go.

Chapter Six

Hunter snarled at me when I opened the passenger-side door of my car to get him. He hadn't recovered from his ordeal, and as it turned out, he wasn't very nice when he was hurting.

He'd wanted to go back to somewhere else—no doubt to lick his wounds in private—but I'd strong-armed him into my car.

By strong-armed, I meant that I'd threatened to come looking for him if he went elsewhere, and it seemed he didn't like the idea of me being out on my own for no good reason.

"I'm fine." The pained words called him a liar.

"Yeah, I can tell. You're doing awesome," I muttered when I took most of his weight.

He shivered, his feet scraping against the driveway. He lifted his lip, showing off his blunt teeth as if they were still the fangs of his dragon.

And we toppled forward, his legs unable to hold him and me not nearly strong enough to haul his weight on my own.

My elbow hit the concrete, and I let out a soft grunt from the impact. "Yep. You are doing just wonderful, I can tell." Frustration ate at me. Hunter was hurt, he was being difficult and I couldn't seem to do a damned thing to help.

"I leave you for one minute," came Troy's voice a moment before Hunter's heavy body was lifted from me.

Despite Hunter's not-too-happy reaction to the help, Troy didn't appear sorry or apprehensive at manhandling an angry hellhound.

Once Troy got him into the house, he paused and peered at me. "Where do you want him?"

"You know I could tear your throat out," Hunter answered.

Troy ignored him and looked my way, like the hellhound was nothing more than an unruly child having a tantrum.

I hiked my finger toward the bedroom. "In there, I guess."

Troy nodded, all but dumping Hunter into the bed with as little respect as possible.

Hunter shivered, his tattoos moving on his skin as if agitated down to his core. Even so, he growled, a low and dangerous sound.

Troy waved him off, then leaned in close to me near the door. "You sure you want me to leave him here? I can stay if you want."

I glanced over to the bed, to where Hunter had his teeth bared, looking about as frightening as I'd ever seen him.

Even now, however, I wasn't afraid. He was snarling because he was hurt, because he'd been in danger. He reminded me of an animal in the corner of a cage, growling at anyone who dared to come near.

"I'm okay," I said, sure of it.

Troy leaned in, nuzzling his forehead to mine, the scene of the forest hanging on him. "Be careful."

I leaned up and took a quick kiss, with an even more vicious snarl from Hunter saying he didn't appreciate it. It seemed the usually happy-to-share demon felt a bit more possessive at the moment.

I let out a soft laugh. "Guess I should go deal with him."

Troy nodded. "Call me if you need me."

I let my hand fall from his chest before stepping back so Troy could leave.

On the bed, Hunter stared at me, his whiskey-colored eyes odd, shadowed, intense. Still he shivered, until his teeth chattered together, like his body couldn't get warm. I recalled the chill of the abyss, the way it seemed to steal all the heat inside my body.

It had me going into the master bath and twisting the handle to fill the tub with steaming hot water.

I grabbed one of the bath bombs from the shelf above the toilet, then tossed it to the water. It had dehydrated flower petals, and while I hadn't found they made me a more peaceful person, maybe they'd work better on Hunter. If anyone could use a little zen, it was the growling, snarling hellhound on my bed.

"Come on," I said when I got back to the bedroom.

"Stop trying to mother me."

I hauled him against me, helping him to his feet. "Trust me, I don't want to be your mother."

He growled but went with me, and because of the walls, I kept us both upright. He leaned against the counter, not fighting me when I stripped him of his shirt.

The lack of even an inuendo when I undid his jeans and pulled them down his legs told me he wasn't firing on all cylinders. The shivering had worsened, his skin freezing to the touch.

The deep, blissful groan when he lowered into the hot water said I'd made the right choice.

Silence took over the room, steam filling it, fogging the mirror, and I dimmed the lights before sitting on the counter.

Hunter looked better already, as if the heat was helping to ease whatever damage his tracking of Lilith had done.

"She's in purgatory, isn't she?" I asked.

Hunter nodded, eyes closed, sunk down into the water to his chin. "Yeah."

"Is that what happened to you?"

"I'm made in hell. Purgatory is toxic to me, even to my other form." His teeth chattered every so often, as if the heat eased some of the coldness inside him but didn't quite rid him of it all.

"Are you feeling better?"

He opened his eyes, and I was grateful that they had returned to the ones I knew. "Yeah, I am. Thank you." The gratitude seemed ripped from him.

"You don't like help, do you?"

"You saw where I'm from, Ava. In fact, Jerrod was a complete asshole, but he was one of the nicer hellhounds. I haven't lived a life where weakness is exposed." He groaned softly, as if everything hurt. "And it isn't something I deal with often. "

"Well, you just need to get used to it, because I'm not the type to sit back and do nothing when you get hurt."

"So I've found."

"What else can I do?"

He lifted one hand out of the water and reached out to me.

I went over and sat on the edge of the tub, slipping my hand into his, rewarded when he held it tight. It was odd to see him like this, and again, it stung.

I recalled Hunter being so strong that first night. Just like Kase, like Grant, even like Troy. Men who had been larger than life until knowing me had hurt them all.

"Stop blaming yourself." He closed his eyes again.

"You're all worse off than I am. It's like you're taking all the hits instead of me."

"You got yours the first few weeks when I met you. If I remember right, you got your ass handed to you by trying to find Rachel's spirit, then by a poltergeist, then you got thrown around by Olin, a scar from Lilith on your arm and roughed up by werewolves."

"Are you saying I paid my price early?"

He shook his head. "No. I'm saying we were fighting wrong. We were attacking symptoms, not the cause, and we were fighting *our* way. Now? Now we're getting to shit that you're more qualified to deal with."

"That doesn't make me feel any better."

"Wasn't supposed to. Fact is, with where Lilith is, this is going to get uglier before it gets better. You need to get ready for that."

I blew out a slow breath. "I already lost Gran. Isn't that enough?"

He shook his head. "I've found the universe likes to take away something on par with what we want, just like with magic. The more you want, the bigger the price. You're looking to save *everything*, shadow-girl, so there's going to be one hell of a payment."

"I don't have anything else to give," I said.

"Don't you?"

"My life? Fine." Funny how quickly that answer came. When it had all started, I would never have considered putting myself in a position where I could lose my life for a cause, but I also hadn't had anything worth saving.

My life had been empty, just me pretending to be normal, keeping my head in the sand as I moved through time without any attachments.

Then Kase had shown up on my doorstep and everything had changed. I'd been thrust into a world that *needed* me.

One that I needed.

"What if the price isn't your life?"

"What else could it take?"

He lifted an eyebrow as if the point were obvious.

And it *was*. Despite the way my mind refused to think about it at first, even though it avoided that reality or option, that lifted eyebrow forced me to face it.

The price could be not my actual life but the life I'd found, my place in it.

It could be my men…

It almost had been, time and time again, as if the universe were warning me what was coming.

Could I go through with it if that were the price?

It was a far more difficult choice than if it were my own life.

Hunter ended my line of thought by a quick jerk of my hand, one that toppled me into the water, still fully dressed.

I gasped, water splashing in my face, Hunter's naked body spread out before me. I was *sure* I elbowed him, but really, that was his own fault. I refused to feel bad even if he were hurt, because he'd caused it!

Still, he seemed to have bounced back, because he shifted me despite my struggles until I was stretched out across him.

I sputtered and picked a dried flower from my cheek before giving him a chiding look. Not that I could make it too serious, because something about Hunter's nude body turned me to mush every damned time.

"You must be doing better," I said.

"I still have this chill inside me, like I breathed in some of that mist I can't quite get out of my lungs."

That took me back to the day after I'd first found that void, when Gran had pulled mist from me.

I had no idea how she had done it, but I recalled how it had felt when it slid from me. My lips found his, and I drew, calling that same feeling as if I could control it.

When I pulled backward, that same freezing mist left him, escaping his lips and passing between us. It froze my mouth, my tongue, my cheeks, but I didn't swallow it. I didn't take it into my own lungs. Instead, I tilted my head back and blew it out. As it had the last time, it dissipated as if it couldn't exist in our universe unless inside a person.

Hunter's eyes were wide when I looked down, as if I'd yet again surprised him.

The shivering had stopped, and when he put a hand behind my neck to pull me in for an aggressive kiss, it reminded me of his question.

What if he was the price the universe demanded? What if they all were? What if I could manage to stop Lilith, to save everything except what I really wanted?

When Hunter grasped my shirt and pulled the soaking cloth from me, I pushed the worry aside.

I'd worked too hard, suffered too much, to let the universe take away anything else from me — especially the men I was hopelessly in love with.

Chapter Seven

Grant looked a bit more put together than he had the last time I'd seen him. He'd had his hair trimmed, his face shaved and he had no blood on his clothing.

It was sad that *that* was an improvement.

The dark circles beneath his eyes said he still wasn't sleeping well, but then again, neither was I.

"So, purgatory," he said, as if that opened our conversation up.

I nodded. "It's the place I see in my dreams."

He sat on the countertop of the kitchen island in his hotel room. "I figured your dreams weren't just dreams. I'm pretty sure you don't actually sleep — not the way we think of it, at least."

I thought about that choking sensation, and no matter how much I wanted to deny it, it made sense. "I'm actually in purgatory when I sleep?"

"I think a part of you is there, the part that's reaper. It's your connection to purgatory, like a tether."

I thought back to Gran, to her saying I'd be the one to deal with this.

Lilith was in purgatory, and only someone with access there could deal with her. It looked like I was the lucky volunteer for that.

"So how do we get there? When I saw her, I don't think I was really there."

"You weren't. You followed Hunter's trail—think of it like astral projection. In order to deal with Lilith, we'll have to physically go there."

"And how do we do that?"

He swung his feet, his heels striking the front of the island. "I've been researching all night. Purgatory is the sort of place the living and the dead don't just stroll into. It is entirely toxic to us, as you saw from Hunter's reaction. Not to mention the entire *where* it is thing is complicated."

"More complicated than hell?"

"*Much.*"

I blew out a slow breath. "Why is nothing ever easy? Just go here, kill this person, then you get congrats-on-saving-the-world sex. Instead, everything has all these steps and nuances and problems."

Grant chuckled softly, as if my complaining charmed him. "Maybe saving-the-world sex is like make-up sex. It's only good if you *really* fucked up." He kept speaking before I could snark back. "Purgatory is in the space between the living and dead world, and it's surrounded by a layer of protection that helps keep it from spilling into the living or dead realm."

"The void?" At his look, I went on. "When I followed Rachel's spirit that first time, I fell into…" I shuddered when the words wouldn't come at first. "It felt like this deep ocean, freezing and empty and massive."

Grant nodded. "That sounds about right. Normally, when people die, their spirits pass through that abyss in a blink. If they fight it, though, if they have unresolved issues, they get stuck there and it'll drag them into purgatory. Worse, we'll have the same risk."

"Not me. I don't fight anything."

He lifted an eyebrow as if he knew he didn't need to call me out on that bullshit. I'd fought every last thing, anything I didn't like, didn't want to deal with.

"Fine," I muttered. "I get your point."

"The area surrounding purgatory, the path to it, can possibly get us stuck, too."

"Possibly?"

He shrugged. "As far as I know, no one has ever gone to purgatory. All we know is through seers who have managed to peer in. All of this is a best-guess thing, just taking theoretical knowledge and trying to apply it to something no one has ever done. Purgatory traps those who are conflicted, so there's a good chance that when we try and get through, if we've got anything holding us back, we'll end up stuck."

"What do we do if that happens?"

"Try to get unstuck? Look, I know you want all the answers, but I don't have them. All we can do is try and figure it out as we go. No one has gone there, no one knows the details."

"So how is Lilith there?"

"Lilith isn't like anything else, and because of that, it's hard to know what abilities she has. All the time since we've been back, I've been looking into her, finding every record the guild has on her, tracking down every expert I've heard of, and it all points to the same thing—Lilith has a connection to the dead, probably because she was made by Lucifer, who's also connected to them. She's proven herself dangerous over the years, but no one knows exactly what she's capable of." He lifted an eyebrow as he looked at me. "It's a bit like you—we don't know what you can do until you do it."

"So how do we get there if it's toxic and no one can pass the abyss?"

Grant shifted, the first sign of discomfort he'd shown, telling me I wouldn't like his answer. Then again, did I ever? "Well, it's going to take reaper blood. That could bridge the realms and allow us passage, since reapers are tethered to purgatory. As luck would have it, I happen to know one who bleeds."

"Wonderful. Why is it that every plan you have requires making me bleed?"

"Maybe try not to have such useful blood?" He let out a slow breath, as if the rest of the conversation wasn't so pleasant—not that the first part had been full of good news. "Tearing portals into limbo is a dangerous thing to do. It requires access to a huge amount of steady power, and that sort of power is rare and dangerous. I only know of one place where it would be even possible."

I didn't need him to continue to know it was a horrible place. "Let me guess. It's on some haunted mountain with killer yetis or on the ocean floor in the mouth of some huge sea creature? Maybe on the moon?"

"I wish," Grant muttered. "Nope. The only place we have a chance of pulling this off is on the intersection of ancient power lines."

"And where exactly is one of those located?"

"How do you feel about breaking into the guild?"

And boy, that sounded like one hell of a bad idea.

* * * *

The door of Kase's townhouse stood open when I arrived, the handle broken as if someone had twisted it and snapped the lock clean off.

Had someone attacked him in his weakened state? Someone from the coven?

"You need to leave," came Kase's voice—careful, controlled but still weaker than it should have been.

I rushed into the house, fear gripping me. I hadn't gotten to put my nifty and freshly bolstered new tattoos to the test, so if anyone had decided to cause Kase problems, they seemed as good a target as any.

"You don't need to be so damned difficult," came a voice that slowed my steps.

Troy?

"I am not being difficult."

"Yes, you are. Are you going to let yourself just die? For no good reason?"

A deep growl came out—Kase's. "What business is it of yours?"

Heavy steps echoed, but I stayed back far enough that I couldn't see them and hoped they couldn't hear or smell me. It was odd to hear them talk on their own, without me there to play peacemaker. It was like eavesdropping on adults as a kid, when I realized they existed outside of my life.

"How do you think Ava is going to take it if you just waste away? How *dare* you put her through that."

"She'll get over it."

"If you think that, you don't know her all that well."

Another growl. "Can you at least sit across the room if you refuse to leave? Keeping my composure is far more difficult when I can smell your blood."

"No. Maybe the smell of my blood will force you to make a good choice for once. Now stop being stubborn and just agree."

"I will not live my life beholden to you or any other werewolf. I refuse to live as nothing but a junkie."

"Why's that any different from before, since you were already living off human blood?"

Kase made an unhappy noise deep in his throat. "Because at least then I could feed from any number of mortals. Now? It's just you. I won't force you into this."

"Last I checked, I had to *break* your door to get in here. Pretty sure you're not in any position to force me to do anything."

I kept still, hoping they could work this out. Maybe with me out of the way, they'd be less difficult. The reality was that no one could force Kase to do anything he didn't wish to. He was too old and too stubborn. He could resist any of us, and if he was done, if he thought he was losing himself, he'd end his life before doing anything he couldn't control.

The same fear that had gripped me each time I'd left him simmered inside me — the worry that I'd come back and find him gone.

"We need your help," Troy said, his voice softer. "We need every damn one of us to even hope to survive this, to keep her safe."

"So I'm supposed to live like this forever? Because if I feed from you again, it will only make this worse, only prolong the inevitable."

"So? You won't endure it for Ava?"

Silence met that question.

Was it even fair to ask that of him?

I passed the entry, tired of sitting on the sidelines for what seemed to be a conversation that revolved at least partly around me.

Kase turned his gaze my way, his veins impossibly darker, as if the disease had spread, and his cheeks were sunken in. "I should have guessed you'd be lurking about," he said.

"If you weren't in such bad shape, you'd have smelled her from the doorway." Troy sat back, as if my arrival signaled the end of his part.

"I'm not going to try and force you to do anything." I hated the words as I said them. I wanted to force him. I wanted to make it perfectly clear that Kase needed to feed, to beg him to use Troy, to demand it, but that wasn't fair.

I knew how it felt to be forced into things, so I couldn't do the same to him.

Troy rose and nodded, as if letting us know he'd allow us to talk in private but wouldn't go far.

When he left, I took a spot beside Kase, ignoring the way he sat, rigid and distant.

"I thought you'd try to make me," he admitted.

"I doubt it'd work if I did. Besides, it needs to be your choice, because even if I could force you, it would just postpone the inevitable."

He leaned forward, his elbows going to his knees. "My maker was a monster. I've often heard that vampires simply live until they become one."

"And you think feeding from Troy makes you one?" I tried to keep up with that line of thought, but I had to admit, I couldn't connect the dots.

"I've fought a long time to not turn into what made me, to not give in to that. There have been times I thought it would be easier, times when I tired of existence. It drags on for those of us who have been here through so much. It presents a temptation like you wouldn't believe, the desire to feel *something*, anything."

"That's not you."

"Of course it is. I have that in me, and it is so near the surface at times. Feeding from a werewolf, from Troy, it teases a line I have refused to cross."

"But that isn't where the line is. If you attacked Troy, if you forced him, *that* would be crossing the line. If he's offering, what's wrong with that?"

Kase didn't look at me. His gaze was across the room, locked on nothing. "Do you know how I met Gran?"

I shook my head. "I assumed it was at her shop?"

"No. I have known her since I was young. When I went to face the god killer I told you about, it was Gran who stopped me. You asked what happened when I faced the god killer, and I told you it was a story for another time. The reality is that I faced the god killer to die, but when it attacked, Gran stepped between us. She was the reason I didn't die that night."

I crossed my legs and turned toward him, even though he wasn't looking my way. "What happened?"

"Gran told me it wasn't my time. I was so tired, but she said I couldn't give in yet, that I had things to wait for."

"For Lilith?"

He shook his head. "For you. She said I had someone who would not be born for a very long time, that I needed to wait."

I thought about that, about how many people had been touched by Gran, how many lives she'd shaped.

"So why are you giving up now?"

"Because she also said I had to earn it. I had to be worthy of it. I've always held myself to a standard to do just that, and now I see why. If I had let myself fall to my baser urges, I wouldn't be who I needed to be." He finally turned to meet my gaze. "If I do it now, I'm just as bad."

"You're not. You don't become your maker just because you do what you need to do to survive. You aren't hurting anyone."

"Troy?"

"He's here *offering*. Don't try to use him as an excuse for you to give up. Life sucks — trust me, I know. Do you think I *wanted* to be what I am? Because if I could opt out of this whole reaper thing, I would. You really think I didn't have a moment of doubt afterward? That I didn't sit there in my room in Lucifer's palace and wonder if it wouldn't be easier to just…give up?"

Anger flashed in his eyes, as if the thought of me not being there were the worst thing he'd heard.

"When Lilith killed Gran, when I sat in that room alone — so damn alone and feeling like a failure, a freak, useless — I was ready to be done. I didn't care if Lucifer killed me, if Lilith came back. It was too much, and it felt easier to just stop." I tore my gaze from his, the intensity too much. "So, yeah, I get it."

He reached out and set a hand to my cheek, the chill of his skin shocking. "I'm tired, Ava. I've lived longer than I should have already."

"But I haven't gotten you that long. It's not fair."

He pulled me closer until I crawled into his lap and stared into his dark eyes. "I had hoped I'd find you and feel young again, that I'd feel restored. It was foolish to think you would fix everything."

"You're an idiot. It isn't about me fixing it all — it's the fact that we've been dealing with crisis after crisis! If anyone found some sense of peace in the last few months, they're psychotic. You can't be in a warzone and expect some magical calmness."

"I want peace."

"So stick around long enough to make it, because I can assure you, you're not going to find it if you just let yourself fade away." I leaned in and brushed my lips to his slowly enough that he could stop me, willing him to understand. "I was sent to therapy when I was a teenager one time, after yet another family said I was weird and deranged. It was this man who told me something that's always stuck with me. He said that he couldn't promise life would get better, but he could guarantee it wouldn't get better if I didn't stick around. If you want that peaceful life, you won't get it if you let this stupid addiction win."

He returned my kiss. "What would peace even be? If we all lived through this, what would a future look like?"

"I don't know," I admitted. "What would it look like for you?"

His voice was soft, quiet. "I don't want to have to fight, to have to keep up my guard. I would step away from the coven — I only participated to pass the time. I would want a safe home, a place I would not have to keep up pretenses, where I did not have to watch my back."

"And how would I fit into that?"

His lips curled into a smile. "You would be in my bed, of course."

I didn't want to break the moment, but I had to. "And Grant?"

"He would set wards and cause no end of trouble, I am sure."

"Hunter?"

"Lurking about, probably conspiring with Grant to cause mayhem."

The next one was the hardest. "And Troy?"

He exhaled, but instead of the copper-tinted breath I was used to, it was almost sickly sweet. Yet another sign that something was seriously wrong with him.

"He could sleep outside, like a good guard dog."

I chuckled at the half-hearted statement. "That's better than I thought you'd say. I was expecting you to say the pound."

"If I thought I could get away with that, perhaps. Unfortunately, I've come to the conclusion that you need him, and despite my personal feelings about him, he's good for you."

"So does that mean he can curl up at the foot of the bed?"

He smiled, and despite the way his cheeks were sunken in, it charmed me. "Okay."

That made me pause. "Okay? He can sleep in the bed?"

"No. Okay, I'll feed from Troy."

I flattened my hands on his chest as I tried to read past his words. "Really?"

He nodded. "Maybe it's worth sticking around, if for no other reason than to see Troy living in the yard."

"I'm not sleeping in the yard." Troy's voice came from behind me, reminding me of how wrapped up in Kase I had been. I'd entirely forgotten how good his hearing was — or that he was still anywhere around.

I glanced over my shoulder to find Troy there, his eyes bright, the way they turned when his wolf crept toward the surface.

Was it jealousy? Excitement at the feeling of being fed from?

Did it matter?

I went to move but Kase kept a hand on my hip, keeping me in his lap. His gaze was locked on Troy. "You're sure?"

Troy nodded. "Same as last time. We've got mutual goals, and this benefits us both."

Kase's grip remained, the same uncertainty. For a moment I thought he'd back out, that he'd decide against it.

Instead, he returned his gaze to mine. "And you? You want this again?"

Wasn't that an easy answer? Get to feel Kase and Troy together again? Get lost in the feeling of their hands, their mouths, their cocks?

It was almost enough to make saving Kase's life a distant second.

"Fuck, yes," I said, because there wasn't any other answer to an offer like that.

Chapter Eight

Kase's lips were cold, but they heated me up just fine. He kissed me with that methodical build-up he always had, as if it were a game he excelled at playing.

The shuffle of fabric behind me told me Troy was disrobing.

Maybe I should have been annoyed at the expectation, but what was the point in that? We all knew damn well where this was headed. Even if I could have pretended that a feeding could have been entirely platonic — like two people in a book who had to share a bed and think they can manage without getting frisky — our last attempt had shot that theory to hell.

Kase's bite produced the sort of lust a person couldn't just ignore, and the effect of Troy's blood on him was just as strong.

And I planned to fully enjoy all of that being directed at me. I mean, why not? *Waste not, want not.*

Large, warm hands dipped beneath the back of my tank top, running up my sides. They were already so familiar to me, the callouses on Troy's palms, the way the nails started out blunt until his wolf took more control and they sharpened.

And damn, how I loved when he used those nails on me, when he curled his fingers in and pressed the points against me, when he used them to cling to me.

Kase broke the kiss, and as selfish as it was, I missed it.

Not that I had much time to worry. Troy shifted his hand in front of Kase, and it took only a moment before Kase bared his fangs—they seemed longer and more lethal than ever—and struck into Troy's wrist.

Kase's reaction was immediate. He released a growl so low and dangerous that it drew goosebumps from me, and an instant erection pressed against where I rested in his lap.

I wanted to reach down, to grind against him, but I didn't. I'd seen his reaction to such things before, to being touched, so I waited.

He glanced over Troy's wrist, over where he pulled steadily, drawing and swallowing.

The meaning was clear. There wasn't room for any bull from our past, not here.

He didn't give me a chance to do anything, though. Instead, he reached for his own slacks, undoing them with an easy flick, then grabbed my jeans. I shifted to help him pull them down when a tearing sound told me he had no intention of waiting.

"I liked those," I complained a breath before he did the same to my panties, then distracted me with the press of his thick cock against my bare pussy.

So much for methodical and careful. Kase used a hand on my hip to pull me down, to sink each inch of his hard cock into me until I whined at the stretch.

He lifted his lips, red coating them, before biting down again and using his grip to make me rise and fall over him.

Troy pressed against my back, his weight and heat surrounding me. I felt every inch of his skin, telling me he'd gotten entirely naked.

Which was exactly the right choice, I figured.

He was stretched out so Kase could reach his wrist, and he ground his shaft against my back as if he couldn't help it, as if he couldn't just *not* move, not touch me.

In fact, I was pretty sure that, given the chance, he'd have gotten off exactly like that, and some part of me *loved* the idea. Sure, I'd grown as a person, learned to be a bad-ass when I needed to be, but having someone as strong as Troy grinding against me until he came, using me like that...it ticked boxes I didn't even know I had.

Troy's lips found my shoulder, his teeth teasing my neck, anywhere he could reach. He didn't break the skin, never had, but I could feel the desire to.

It reminded me of when they'd argued before, when Kase and Troy had fought about me not carrying anyone's bite.

Did Troy want to do that?

Did I want him to?

I tilted my head without thinking about it, exposing my neck like an offer.

I guess that answers it, doesn't it?

He growled, rocking his hips more, telling me he understood the offer for what it was.

Kase released Troy's wrist, the wounds healing as quickly as they had the last time. *Lucky werewolf.*

I kissed away the smudge of red from Kase's lips, the taste of that copper and venom the same as before, and the shot of lust it offered was staggering.

Kase broke the kiss to look at Troy, then tipped up the corner of his lips as if enjoying the sight of the no doubt mindless wolf, of how Troy sought any relief he could from the desire Kase had created.

"One of these days," Kase whispered, his voice already sounding stronger, "I'm going to get Troy drunk on my venom, then I'm going to watch him fuck you for *hours*. Each time either of you feel sated, I'll bite him again, watch you two exhaust yourselves."

The idea made me cry out, especially when Kase thrust in deeper, when he bottomed out and reminded me just how *good* he felt.

It wasn't just the idea alone—which was no doubt as hot as fuck—but the fact that we were talking about a future, about a tomorrow that included us all. It was as if Kase had finally accepted that we *could* all work.

"But the poor wolf looks rather feral right now," Kase said as he shifted me so his dick slipped from my needy cunt. "So move back, give him what he needs, and I want to feel your sweet mouth around me while he fucks you." Why was it that the crude words from him were so hot?

Sure, Hunter and Grant could talk like that and I enjoyed it, but coming from Kase or Troy, two men who were always precise and rarely vulgar, it heightened my need to a whole new level.

I shifted back so my knees hit the ground, Troy going with me, until I felt caged by his massive body. His skin wasn't as smooth as it had been, and when he nipped my shoulder, the sharp points of fangs told me he'd shifted more.

And boy, did I love that. His wolf, his other form, excited me beyond measure. It was a part of him I loved just as much as the rest, and it was as much my mate as his human side.

Kase carded his fingers through my hair, then tightened his hand into a fist. It reminded me of the way he took control, of how much I got off on that, too.

I darted my tongue out to lick up the side of his hard cock.

He groaned deeply. "Do you taste yourself? Because I'm covered in your wetness, Ava. Are you going to swallow it down, get to taste just how sweet you are?"

Yes.

The idea might have grossed me out any other time. I would have said that was too far, some line I wasn't willing to cross, but when he said it like that? When he asked with so much lust?

I was pretty sure I'd have done anything he suggested.

I parted my lips, sliding them around his thick shaft, and sure enough, I could taste myself. Not sweet, at least not like I'd expect, but powerful and tempting. I wasn't planning on going to town on a woman any time soon, but in that moment, I understood how they'd told me they enjoyed it so much.

But...maybe that was simply because of the moment, because it was *them*, because I needed them so badly.

Kase used his grip on my hair to pull me forward, to sink more of his length past my waiting lips.

As for Troy, the weight of his body settled against me, over me, and he sank into my cunt with a rough, powerful thrust.

I *loved* when this happened, when he lost his careful control and just gave in to the moment, in to me.

It happened when his wolf surfaced, but never did it happen so much as when Kase's venom rushed through him.

That moment of almost-pain hit me as it always did when he filled me, when his cock stretched my cunt, even better because he didn't pause, didn't wait, didn't wonder if I could handle it.

He knew damned well I could, and he planned to make me.

He fucked me with hard, deep thrusts, ones that knocked me forward and forced Kase farther into my mouth.

Troy didn't grasp my hips, instead choosing to lean over me, something so primal in the position, in the way he took me.

He'd mentioned full moons, but thus far had stayed away when they actually happened, telling me he worried it'd be too much for me.

It made me desperate to experience it, to feel him even more overwhelmed, even more passionate and hungry for me, as if nothing in the world existed beyond me, nothing was more important to him than the feel of me.

"Look at me," Kase said, drawing my gaze up to his dark eyes.

Funny how he could look so much better yet *so* much scarier at the same time. Maybe it was the position, being on all fours in front of him and at his mercy, but the curl of his lips said I was safe.

Even with the two men who could snap me easily if they wanted to, I'd never felt safer or more protected.

"You make a lovely sight like this," Kase said, his grip in my hair still tight, not giving me any control or power as Troy fucked me with wild, hard thrusts. "I think I like it even more than I did before, now that I know exactly how powerful you are. The reality is that you could stop us anytime you wanted."

The words sank in slowly, my lust-clouded brain needing to make sense of them.

When they did? When I recalled how I'd *just* thought about how they could break me if they chose to, I realized his meaning.

In my other form, I could hurt them. They couldn't do a damn thing to stop me. The same rush of power I got from being between them, Kase felt as well. He liked that even though I was so much more than any of them had realized, I still gave in to them.

I shuddered, pleasuring coursing through me from the moment, from the drag of Troy's cock against my sensitive pussy, from Kase's intense eyes and the way he fucked my mouth.

I came hard, the sort of orgasm that sneaks up on a person and pulls them under.

Kase didn't look away, that smirk he had spreading, as if seeing me even more helpless were an aphrodisiac.

I never would have expected *this* from the vampire who I'd seen in Gran's shop, from the untouchable man who never dared to smile or speak to someone like me, which made me cherish it all the more.

I had a feeling that not many had seen this side of him.

When I whimpered as my body came down from its high, Kase tightened his hand in my hair, a sting in my scalp that traveled straight to my clit. "I'm close, Ava," he said, my name something between a growl and a prayer. He didn't ask me if I could take him deeper, if I wanted to, but instead used his grasp on my hair to pull me in closer.

I swallowed so I didn't gag, closing my eyes to block out anything except for the extraordinary sensation of his hot dick so deep in my mouth that he teased my throat.

He let out a groan, his cock twitching, and again I found myself surprised and disappointed when he left nothing for me to swallow, as if I'd been denied something.

Which was stupid.

I tightened my lips and sucked hard as he softened, rewarded with a ragged curse before he yanked me off him. A cutting look said he *knew* I'd been being a brat. He grabbed my chin. "You're lucky I'm a patient man," he threatened, and I had a moment of questioning my life choices when my cunt tightened around Troy's cock at his words.

It was as if him threatening me cranked up my need another few notches.

Kase's smirk said he knew it.

Arrogant asshole.

Still, he sat back, his gaze moving over my body to watch Troy fuck me.

Troy had picked up speed, and the roughness of his skin against my back said he had shifted quite a bit, as if he'd given in even more than he had in the past.

I suspected that each time we had sex, his wolf gained another inch or two of control, and this time? He seemed entirely lost.

There was no doubt that Troy was close—I felt it in the quick rhythm, in the nearly constant growl that left his chest.

Sharp teeth scraped against my shoulder — a warning and a question.

Again, I tilted my head, my answer clear.

Troy let out one of those deep, terrifying roars — I hoped Kase had understanding neighbors, because there was no way they hadn't heard that — before he plunged deep into my cunt and stilled, his hot seed filling me as his knot swelled.

That was normal, or as normal as my life was anymore. The part I hadn't expected?

A shocking stab of pain in my shoulder as he bit down. He didn't just *bite*, though, but rather sank his fangs in and held me still. Even as he rocked his hips, as he tried to get even deeper into me, the bite kept me still for him.

And while it wasn't a reaction like it was with Kase's venom, it wasn't a drugging aphrodisiac — Troy's bite was something *else.*

It was as though I could feel that bond snapping into place, like we'd been dancing around the whole 'mate' thing prior to that. It wasn't physical, at least not entirely.

I wasn't some young girl who believed in fate or romantic nonsense, but I could *feel* something so much deeper than just the physical connecting us.

It sent me over the edge again, my cunt squeezing down on not only Troy's cock but his knot as well, reminding me that I was entirely trapped. A deep, animalistic growl left him, but he didn't release his bite. If anything, he held tighter, determined to not let me get away.

As if I want to go anywhere.

The feelings rushed through me until I gasped brokenly, exhausted and overwhelmed.

Eventually he released the bite, his chest heaving against my back as he breathed roughly. Even when I shifted, his knot tugged at my overstimulated cunt, telling me I was trapped.

He grumbled then moved, wrapping his arm around my waist to keep me against him. He twisted so he rested behind me, us on the ground, then licked at the bite wound. It soothed the burn and teased me.

I glanced up at Kase, grateful to see those horrible black veins gone, to find him looking like his old self again. He looked back, with a softness to his expression that always surprised me.

He reached down, sliding his fingers through my hair—a gentle, sweet touch so at odds with how rough the sex had been—before he grabbed a cushion from the couch and put it down, beneath Troy's and my heads. Afterward, he rose, walking from the room, probably to clean up.

It left Troy locked inside me, his arm tight around me, as he nuzzled at the wound on my neck.

This was worth sticking around for, and I could only hope Kase had decided that as well.

Chapter Nine

"What's the guild like?" I pulled at the leather jacket Grant had brought me as I sat in the car — one I was sure didn't belong to Grant, though I had no idea how he'd gotten it. I'd learned that such things weren't that important, especially because I rarely liked the answers.

"Noisy, but in the most silent way."

I offered him a look that I hoped explained how little that made sense to me. "I don't need anyone taking Gran's place to tell me things that I can't possibly understand."

He peered out of the window, as he'd done for the past five minutes since we'd parked. "The guild is all about posturing. Everything is a power play. It means *everything* means more than it seems, so even when people are quiet, it's still loud."

I frowned as I thought about that, about what it must feel like. "So you're always having to figure out what people really mean?"

He nodded, his expression somewhere between exhaustion and excitement. "I don't mind it. I get off on the battle, on the struggle. It's a game. It's like always playing chess and having to figure out your opponent's moves before they can use them against you."

"But doesn't that mean you're always on guard? Always trying to figure out what people mean? Doesn't that wear you out?"

He paused, as if he hadn't thought about it before. "It's all I know."

"And you never want something different?"

"Like what?"

"Like being able to just relax? To talk to people who aren't trying to screw you over?"

"I don't think that exists," he admitted softly. "People *always* want something, and if they can get it from you? They will."

I thought about the way I'd relaxed when I'd been around Gran, or the way I sank into Troy's arms, or how I closed my eyes when Hunter pulled me against him.

Despite my life not being ideal, when I'd had so few people to trust, I'd still found some.

And even when I hadn't had people to trust, I certainly hadn't had to worry about them actively trying to hurt me.

It sounded horribly lonely.

Then I thought about Grant, about how he spoke to even me.

He was always careful with what he said. I recalled how he'd told me he didn't like to ask in case a person said no.

Maybe it wasn't about him wanting his way and more about not trusting people to know what the plan was? Even when he'd suspected what I was, he hadn't said it, hadn't told me.

It forced me to look at Grant — to *really* look at him. His lips were pulled into that smirk, his jean jacket making him look so much like the first time I'd met him, when he'd come to the house in a similar outfit.

Except, even if he didn't admit to ever letting down his guard, I could see something different with him.

That first day he'd guarded his words more, speaking with the edge of a man protecting himself.

He might not tell me everything even now, but I didn't feel he was hiding as much, either.

"How do I look?" I asked to change the subject, because a few minutes in a car before planning some sort of heist at the mage's guild wasn't the best time to untangle his knot of emotional baggage.

His gaze moved over me, slow and teasing. "I'm usually partial to the whole naked look for you, but I have to admit, you look good in leather."

"Well, enjoy it, because it's not something I'm going to try again." I tugged at the thighs of the pants, wondering how on earth singers dressed in tight leather pants and danced around a stage. I didn't even have testicles to fit inside the thing, but it seemed there wasn't nearly enough room.

Still, when I'd seen myself in the mirror of the hotel room we had gotten ready at, I had to admit...

I looked good. I reminded myself of one of those kick-ass women I'd seen in hell, the ones who had seemed ready to put anyone on their back for looking at them wrong. That wasn't me, but it was nice to play that part.

When I'd arrived, Grant had had an outfit already there for me. A white tank top, a pair of black leather pants and a matching jacket.

It made my hair stand out, the way its black sheen wasn't as dark as the leather, that it was instead an almost charcoal tone. The smart man had put me in a pair of boots rather than heels, and I had a feeling it was because he knew damn well there might end up being running involved.

If I died because I tripped wearing heels he'd picked out, well, I'd have had to haunt him for years. Every time he wanted to masturbate, I'd remind him about how his grandmother looked naked to ruin it.

"You're sure the others will be able to meet us?"

Grant nodded. "I made sure they all had the marks for transport. As soon as we get to the right place, I'll activate the spell, and they'll portal right to us." He offered me a chiding look. "I'd have preferred to do the same with you, but you don't portal well."

"Too bad. Now you have back-up." And the more I heard about the guild, the more his tension had increased, the more grateful I was to be there. He was tough, but I didn't want him facing who knew what alone. "And I finally get to see the guild."

Grant gave me a less than enthused look, as if he could think of no worse way to spend his time. "This isn't a field trip, Ava."

I waved him off. "We've been to *hell*, Grant. I don't think a building full of mages is a big risk."

He snorted softly. "Trust me — hell was a cakewalk compared to the guild. It isn't just a building with some mages — it's a building full of all the most dangerous secrets and the only people on earth who know them.

Not to mention, the majority of those people would love to get a hold of you."

"Me?" I frowned. "What do they want me for?"

"Because if there is one truth to the guild, it's that power is always in high demand. Power is gained from things no one else has or knows, and that's exactly what you are, Ava. You're something that hasn't ever been. Trust me, there have been more than a few mages who have considered trying to grab you, to experiment on you, to figure out if you could be useful."

I swallowed down the anxiety at that thought, at the idea that I had even more enemies than I knew of, that people were wanting to *experiment* on me.

Sure, like any normal girl, I'd had alien abduction fantasies now and then, but I had a feeling that if what Grant implied happened, it would be far less sexy than my mind had conjured up. "Well," I said, trying for false bravado, "too bad they don't realize just how not-useful I really am."

He gave me a look that said we both knew it wasn't true, but in true Grant style, he played along. "Right. If only they saw the time you tried to climb that boulder in hell, when you slipped in the mud."

I let out a soft laugh as I recalled that, when I'd been trying to keep up with the big boys on our endless hiking and had ended up on my ass in a puddle of something that for sure wasn't water.

He leaned in closer, his laugher drifting away. "I'm serious, though, Ava. You need to be careful. Keep your eyes open and don't trust *anyone*. Let's go."

The building we'd parked across from appeared like any old office building — square, depressing and beige.

"I have to admit, my expectations were a lot higher," I said.

Grant shut the door to the car as we exited. "You should know better than to trust what something looks like by now."

Which was fair. Hadn't Troy taught me that? He looked as normal as could be, if a little stuffy, and he turned into a werewolf—maybe looks weren't that useful.

"Couldn't you still make it look a little more impressive?"

"Why? People want to look closely at things that are special. No one wants to get any closer to a place like this."

I wrinkled my nose when I approached the front. "Does it smell of fish?"

Grant nodded.

"Why fish? Why not something worse?"

"Because if something smells like rot, people are going to wonder why. Smelling just a bit of fish makes people assume it's nothing dangerous, but unpleasant enough they'll stay away."

At the door, Grant waved his hand across the intercom, and a blue glow started like some strange security system before the door opened.

"So if you can't do that nifty open-the-door thing, does the door just stay closed?"

Grant held his hand out for me to go before him. "Of course not. The door opens, but it goes into the regular building."

"Then where does it go this way?" I stepped through the entry way, and it was as if the air was stolen from my lungs, an electrical charge running over me. I stumbled, and strong hands caught me before I faceplanted.

Grant stood in front of me somehow, when I was positive that he'd been behind me moments before. He had my chin between his fingers and his other hand on my side, his green eyes locked on mine. "You really don't deal with portal travel well, do you?"

I drew in a deep breath before shoving his hands off me. "You could have *warned* me."

"When people tense, it's worse."

"It's always about not telling me stuff with you. Haven't you learned that isn't a good idea?" I forced myself upright, ignoring the swirling in my stomach that said I'd nearly left my breakfast there on the threshold.

When I peered around, however, it became even clearer that I wasn't where I had been.

I stood in a room so large that it could never have fit inside the building on the street. It reminded me of a mall, with a central space, doorways along the sides and people walking everywhere.

A few looked our way, but most kept moving as if people appearing happened all the time.

Which I guess it probably did...

I pulled the leather jacket around me, straightening it, trying to make myself look more put together, as if they hadn't all just watched me almost throw up from one little portal.

"You good?" Grant asked.

I nodded after taking one big breath to settle my stomach. "Yeah. Let's do this."

"Good girl," he whispered before gesturing forward.

"I would have thought, from what you said, that everyone would be staring at you like some celebrity."

He chuckled, but I noticed that no matter how relaxed he appeared at first glance, his gaze held a wealth of tension. "We're on the first level, which is open to anyone with magic, even the humans who haven't gone through the rituals yet and their close family. Basically? This is the least restrictive area. You've got your weaker mages, your mortals, even a few non-magical people who are part of our world. They don't know much down here." He nodded at a series of doorways toward the end. "That's the pathway to the upper levels, and as we go through them, more people will recognize us both."

"It's nice to see you here," came a female's voice that said it was *not* nice to see him.

A woman stood there, dressed in a pair of black slacks and a white button-up shirt that made her look sleek and professional. Her blonde hair was pulled back into a neat bun and her lips were painted bright red.

"Maya," Grant said, his tone friendly on the surface, but with warning beneath that.

"I wasn't expecting you today," Maya said. Her gaze moved over to me. "And I certainly wasn't expecting *her*."

Grant shrugged. "You know me—I like to do the unexpected."

"You're here for the council meeting?"

"Is there a problem with that?"

Maya looked as if she wanted to say there was, but shut her mouth before any actual complaint escaped.

Grant didn't seem the least bit worried about Maya.

He was on guard, with an edge to his words and a caution to his gaze others might not notice, but he wasn't *afraid* of her.

Was that because he knew he was safe or because he knew he wasn't? Funny that the two could be so different but end up at the same place.

"This way." She held out a hand.

"I can find my own way." Grant didn't move, his refusal clear.

"I am sure you can," she answered, "but if anything happened to the Magistrate under my care, it would fall on me."

Well, that made sense—

Her words hit me, and I turned a surprised look on Grant. Maybe I was supposed to play things close to the chest, to pretend that I knew everything, that he and I were on the same page for all topics of conversation. Too bad my poker face sucked. Or at least, I assumed it did. I hadn't ever played.

Maya let out a soft laugh. "You left that out, did you?"

Grant didn't appear rattled by the conversation or my look. "Because it isn't true."

"It is. You were next in line. The old Magistrate died, and that left the position to you."

"I never accepted it."

"Acceptance is nothing more than a technical issue. So long as you're alive, the position is yours by right."

Grant narrowed his eyes, the first sign of real annoyance from him, as if the talk had moved from unpleasant to downright objectionable.

Maya took a step backward, her back straightening as if she'd *just* realized she was poking something she really didn't want to get a reaction from. "I'm sorry," she rushed out, "I was just talking."

"I can find my own way to the council room. I remember where it is, and nothing here is more dangerous than I am."

"Of course." Maya said it with the hesitation of someone who didn't like the idea but knew better than to argue any further.

We left her standing there, though it took a moment for me to follow Grant. I felt rooted in place by the bombshell they'd just dropped.

I went back in my mind to everything Grant had told me, all the times we'd talked about the guild and his past. I would have remembered if he'd said *he* was the Magistrate, wouldn't I?

Though, suddenly the acting Magistrate showing up to the fight in hell, and Grant being unable to fully separate from the guild made a lot more sense.

We went to a large doorway near the end of the open space, and by that point people *were* looking. I didn't get the sense that it was because they knew who he was, but rather the exchange with Maya had clued them into something being amiss.

It would have been like someone dressing down the President of the United States. I didn't need to know who that other person was to know that they weren't someone to screw with.

Another piece of metal, similar to the intercom at the entrance but not as modern looking, sat beside the doorway at the end. Grant slid his fingers over the front of it as if drawing a sigil, and when he finished, it glowed red.

The door opened, and I frowned.

We were clearly on the bottom floor. I recalled walking into a ground floor building. However, through that doorway, a stretching skyline said the new space was farther up, and through the far side, I caught sight of a mountain.

There was no mountain near the building we'd walked into.

It seemed I outlasted Grant's patience, because he set a hand on my lower back and pressed me through the opening. "Come on."

"But..."

"Yes, each of these doorways are actually a portal."

"So how can I pass through them? When Lucifer called for me, it didn't work."

Grant stopped, as if he realized I wasn't going to be quiet until he explained it. "Lucifer created a transient portal. They're less stable magic because they bridge two places temporarily. The kind used here connects two places permanently. Arches at each end stand as fixed points."

"Why did the first door affect me more than these?"

"Because the first one had wards to keep out unwanted visitors, so you were reacting to more types of magic. These are simple passageways."

"And?" I crossed my arms, refusing to move any farther into the empty room we'd entered, the portal fading away behind us until the noise from the large open area had disappeared. We had other things to talk about than just how magic doors worked.

"And nothing. They clearly work for you."

I lifted my eyebrow, telling him that wasn't even close to what I meant.

He set his hands on his hips and let his head fall back, releasing the loudest, most long-suffering sigh. "Do we have to do this *now*?"

"We talked about you not lying to me."

"I didn't lie—I just didn't mention it."

"I feel like *you* running this entire place is something you should have disclosed, like an STD."

"I'd rather have magical gonorrhea than this, trust me."

I still didn't move an inch. He *owed* me at least this.

He cut me a chilling look.

"Nice try, but if Troy's wolf doesn't scare me off, do you really think you could manage it?"

He snorted softly. "You fuck a werewolf and his knot—willingly. Who am I kidding? Nothing scares you." He rubbed his hands over his face, as if he could get his mind working and the words out.

We stood there alone, in silence, for a long moment before he answered. "The Magistrate position transfers in one of two ways. First, the current one claims a successor."

"And that was you?"

He nodded, a quick jerk of his head that screamed he didn't like the topic. "The second way is that someone can claim the title by killing the current Magistrate. There must be witnesses that they were the one to kill the Magistrate, and it really just depends on if they can keep their head after they do it. See, some of the time others will stand up if the old Magistrate was better liked, or people suspect it was a fluke, so it is a risk to try that."

And that made things clear.

"So you were the named successor, *and* you killed the old Magistrate, meaning you're the only option."

"Until someone takes my head, yeah. They don't have any rules in place to deal with this because no one has ever not wanted the job before, and without an official Magistrate, they can't change it."

"But you don't want to be in charge here?" I thought about all the benefits this sort of power could give a person...

Grant was a man who *loved* power. How could he turn around and just walk away from the potential here?

"This place," Grant said, voice soft, "it's ugly, Ava. It's diseased. Try to take it and you'll just catch the illness yourself."

"Couldn't you change it, though? Turn it into whatever you want?"

"No. Some sicknesses are too deep to cut out. You have to let the whole fucking animal die."

I set my hand on his arm when his expression turned dark and cold. I *wished* he talked to me, that he actually told me what the hell he was thinking. It was like an entire lifetime of sorrow filled his head, but he wouldn't let any of it out.

He looked down at where my hand was on his, as if he didn't understand the touch, like it was something he couldn't come to terms with. "You know I killed the council — you know what I've done."

"So?"

"So, why are you sitting here trying to comfort me like I'm some victim?"

I frowned as I thought about it.

"Because I know you."

"What do you know, exactly? Last I checked, I keep things from you, I've not told you important information, and you've *seen* some of what I am capable of." He lifted his gaze to mine, having lost that humor of his, the way he normally made everything into a joke. Instead, he had an intensity in his eyes that made me almost want to shrink back, to pull away.

I didn't, though. "I know that when you could have saved yourself in hell, you didn't. You barred a door and put yourself on the dangerous side of it. I know that you're going to a place which is the last place you want to be now to help me and to help everyone else." I held his arm tighter, as if trying to drive home to point. "So I know that if you killed those people, you had a damned good reason for it."

He said nothing at first, his green eyes locked on mine, before he came forward in a rush and his lips were against mine. He carded his fingers in my hair to keep me still as he kissed me, his body crowding mine until something pressed against my back.

A wall?

Did I care? *Not one bit.*

I kissed him back, meeting all his urgency and need with my own. I curled my hands in the edges of his jacket, clinging to him, wrapping a leg around his hip.

He *was* good. I didn't care how these people saw him, or what he'd done. He wasn't someone struggling with change, with trying to be anything, but the truth was that whatever he'd done, I believed he had a good reason for it.

A throat cleared, and I dropped my forehead to his shoulder.

Other people got to have quickies in hallways.

Me? I got cock-blocked by *everyone.*

"Really wishing I hadn't had you remove that spell," I whispered to his chest. "Maybe they wouldn't have noticed me here and we could have finished."

Grant chuckled, but the sound was strained. The erection pressed against me through his jeans said he'd been on board for the same thing I'd wanted.

Good. Somehow suffering together sounded better than me suffering alone.

Grant took a step back and turned toward the sound.

Jameson stood there, the acting Magistrate I'd already met in hell.

His gaze slid impassively from one of us to the other. When I'd met him at Lucifer's Court, he'd hardly noticed me, but this time?

He watched me with the same level of wariness as he did Grant.

It seemed like my little turn-into-a-reaper trick had earned me a reputation.

"Yes?" Grant asked dismissively, as if he hadn't been nearly screwing me in the hallway a moment earlier, or perhaps had been but didn't see a problem with it.

"I heard you had come. I didn't quite believe it."

"Why not? Aren't you the one who always wants me to come?"

"Yes," he said, voice careful. "But I have to wonder why you've chosen today of all days to attend."

Grant shrugged. "Maybe I'm tired of sitting on the sidelines. This *is* my place, isn't it?"

Jameson's lips flattened. I had to give him credit, though, because when he answered, it was without all the *fuck you* he no doubted wanted to add. "Of course. You *are* the Magistrate."

For now.

It seemed I understood mages better, because I could translate that threat without any help from Grant.

"Well, when it was discovered you would attend this meeting, word was sent out. We've moved the meeting back a few hours, to allow for those who had chosen to miss this meeting to attend. You coming changes the dynamic, of course, so those who had opted to miss it wished to change that decision."

A tension started in Grant's shoulder, as if the news wasn't what he would have hoped for. "I have other matters to attend to. Moving a meeting is highly improper."

Jameson's eyes narrowed, as if picking up on something in Grant's tone. "Your presence is unheard of. It has been over a hundred years since we have had a Magistrate attend a council meeting."

Again, another tidbit of information.

Grant's that old?

He looked like a college student most of the time, so the idea that he was actually over a century old sent me for a loop.

At least this time I didn't have my mouth hanging open.

See, I'm learning.

Grant nodded. "Very well. I can return at that time."

"Nonsense. Your quarters have been prepared."

"I don't have quarters."

"The Magistrate quarters are yours."

Grant's cheek twitched, not in humor but as if he were trying his hardest to not show anything in his expression.

Or incinerate the man before him.

"Thank you," Grant bit out from between clenched teeth.

It was the least grateful thanks I'd ever heard. Well, at least since the times I'd had to thank a gynecologist for an exam.

Jameson nodded, then extended his hand toward the end of the large room, to where a number of other doorways sat. "I have ensured the room is clean and well stocked. It is still coded for your entry. At this point, the meeting is scheduled for nine this evening. I will alert you should that change."

"And we will be in the Jade Room, won't we?"

Jameson again stilled. "We have been meeting in the Amber Room since..." He trailed off.

Since what? It only took a moment for me to piece it all together. *Since Grant killed the whole council, probably.*

"Yes, but if we are to return to normalcy, shouldn't we do it in the right place? What better sign that the guild is functioning again than a Magistrate ruling in the Jade Room, as was always the tradition?"

Jameson didn't look all that convinced, but at the word *Magistrate*, he pulled back as if slapped. Then again, he'd been acting as one, hadn't he? It was a reminder that he wasn't, and that Grant was in charge.

"Of course, *Magistrate*," Jameson said in a smooth voice before nodding again. "I will arrange to have the meeting held there."

With that, he walked away, though Grant didn't move his gaze from the other man, not until Jameson disappeared through a doorway.

"Well fuck," Grant said, his voice losing some of that tension. "A change in a plan as complex as ours is always bad."

"But he's going to use the Jade Room. Look for the silver lining," I argued, surprising the hell out of myself. I wasn't a look-on-the-bright-side sort of girl myself.

He blew out a breath, the tension in his expression loosening and disappearing. Instead, he let his gaze travel down my body, taking special interest in the way my thighs looked in the tight leather. "Silver lining, huh? How about the fact that it seems we will have uninterrupted access to a private suite for a few hours?"

"Sorry," I said. "Not going to happen. Do you know how hard it was to get these pants on? There is no chance I'm going to take them off until I can leave them off."

He lifted an eyebrow. "Oh, Ava, you forget—I'm magic. The work it'll take to get you out of those pants will be *well* worth it."

And suddenly the change in plans didn't sound so bad…

Chapter Ten

"Are you a magistrate or a king?" The words came out of my mouth before I had time to think about them when I walked into the room.

The skyline stretched out, and it seemed the quarters took up the entire top floor, given the expensive windows that surrounded it. A huge balcony surrounded it on all sides, and the massive living room could easily fit a party of thirty or more.

Grant huffed, shoving his hands into the pockets of his jacket. "Trust me, it isn't all it's cracked up to be."

"How can you say that? I've only ever seen you sleep in hotel rooms or by-the-hour motels in hell. This is an upgrade."

"*This* is a perfect example of a golden cage, Ava. It looks pretty, but it's a trap."

When I turned, I found Grant staring at a picture that hung above the mantel of a huge stone fireplace. The painting was like those fancy ones people commissioned in the past. He didn't glance and it and move on, though. He seemed frozen in place.

The painting was old, and the dress of the two people in it made me suspect it had been painted in the eighteen hundreds. A man in a suit had a cruel, stern look on his face and a cane clutched in his hand. He looked no older than his late twenties, but there was a twisted nature to his expression that made me sure he was *far* older.

Beside him was a young boy, not even ten. He had blond hair and was thin enough that it seemed he hadn't eaten much in his life.

The thing that stopped me were the kid's eyes.

I *knew* those eyes. The piercing green were a familiar set I'd stared into plenty of times.

I didn't need to ask.

The painting was of the old Magistrate and Grant.

Grant nodded as if he knew what I was thinking. "He had that done just a week after accepting me into the guild."

"Accepting? I thought he was your father?"

Grant let out a slow breath. "He raised me, took me in. Mages can't have children, so heirs are *claimed* most often, sometimes from descendants of the mage's line who didn't take the immortality rituals."

"So you were related to him?"

"No. I was an orphan, just another vagrant mage they found."

"I'm sorry," I said, as empty as the platitude was. Saying sorry didn't change shit.

"Back then, there weren't a lot of options for kids without parents. I lived on the streets, stole what I needed to in order to get by. I knew I had powers but didn't understand them. That didn't stop me from using them the best I could, and that's what got me noticed."

"Isn't living here better than the streets?" Maybe I should have kept my mouth shut, but I *remembered* how badly I'd wanted a home – any home – when I'd grown up.

I remembered falling asleep, unwanted, and praying for nothing except to find someone who lived in a place like this to take me in.

It *had* to be better than the alternative, and I hadn't even lived on the streets.

Grant shook his head, though he still hadn't moved his gaze from the painting, as if he couldn't. "No." He rubbed the heel of his hand against his chest as though there were some deep ache there he couldn't rid himself of. "Jameson is playing a game by putting us here."

"What sort of game?"

"The kind he plans to win. He's been wanting to kill me for years."

I paused. "That's why he came to the competition, right?"

He nodded. "He probably hoped I'd be wounded enough that he could finish me off and take my place."

"What would putting you here matter?"

"Because he knows I had a complicated history with my father. I'd guess this is a way to unnerve me, to throw me off balance."

And judging by Grant not taking his eyes off the painting, I'd say it had worked.

He wasn't focused on what we needed to do, on what was coming, on our plan. He stared at the painting as if the meaning of everything were there, as if he could understand the world if he only studied it long enough. Hadn't I done that too, though? How many times had I sat on the bench outside the fire station where I'd been left as a child, watching it like I'd come to some great epiphany?

Jameson wanted to get under Grant's skin, and he'd achieved it.

But I wasn't about to let Grant get lost so easily. I shifted around him, standing between him and the painting, before I set my hands on his chest and waited for him to look down at me.

Even when those green eyes locked on me, he was miles away.

"Pretty sure you mentioned being able to help me with these pants. If you can't even manage that, what sort of mage are you?"

He didn't move for a moment, and the shadows of his past crept over him like spiders. Then, after blinking slowly, he offered me a smile.

A *real* smile. It wasn't mocking, it wasn't hiding—it was like some gratitude he *had* to get out right then.

So I took it, and when he grabbed my thighs, when he lifted me against him, I gave him everything I had right back.

He all but dropped me on the bed, and I scooted back to make room for him. He pulled his shirt off, giving me the look at all that tattooed skin that I'd craved. He didn't have the physique of Hunter or Troy, but that had never stopped me from wanting him. He was different, lithe and dangerous in an entirely distinct way.

I shrugged off my leather jacket, then tossed it aside. The warm air of the room slid over my bare skin when my shirt joined the jacket, when I wanted to strip off everything to feel him.

It made me pause for a moment, thinking back. Had I ever been with Grant on his own?

I'd been with him with Hunter, but somehow, I hadn't slept with Grant alone.

And why exactly did that get my nerves going?

He paused, his fingers on the button of his pants. "Second thoughts?"

Are they?

I shook my head. "I just realized I haven't slept with you alone."

He let out a soft laugh, but it lacked humor. "I don't plan on doing any sleeping. Still, if you don't want to, if it's weird without Hunter..."

The statement hung between us, him giving me an out, as if he thought Hunter was the only reason that I'd accepted him. And despite the way he hid, the way he was so hard to read some of the time, I could see right through his statement.

He worried that he wasn't enough by himself, that he'd somehow snuck into a relationship on Hunter's heels, as though maybe on his own, I wouldn't want him, that he wasn't enough.

Which was a stupid thought, really.

Hunter was a lot of things — more than a few of them insults — but he was hardly the glue that kept Grant with me.

I rose to my knees and slipped my fingers behind the button of his jeans, beside his fingers, then tugged him a step closer so he stood just before the bed. I could have told him I wanted him, that it had nothing to do with Hunter, that Grant and I had our own bond between just us, but Grant was a stubborn asshole who wouldn't listen.

However, I didn't mind giving him a more hands-on lesson about how I felt.

I flicked the button of his jeans, then pulled the zipper down. I wish I could say I was sultry about it, that I was like the strippers he'd talked about in hell—sexy and totally controlled.

Instead, I had a feeling I looked more like I did at two in the morning when I broke into that bag of cookies I liked to hide away on top of my fridge. Even knowing that didn't stop me, however. Grant had seen me through a lot, so if he knew that I removed his pants with the same excitement normally reserved for sugary treats, well, I was fine with that.

He groaned when I yanked his jeans down, when the action gave me access to his cock, since Grant was exactly the sort of man to forgo underwear. He was hard, his shaft resting against his lower stomach and all *mine*.

I wasn't a possessive person, but something about this moment made me want to claim him, even more so because he seemed uncertain of whether I'd want that. I wrapped my hand around him, the heat of his cock searing.

The sound he let out was anything but controlled. It was deep and desperate and made me wish we'd already worked at getting those absurdly tight pants off me.

He slid his fingers through my hair, a reverent touch, as if he couldn't believe I'd let him. I rewarded him by dragging my tongue up his shaft, tracing the thick vein, teasing where the foreskin gathered. He tasted of fire and lightning, and it lingered on my tongue as I pressed kisses along his length.

I toyed with him, enjoying the way the muscles of his thighs, of his stomach, all tensed with want. Even so, he didn't move. He let me have him, let me please him and play.

Of course, the disgruntled noise he made when I pressed my lips to his hip, to a rose tattooed there, made me grin. It felt like playing a game with a mountain lion I was for sure going to lose.

Though, I had a feeling that even losing to Grant would be winning for me...

I traced the petals of the rose, nipping at the stem which rested on his groin, so close to his cock I could only imagine the look his tattoo artist must have gotten.

"You're killing me, Ava," he groaned.

"You're impatient," I countered before blowing cold air over his hard length. "Good things come to those who wait."

"'Don't play with fire' is an idiom you should take to heart more," he threatened.

I snorted—not the sexiest sound, but whatever. "*Puhlease.*" I drew out the word with as much mockery as I could. "What are you going to do about it?"

I was pushing him. I knew it. He knew it. If the windows were open, people close by might just know it.

That was fine by me. As it turned out, I was a bit of an exhibitionist when it came to my men. It was like after I'd gotten a taste of what they did, of how it felt to have them, I didn't really care if Suzy-Prude down the way knew all about it.

He tightened his grip in my hair, forcing my eyes up to his. The green in them seemed darker than usual, almost molten. "What game are you playing?"

"No idea what you mean." I reached my tongue out as far as I could, just barely able to dart the tip against the head of his cock. Why the hell did that do it for me? Why did it make the want inside me grow more, consume me?

Because Grant had been playful, and he'd teased me, and he'd given me pleasure, but it had *always* been with hesitation. It had been a game, a team sport with Hunter. He'd never really given in to what he wanted from me, had never let it be just us, let it be real.

Push a man far enough, and their truth always comes out.

He narrowed his eyes, looking downright terrifying from that angle. I stared at his tattooed body, his toned stomach, the ink over his chest, the way his bicep moved as he gripped my hair. "I knew when I met you on your front porch, you'd be trouble," he admitted.

"But you stuck around."

That made his lip curl up and into a smirk, one that was not in the least bit reassuring. "Yeah, I did."

"So it must not bother you that much."

"Believe it or not, I like that you're trouble. I like that you're tough and stubborn and that I always know where I stand with you."

That hit me, forced me to focus in on his eyes. He'd spent his life having to read people, having to guess their true intentions, never sure he could trust what they said.

"I like that if you're mad enough to stab me, you'll damn well bury the knife in my chest and not my back." His words came out soft, and even though the statement was pretty bleak, I got the sentiment.

It wasn't that he believed I'd never turn on him, that I'd never go against him, but he trusted that if I did, I'd let him know I was coming for him. It was a weird declaration, but with him, it made sense. He hadn't lived a life where people had each other's backs for good, so even thinking I just wouldn't betray him was enough.

He let out a soft laugh, some of the fierceness of his expression fading away. "Besides, let's be real—I think I'd let you sink that knife in anyway."

That didn't sit right. I opened my mouth, ready to tell him that I wouldn't do that and he was an idiot for saying he'd allow it. He shouldn't allow anyone to stab him, including me!

However, he took advantage of the moment, using my hair and pressing the head of his cock past my open lips, into the heat of my mouth, then gave me a hell of a pleased smirk.

It seemed like an empty win—I was planning to suck his cock anyway—but any desire to brat disappeared at the taste of him, at the way his dick felt against my eager tongue.

He could have his win if I got this. It sounded like a pretty good consolation prize.

I lavished attention to the head of his cock, not caring about taking him deep. I slid my lips forward and back, my hand wrapped around his shaft and my tongue stroking the sensitive area underneath.

The world drifted away, blocked out when I closed my eyes and focused only on him, on his length, on his fingers in my hair. I sucked hard, tilting my head to tease more of him, pulling back to slide my tongue against the slit at the top. Pre-cum escaped, like a promise of what was to come.

"Fuck," he whispered, voice rough and strained. "Every time I think I can't want you more, you go and prove me wrong."

Which was exactly how I felt about him. He overwhelmed me, made me need things I'd never needed, made me feel free in a way I wasn't used to.

When I sucked harder, wanting him to let go of everything, wanting him as desperate as I felt, wanting to swallow down his cum as I had before, he pulled at my hair.

I wasn't *about* to let go, though.

He released a deep sound, something from his chest. "Trouble," he panted before pulling again, with no more luck. "I haven't had you yet, and I sure as fuck don't want to waste this."

He left the rest unsaid, that his real fear was that we wouldn't have another chance. We were headed into purgatory, and that wasn't the sort of place people came back from.

That made me give up my prize, had me tightening my lips once more before pulling back and releasing him. Having sex with Grant felt like finishing something, like completing a bond that had been uncertain before.

He moved quickly, kicking off his shoes and stripping off his jeans. Each time I thought of him as weaker than the others, he reminded me that even if he wasn't as physically strong, he had his own methods. I found myself twisted and on my back, though his hands were busy on my pants.

He'd used his magic to move me, effortlessly flipping me while focusing his attention where he wanted it—which was on trying to get my pants off.

And despite how much I enjoyed his little show of power, it turned out that even he wasn't a match for tight leather.

"What black magic is this?" he muttered as the fabric stuck to my skin, especially since what we'd already done had heated me up and sweat did *not* make for easy removal.

"I told you these were a horrible idea."

"I once killed a *dragon*, you know. Not just Hunter's smoke creature, but a real fire-breathing dragon. I will not be made to look like an idiot because of clothing."

"Well, next time you kill one, you can turn them into a pair of pants to show them who's boss." I let out a gasp when he tugged hard, the leather sticking and refusing to go past my ass.

These were great-looking, but they had not been made with my generous ass in mind.

He let out a frustrated sound before his lips moved, quiet words falling from them. Before I had a chance to complain, the fabric loosened considerably, and Grant pulled the scraps free, a look of victory on his features.

"You cheater!" I peered down at my bare legs, at the black lace of my underwear that, while cute, was probably not appropriate for guild business. "And now what am I supposed to wear?"

"You doubt my ability to get you another pair?"

"Well, you couldn't get these off. My faith in your abilities isn't that strong."

He let out a long-suffering sigh before slipping his fingers into the waist of my underwear and tugging them down my legs. I shifted, helping him, wanting nothing more than to get rid of every bit of cloth that covered either of us. In fact, I arched my back and reached behind me to undo my bra, not at all confident that he'd manage to get that off by himself.

And all I really cared about was him getting *me* off anyway.

He leaned forward, over me, and I spread my legs around his hips. The moment felt oddly sweet and intimate, something closer than what we usually were. It felt personal.

He paused, staring down at me as if he'd realized the same thing. Resting as he was on his forearms, his skin stood out against mine, the bright colors and deep blacks of his tattoos stark against the blankness of mine. "You know why I got all these?"

I swallowed down a joke, refused to go there when it seemed he actually wanted to tell me something. "Why?"

"Because I was nothing growing up. I had nothing, not even a last name. People didn't see me, never looked at me. They did this thing where they'd look past me, where even if I was there, right in front of them, they'd pretend not to see me."

Boy did I understand *that*. It also made sense as to why he'd helped me get my protection spell removed — he knew how it felt to not be seen.

"That doesn't explain the tattoos," I said when I couldn't follow the train of thought that went from point A to point B.

"After I gained my immortality, when I accepted my own power, people saw me for how they could use me, for what they could get from me. People have looked at me all my life and seen what they wanted. So, I figured, fuck that. I want them to see what *I* choose." He lifted one of his hands, bracing himself with the other, to tap at the large tattoo on the left side of his chest, where it wrapped over his shoulder and his ribs. "This was my first. I went in just after I killed the council and my father, spent hours in the chair with Hayleen."

I peered at the image, taking the time to study it. Before, it had been just color and chaos, but as I traced the lines, it came into focus and I found meaning in it. It depicted Grant killing the council.

Beings arched, with lines of power reaching toward them. The tattoo was messy, dense, requiring me to study closely to make sense if it. At the center, where the swirling tendrils of magic convened, was darkness. It wasn't a figure, but a monster of some sort. Was that how Grant saw himself?

Of course it was. Despite him saying he didn't regret his actions, there had never been a question about the deep divide inside him, as if it were a choice he could never fully be comfortable with.

And the tattoo showed it. While I didn't understand it all, I didn't need to.

"When Hayleen puts on tattoos, she uses a form of empathy, where she pulls things from the person, that guide what the finished image will be. This is what she put for me. Each tattoo was created from *me*, from my memory, from my feelings. It was putting right on my skin who I am, even when people refuse to see it."

I slid my fingers over the image, hating it more than a little because of the way he saw himself. Still, I scooted down then leaned up, until I could press my lips to the center of the tattoo, to where the swirling darkness sat, as if I could clear the hatred that had gone into its creation.

He shuddered before he caught my chin, lifting my gaze to his, trapping me in those deep green eyes. "I don't know how this will all go, Ava. I'm a realist, and what we're planning on doing, no one has ever done. I've wanted nothing more than to gain power, to secure my safety and survive. The idea that I'm headed to a place that is probably going to kill me is insane, but you know what? If this is my last time I have — " He leaned in to brush his lips against mine. "I don't think I've got any complaints about that."

I slid my leg up and around his thigh, trying to pull him closer as I deepened the kiss. His words reminded me how little time we might have left, and damn it, I wasn't about to die without having had Grant like this, fully and all to myself.

He groaned, then brought his hand down my body, teasing my breast, my heated and sensitive skin, before wrapping his hand around his cock. When the blunt head pressed against my wet cunt, I was beyond ready.

It turned out that Grant alone was foreplay, that I'd been desperate for him from the moment I got him alone. Even with the serious talk, even with how sad discussions tended to dry my vagina right up, it only made this moment better, more important.

Grant paused, not as if waiting for permission again but as if savoring that split second before things changed, before he got what he wanted most. When he pressed forward, plunging deep into my pussy, the sparks that rushed through me made me gasp.

He felt perfect — thick and hot and wild. He rested his weight on his left forearm, his other hand grasping my back to hold me to him tighter. He withdrew only an inch or two before delving in again, taking me as deep as he could, his lips to mine. His kiss was all-consuming, breathing me in and keeping me there, with him.

I rolled my hips, straining for the same thing he was — to forget everything else going on, to shove our pasts away, to force our futures to hold off for just a little longer. Grant could do anything, or so it seemed.

I didn't understand his power well, and he constantly showed me that he was capable of far more than I could imagine. This moment held that same magic because of how time seemed to slow, how the world shrank down until it was just the two of us.

We moved together, feeding off each other, off the lust and the need that had brewed from the moment we'd met. Where Hunter usually helped to translate that between us, like a buffer that allowed Grant to use jokes to create distance, nothing could do that now.

And he didn't seem bothered by it. He took me hard, as if driven to possess me entirely, to prove something with his actions alone. I let myself become lost in the same madness as him. I curled my fingers in, digging my nails into his marked skin, anything to have *more*.

He groaned against my lips, and I could swear a current rushed across him, as if electricity danced over his skin. I broke the kiss to look down, to find a blueish-white light covering him, like the sparks inside those orbs I'd seen as a kid. It was sharp, almost painful, but deceptively beautiful — just like him.

He buried his face in my throat, his lips soft but demanding as he traced the curve of my shoulder. "I can't help it," he said, as if in apology. "You undo my self-control."

I went to say I didn't mind, but when I pulled back just a little, the sparks shifted from him to me, catching the hardened tips of my nipples. The sting shocked me, unlike anything I'd felt before, and my cunt squeezed down around him when the touch nearly threw me headfirst into an orgasm.

Well, fuck. That sure as hell said I didn't mind it a bit.

He let out a chuckle before shifting his weight up to his arm, putting room between us even as he never lost that punishing rhythm, as his thick cock plunged into me without hesitation. "I swear, you were made for me. Each time I think you're going to wake up and realize this is a bad idea, you end up just as twisted as I am."

I could have argued, but was there a point?

Besides, when he lifted the hand not bracing him, when those sparks arced forward as he moved his hand over me without touch, instead teasing me with those powers, I didn't care to fight him.

It was absolutely sinful what he did with that electricity, the way it made me cry out, how he dragged it across my sensitive breasts, my ribs, my stomach. Each place drove my need higher, drew my body tighter, like some elastic band I was terrified of snapping.

He kept moving that hand down, and when I met his gaze, he *smirked*. It was the confidence I knew from him. He might be nervous about me, about how to view himself, but when it came to dealing with his power, he had no doubts in his abilities.

And, while allowing him to get those powers anywhere near my more sensitive parts seemed like one of those horrible choices I couldn't take back, I didn't stop him. We *both* needed me to give in, to trust him.

Sure enough, when he dropped his hand lower, when those arcing currents passed between my mound and his hand, then shifted to my clit, the world came to life around me. It hurt in the best possible way, and even without pulling the hood back, without touching my clit, it felt as if his lips were latched on to me, as though he were stroking me directly.

That overwhelming, tightening, *I just might die if this keeps going* feeling consumed me so fast that I stood no chance against the rush of sensation. It swarmed over me like the power across his skin, taking me over, shoving me into an orgasm that felt foundational. It stole my breath, my thoughts and my doubts. It left me hollow and weak, even as he fucked me through it, as he tried to hold off, to make the moment last since we both knew the real world would come back when it was over.

When I came down from the initial wave and caught my breath, I shoved at Grant's chest. The drag of his cock against my overly sensitive pussy was too much of a good thing. It was like trying to take another bite of cake when I was already beyond stuffed.

He sank into me as deep as possible, taking my thigh in his hand to pin me down, before he shuddered and let out a sound that I knew I'd hear in my dreams. It was full of want, of a satisfaction that came from his core, as if he'd waited for *this* his entire life.

Afterward, when his cock stopped twitching, he collapsed forward, sweat coating both of us. The rise and fall of his chest was erratic, as crazy as the sex had been.

A few long moments later — though I still had zero desire to move — he pressed himself up so he could look into my eyes. It turned out that felt far too intimate with him still inside me...

He set his hand on my cheek, then tilted my head so he could offer the sweetest of kisses. Without pulling back, so his lips still brushed mine as he spoke, he whispered, "I don't care about saving the world for anyone or anything else. It can all burn as far as I'm concerned. You, though? You're the only thing in it worth saving, and I swear I'll do whatever it takes for that alone."

The promise meant something, spoken with a certainty that said he'd put everything into it, that he wouldn't fail.

And so, even though he'd balk if I said it out loud, I made him a similar promise.

It didn't matter what we would face, what would happen. I wouldn't let this damn trip be the end of him, either.

Chapter Eleven

The Jade Room was impressive, but in a very different way from the rest of the guild I'd seen. So far, most of what I'd gone through were skyscraper-type buildings. The quarters I'd stayed in with Grant had sat at the top of a tall building with an expansive skyline. They were modern, sparce and expensive-looking.

The Jade Room was different. Instead of the modern decor of the other places, rather than a building that could have existed anywhere, in any big city in the world, I felt as if I'd been thrown backward a few hundred years.

Is this a castle?

I always thought I was different from other women, but in that moment, I became every little girl who wanted to be a princess.

Well, I wanted to be queen — the evil sort who got to run everything and who no one questioned.

Still, this sort of place would work well for it.

I was back in a pair of leather pants that were *far* too tight to be reasonable. Grant had summoned them up from whatever little hidey-hole he had, then made a comment about the sight of my ass in them when I'd asked why he couldn't have just gotten me sweats.

A delicious ache reminded me of how I'd spent my time with Grant, of how we hadn't stopped at just one round. It turned out that despite his age, he had a libido and recovery time that matched his youthful appearance. I didn't mind putting those to use at all.

"Grant," Maya said from ahead of us, pulling me from my musing. She wore a full suit this time, and appeared far more in control. I wasn't sure if that was because she had backup close by or because she'd been able to school her features, since she expected Grant this time.

"Everyone able to move the time?" Grant asked.

"Yes, Magistrate. We have a full attendance."

"How many is that now?"

"Forty-seven."

Grant stopped so quickly, I ran into his back. He kept his attention on Maya, though. "Forty-seven? Why are there so many more?"

"You've been out of touch for a long time."

"So? I doubt there are that many more mages."

She shifted as though she didn't care for his scrutiny. "No, our numbers haven't increased."

"So why?"

"Because without someone to cast breaking votes, many of the disagreements ended with splitting territory."

Grant rubbed at the bridge of his nose. "You're telling me that mages got into petty arguments and instead of working them out, they simply decided to take their toys and go home? To split up previously defined territory into even more chunks for no good reason?"

Maya nodded, swallowing hard, the whole cool-and-collected thing going right out of the window. "It seemed a better idea than war."

Grant shook his head. "At least with a war, there'd be less bickering. How does it even work to have that many people on the council?"

"It works like it did before."

"Except there are now *forty-seven* different heads of council, each with, what, thirty other mages below them, so the entire bureaucracy of it means nothing ever gets done?"

"I didn't think you cared much about how things were run." Jameson walked up, and Maya had the face of a woman who *knew* she'd been saved.

Then again, it didn't seem like Maya had a whole lot of power in the scheme of things, so I was thankful Grant could take his anger out on the acting Magistrate rather than her.

"That's because I didn't know you all would take not having a Magistrate as a ticket to act like idiots and screw up an already bad system."

"Is that why you returned?"

Grant snapped his mouth shut, as if he loathed the very idea of coming back into the fold. Sure, that was the story we were peddling, but it didn't mean he had to *like* it.

And clearly, he didn't.

"You're making people nervous," Jameson said as he gestured farther into the space.

Grant walked beside him while I trailed behind both. It gave me a chance to survey our surroundings, and I didn't have to keep up any of the conversation.

"Why would that be?"

"Because you show up without a word, ready to step back into a position you've rejected for over a century. Would you not find that curious? Especially given your last interaction with the guild?"

"You spend a century trying to get me to come back, then act surprised when I do it?"

Jameson made a noncommittal sound, as if he didn't want to call Grant out but knew there was more to it. Then again, even if he knew Grant was up to something, I doubted he had the power to do anything about it.

Other people stood in the hallways and rooms we passed through. It wasn't open in the way the last places had been, and the stone walls showed signs of aging. I felt like I was in some old castle that had withstood thousands of years, as though I were walking through history itself.

The people did *not* look happy to see us. On the plus side, for once, their censure wasn't reserved just for me. I got plenty of it, sure, but Grant had his own hate. That made me happy, since for whatever reason most of our interactions had me as the unwanted one.

The mages dressed in varying types of clothing, some looking like they'd stepped right out of boardrooms and others as if someone had pulled them in from a surfing trip. One girl seemed no older than ten, blunt bangs hanging across her forehead as if she had to take her school picture in a few hours. The knowledge in her dark eyes told me her youthful face was a lie and cautioned me against trusting her.

"I believe some are worried you may have decided to remove the council again," Jameson said, drawing my focus back to them.

I quickened my steps to keep up, reminded that my short legs were still a problem.

"And why would I do that?"

"You did it before."

"Are you telling me there is a repeat of the situation that caused that?" A catch in Grant's voice drew me closer. He spoke as if it were a warning, not a question.

Jameson paused a hair too long before answering. "I have no idea what you're talking about."

"*Sure.*" Grant peered over his shoulder at me, his eyebrow lifted as if passing some message.

What it was, I had no idea. Maybe just to stay on my toes?

Through a final large archway was a massive room with stone tables and benches that all faced the same direction. There, at the side, was a raised area that was carved directly from the stone, as if the entire room had been built around this one spot. A stone chair at the center was likewise carved, and openings to each side of it were shrouded in darkness, not allowing me to tell how far back the paths went.

Jameson nodded at people as we passed them, the groups moving about as they took seats at the tables and benches around the large room.

Still, they spared him hardly a glance before gawking at me and Grant. It seemed we were the real show they'd come to see.

I expected to take a seat at one of the benches, but we passed them all and headed for the front, for the carved seat. It reminded me of the other thrones I'd seen so far—Colter's at the coven, Lucifer's in hell. It seemed every person and group needed some obvious seat of power, as if being ruler alone didn't mean much without the nifty furniture to prove it. I could almost picture these arrogant men looking through catalogs — *ah, yes, the maple one is nice and all, but nothing says 'my dick is really big' like skulls.*

Jameson peered at the seat, his longing making me take a step toward Grant. Desire like that did nothing good for a person. It twisted them, made them do things they never expected just to get or keep what it was they really wanted.

Jameson *wanted* that throne. He craved the power, the right to sit there, and I had no doubt that if he thought he could, he'd take out Grant to get it.

The shrewd look in Grant's eye said he knew it, too.

"Do you have an agenda?" Jameson asked as Grant stood beside the seat. "We had scheduled to discuss the ongoing issue with feral mages and convene additional resources to properly locate and put down any mage who shows signs of infection."

"It isn't an infection," I broke in.

He gave me a look that said he wanted to be dismissive but wasn't sure he could get away with it. He saw me as a little girl, an outsider, and he didn't care for me having opinions. Still, I'd guess my whole reaper trick warned him off it. "It operates as one."

"But I can cure them. I've been doing it for the werewolves and the vampires." I pressed. "And when we deal with Lilith, they'll be freed from it anyway."

"And in the meanwhile? Do you have any idea how dangerous mages in this condition are?"

I thought back to seeing Troy affected by Lilith, to how his eyes had blackened and his body had twisted to his wolf form. I'd seen it plenty of times since then, when I'd used my power to tear Lilith's influence from the afflicted one at a time. I gulped, hard. "Yeah, I've got a pretty good idea and the marks to show for it. There's no reason to be killing off people who can be saved."

He did everything up to rolling his eyes at me, as if I were an idiot who had no idea about the real world.

"What group is hit the hardest by Lilith's influence?" Grant asked.

"The southern mages have had to be dealt with most severely."

Grant cracked his knuckles, and I dropped my gaze to find he'd drawn his hand into a fist. "And let me guess?" he said. "Those mages nearer to your own status have been placed in special cells to keep them safe?"

Jameson fidgeted. "We lack the resources to properly restrain *all* mages in that condition. Hard choices had to be made."

Grant lifted his hand, palm out, to silence Jameson as if the acting Magistrate were nothing but a complaining child. "Not a single mage will be put down without one of your own caste and group going as well. If you have room for the rich and powerful, you have room for the ones who aren't."

Jameson pressed his lips together, as though he had to hold in the words that wanted to escape. Still, whether it was fear, pragmatics or bureaucracy, he managed to keep himself silent before nodded and walking away.

"Southern mages?" I asked.

"It's a polite way to say mages without money, power or influence."

I frowned as I pieced it together. "So Jameson is just killing off the mages he sees as unimportant?"

"While saving his friends or those who he thinks can give him something in return. I'd love to say this is new behavior, but it isn't." He sighed before taking a moment to unclench his first. "The fact is that the guild's built on the idea of politics and power. It isn't here to help but to rule, to drain the people beneath it of everything they have."

I set my hand on his arm. "I happen to know someone who could burn it to the ground."

He twisted slightly to meet my gaze. "Sorry, Ava, but stone walls don't burn." Still, his tone sounded eased, as if the joke were what he'd really needed.

"I'm serious. Isn't there something we can do?"

"We?"

"Well, I don't have a lot of tricks, but the couple I have are a doozy. You went to hell for me. What's a little war and genocide for you?"

He reached out and caught the front of my jacket before tugging it, pulling me forward and claiming a kiss.

It was odd, as he didn't tend to kiss me in public, not around the guild at least. Jameson had walked up on us, but that had been an accident. I hadn't felt like a dirty secret, more like something valuable that he didn't want others to take advantage of.

Whether he didn't care anymore or just couldn't resist, I wasn't sure.

And when his lips took mine? I didn't care.

Too soon, we broke apart, and a look to my side dried up the lust he'd stoked inside me.

The *entire* room stood there, mouths open, staring at us.

"What are they looking at?" I asked Grant, as if we'd broken an unwritten rule I didn't know about. Was there some prudish no PDA thing in the bylaws? "Am I going to be killed for molesting their precious Magistrate or something?"

Grant laughed, then nodded at the seat beside the main throne. "Well, that little display makes it clear you and I are a set package, that they'd be stupid to try and come against either of us."

"So?"

"So, any hopes they had about trying to backstab me just crumbled away, because now they know I have a reaper guarding my back."

Even though I still hated the term 'reaper', something warm filled me. As I took my spot, as the council stared at Grant and me, and I sat tall, I realized what it was.

Pride.

Maybe I didn't love what I'd become — or what I'd learned I always was — but the looks on their faces screamed the truth loud and clear.

I finally felt useful, as if I had a place that mattered.

Maybe being a reaper wasn't all bad...

Chapter Twelve

The council meeting was far more tedious than I'd prepared myself for. I had thought a room full of magic users would at least have cool special effects. If nothing else, I wanted magical slide shows or *something*. Points made with fireworks and flames and people getting turned to dust.

Instead, as person after person aired their grievances, I had to admit, this was as much fun as an HOA meeting at a senior community.

Tim doesn't cut his hedges enough. Karen lets her kids play outside at seven in the morning on a Sunday and wakes me up. The Kalvery territory keeps creating protection potions to sell and they stink of onions and the scent comes into our territory.

Basically? Adults — or in this case immortals — with the complaints of kindergarten students.

They wanted the council to fix everything, and it was obvious there would be no fix that would actually satisfy them.

Grant remained silent for most of it, though the deep lines in his cheeks said he wasn't a fan of the majority of rulings.

When one group felt another took too many of the new mages, leaving their numbers dwindling, Jameson announced the creation of a sub-committee to look into the problem. When another group complained about vampires killing a few of their members, Jameson said he'd set up a meeting with a representative from the coven.

All in all? After three hours of listening to complaints *no one* looked any happier than they'd been when the thing started. In fact, everyone just seemed worn out. Was this how the guild kept power? By exhausting everyone with so much pointless bureaucracy that they were too annoyed to revolt?

I'd been a life insurance saleswoman before everything had fallen apart in *my* life, so I understood bureaucracy. It wasn't as if I'd never dealt with red tape before. I'd done my share of pointless running around over dumb forms and duplicates and nonsense.

Still, I wasn't sure I'd ever experienced anything as mind-numbingly unproductive as *this* meeting. In fact, at that moment, I would have happily skipped away to fill out a P-147 form in triplicate with notarization if it saved me another minute *here*.

A glance in Grant's direction told me he felt the same, although he had a lot more anger about it than I did. Then again, these weren't *my* people. It was easy to see it and almost laugh at the stupidity, but I hadn't lived it. I hadn't witnessed what it did to the mages not lucky enough to be here, to have the clout to have their voices heard.

Still, the monotony of it all had me yawning.

Sure, it was rude, but I couldn't help it. I'd thought the damn meeting part of our plan would last all of ten minutes before we could escape and get to the *real* action.

I hadn't been prepared to deal with *this*.

Grant offered me a side-eye before rising from his seat.

The room fell silent, the speaking mage freezing as if suddenly in the sights of a much larger predator.

"Let's take a break," Grant said.

"But, Magistrate," Jameson argued before a stern look from Grant stopped whatever he planned to say. Jameson nodded, though he didn't look put in his place. "Of course. I forget you lack the stamina as we have for such meetings."

The subtle-as-a-brick-to-the-face jab didn't faze Grant. "My companion doesn't portal well. I'll make use of the personal chambers here, and we'll meet again in an hour."

Jameson narrowed his eyes, as if he knew it was a ploy but didn't dare say anything.

Grant didn't wait for an answer. He held out a hand to me, which I took happily. *Anything* to get us out of that damn council room.

"Hasn't anyone heard of cushions? I get that the whole 'carved from rock or made from bones' gives a certain aesthetic to things, but I'm telling you, a few throw pillows could really make these things more comfortable." When we were safely down the hallway, away from prying eyes, I rubbed my ass, which had fallen asleep a very long time ago.

Grant reached down to cop a feel that he didn't try to disguise as helping at all. "The meetings didn't always take so long, not when the council was first made."

"Really?"

He nodded. "Believe it or not, the guild was good when they created it. At least, that's what the records say. They had a council of four and the Magistrate. The Magistrate broke ties, kept people on task and the council was made up of mage specialization. Destruction, healing, artifacts and dark. It gave everyone an equal say in how disputes were handled. Below those four were others, who typically handled physical territories, and thus the mages of that type within those areas. They delegated smaller matters so they didn't waste council time on things the lower groups could fix themselves."

I thought back to the squabbling, to the petty problems that all sounded like those annoying first-world issues instead of real complaints. "What happened?"

"What always happens. Some people became entrenched in the system, twisted it for their own gains. Even when I joined, the council only had seven, based on political dealings rather than magic type and territory. Now council members have to have serious connections to get a spot and *never* see those they supposedly represent. It leaves us with a few powerful, untouchable mages and a whole lot of people who get no say."

"Can't it get changed back?"

"Probably not. Even after I took out the entire council, when they could have built *anything* in its place, they twisted the system even more, made it worse than ever. Places of power create vacuums, and they're always filled by people who *want* that power."

He sighed as he waved his hand in front of a large archway in the stone. The action made the rocks float apart to let us pass before reassembling into a solid wall. "I've realized the only people who should lead are ones who don't want to, which is the dig of it all. Anyone who wants to rule isn't qualified, and good luck forcing someone who doesn't want to into that seat."

"You were forced into it…"

He lifted his eyebrow. "And look how well that's gone."

I ignored his good point, especially when I got a look at the place we'd arrived at. Again, it was stone, carved from the rock. Where the council room had been closed in, however, here a large window led to a balcony. There was no glass, and a heated breeze blew into the room.

I went toward it, drawn to see where we might be. Grant had explained that much of mage territory didn't exist in real *places*. At least, not like I understood, on a map of the world. I couldn't point just south of Phoenix and say, 'there it is!' They sat in small pocket universes, places the mages of the old days had carved out. It meant nothing could attack them or gain access.

There was no horizon like I was used to, and the reddish hue of the sky reminded me too much of hell. Beyond where we were, I could see no land, no sea, *nothing*. Peering down and up, I found the face of a mountain rather than the castle I expected. It seemed they'd created the place right inside the rock, carving it out and making rooms from stone inside it.

Grant set a hand on my lower back as he came up beside me. "I remember these halls. I might have lived in that penthouse, but I grew up *here*, in this place, with this sky."

"Why?"

"My father was always working, and I spent my time inside books. I wanted to learn everything I could, to make the most of what I had. This place is the seat of mage power. Not the penthouse, not the place where mages bicker and think that the right last name is power. *Here* is where our ancestors unlocked real power, where they learned how to harness energy, where they wrote it all down. There are whole libraries in this place that haven't been visited in hundreds of years because we've forgotten what real power is."

"You're telling me you haven't gone to see them?"

He shook his head. "There's too much here, more than even an immortal life could ever hope to read. I've probably seen more than any other mage alive, but even for me, it's too much—too vast. It's made for an entire people, not for one person." He blew out a sigh. "Sometimes that's the worst thing for me, knowing how much is here, knowing what we were and what we *could* be again, but then to realize that no one else cares. No one else wants that. They're too busy fighting each other."

I slid my arm around him, staring out at the bleak landscape and the fathomless depths of it. "It could change."

"Maybe. I remember something my father said to me, something that stuck with me. He closed a book I was reading once, snapping it right on my fingers. *'Get your head out of the books and look around,'* he snapped. *'You'll miss everything important.'* I looked at him and told him, *'The man who refuses to read has no benefit over the man who can't read.'* It was something I'd heard when

I was still on the streets, from this old woman who had handed out books to any kid who wanted to read, who had sat there and taught me to read. My father stared at me, as if he hadn't expected me to talk back, and said, *'Things are the way they are, and only a fool tries to go backward.'"* He sighed. "I guess he learned it in the end, though."

I opened my mouth, ready to say something to him. I wanted to reassure him, to tell him I understood, but before I could, he turned around. "All right, let's summon them."

I tore my gaze from the eerie sight outside the window, following Grant back inside.

He held out his arm, and three marks rested on his skin. It was hard to say they hadn't been there before, what with the huge amount of other tattoos present, but it seemed I'd had enough time to memorize each part of his body, because I knew they were different.

He whispered words as he ran his fingers over each mark, a different design for each.

A shimmering circle appeared, one for each mark as he activated them, and through them stepped the three men.

Kase looked as he always did, but *much* better than he had before feeding from Troy. It reassured me that we'd done the right thing. He wore a suit, as always, with his hair pushed back and his skin its normal color. He took a moment to straighten the cuffs on his shirt, an action that made me smile. We were ready to head to a place no one should *ever* go, and there Kase was, still trying to look his best.

Troy, on the other hand, was dressed down. He wore a pair of faded blue jeans and a loose black T-shirt, the sort of thing he'd worn to do yard work — at least when I wasn't lucky enough to see him shirtless. He caught my gaze, his silver eyes intense as if he had *hated* me being somewhere he couldn't get to before.

An answering surge of want ran through me, reminding me that whole mate thing wasn't something to take lightly.

Finally, Hunter walked over to Grant, wearing a T-shirt and jeans with holes in them, looking like a man who really believed his band would take off any day now.

"Everything go well?" Hunter asked.

Grant nodded before rubbing his hand over the marks on his forearm, which disappeared as if they'd never been there in the first place. "Almost perfectly. We've got about forty-five minutes before we're supposed to get back."

"And how far is the circle?"

"From here? Thirty minutes."

"Couldn't you have summoned them directly to the circle?" I asked. "If anyone sees them, I feel like it sort of does away with our whole secrecy thing, and in case you haven't looked in the mirror lately, you all aren't inconspicuous."

Grant shook his head. "The closer to the circle we get, the less reliable portal magic is. The circle at the roof rests on some of the most unstable power lines anywhere. It's why the old mages created this place *here*. Things get weird the closer we get, and magic becomes less predictable."

I frowned. "If there's *more* magic available, why would it work less well?"

"It's like having a blender that needs a certain amount of power to work. If you overload it, if you send too much electricity through, you end up with a spark and maybe a fire."

"So why do you think you can use that power to get us to purgatory, then? If it's that dangerous, why do you think you can do it any better?"

"Worried?" Grant gave me a smirk until I didn't answer. It slid away, as though he'd never considered someone might really worry for him. "Well, I'm not just any mage, Ava. I can handle a lot more volts than your normal magic-wielder."

I wanted to feel reassured, but I really didn't. I'd learned Grant was capable of a lot, but one thing he couldn't seem to do was admit when something was beyond him.

Still, we were here, and there weren't any other options. I had to trust that he could handle it.

Grant went to the back of the room, on the far wall across from the doorway where we'd entered. A picture sat there of someone I didn't recognize but who wore the sort of robes people used for cosplays of Merlin.

Grant set his palm flat against the wall and slid it along the edge of the painting, his expression focused. Finally, he shifted his hand, moving his thumb up along the wall, and a groaning of stones answered him.

The picture faded away, as if it had never been there, and behind it, a darkness so deep, I had an instant moment of '*fuck that nonsense.*' It reminded me of the void, of that crushing moment I'd fallen into it after trying to find Rachel's spirit.

He caught the look. "It's fine, Ava."

"Dark, scary tunnels are rarely fine. In those choose-your-own adventure books, this is considered the obviously bad choice."

He twisted his hand, palm side up, so a small ball of light rested there. He held it out to me, and it rolled from his palm to mine. It was warm and reminded me of a levitating bouncy ball. "The darkness isn't so bad," he told me.

"In my experience, some pretty horrible things happen in the dark." I remembered the nights I'd fallen asleep as a kid, in beds I didn't feel safe in, the times night felt too empty and full at the same time.

He caught my chin so I looked into his green eyes. "Trust me, Ava. I've been through this place a thousand times. *You* are the scariest thing that's been in these tunnels."

I took a deep breath before nodding. I didn't feel like the badass he seemed to think I was, but when had that ever stopped me before? "Into the creepy tunnel we go."

Chapter Thirteen

We walked in the darkness for what felt like forever. The light of the ball Grant had given me didn't stretch far, just enough to see Troy's back. Grant had taken the front, then Troy, me, Kase and Hunter at the back. I suspected it was because Hunter could easily shift into his smoke form to end up wherever he might be needed, and Grant knew the way. The rest of us just piled in between those two.

The tunnels were silent.

Well, silent other than a horrible skittering I tried hard to ignore. It reminded me of a movie I'd seen, where the legs of a spider tapped against a tile floor. I could only imagine the things that might exist in such a place.

And, yes, maybe I was a big-scary-reaper, as Grant would tell me, but even I had my limits, and spiders seemed to be one.

It wasn't just forward, though. We climbed flight after flight of stairs, my calves killing me partway through. Grant had said we were headed for the roof, but I hadn't realized just how far up that was.

Our feet shuffled against the stone floor, and I clutched the light as if it might get away. It didn't give me much of a view, but something was better than nothing, so I cherished it. Grant didn't speak — no one offered anything other than steady breathing, the stroke of our feet against the floor and whatever crawled along the rocks.

Troy stopped in front of me so fast that I ran into his back, the ball escaping me. When it hit the ground, it shattered, a bright flash before fading to nothing.

Panic struck me when I couldn't see *anything*. I felt adrift, cut off, as if I were alone in the black and lost.

Before it had time to gain any real footing, however, a hand caught the back of my neck and a body pressed against me. "You're okay," Kase's smooth voice told me.

I pulled in a shaky breath, the darkness allowing me to catch the brimstone of Hunter, the scent of the forest from Troy.

I'm not alone. Even in the darkness, even when I had no idea which way was forward, I wasn't there by myself.

It let me release the tension, the fear. As soon as I did, Grant whispered something, and light poured into the tunnel. He hadn't performed another light-ball spell, but rather the wall in front of him — which must have been why Troy had stopped as well — parted.

Stepping out of the tunnel felt like sliding into a warm bath — *heavenly*.

At the end, I peered back just before Grant closed it to find *far* too many eyes staring back at me.

Thankfully, I only caught sight of the glow of eyes, because I really didn't want to see what they were.

The new room we found ourselves in was also made of stone but largely empty. A single staircase went up from the center, and a sealed doorway sat on one side. Shimmering sigils that glowed red told me that was a door I did *not* want to fuck with. I would guess that was the normal way into the room, and all that shiny 'stay away' stuff kept people out.

Instead, Grant took the stairs, and the rest of us followed. The steps wound up, far enough that I got winded again after a few minutes. Grant's whole *thirty-minute* trip must have counted on people who were far more in shape than I was.

The ceiling opened at the top, and when we reached the place where no more steps sat, I let out a gasp.

The world stretched out around us. We stood at the top of the mountain — building — whatever it was. Posts rose in arches around the flat top, built of ancient stone yet somehow not crumbling, as if time couldn't touch them. A circle of rocks sat at the center, and even me, with my ability to not feel most magic, couldn't ignore the way it coursed through this place.

Wind whipped through my hair, but it was hot and heavy.

I swallowed down a sickness that the magic caused in me, a reaction that was probably my body's way of telling me to get the fuck out of there.

Grant walked around the circle, whispering, his hand doing more of those practiced movements that normally entranced me.

Not this time, though. The way the sky melted away, the way *nothing* existed beyond the mountain, kept all my attention.

And for once, the others seemed equally enthralled. I didn't feel like the only person surprised or impressed by something they all found normal, as if I were some caveman gushing over a lightbulb. Instead, Kase froze, his eyes wide, an almost youthful expression on his features. Troy had his thumbs tucked into the pockets of his jeans as he stared out, as well.

Hunter crouched, his head tilted as if he were trying to understand it.

Grant gave us little time to take it in, though, before a blast of power knocked me backward — against Troy, or I'd have ended up on my ass.

At the center, where nothing had been a moment before, a portal of swirling blackness stood, and Grant beckoned me toward him.

I placed my hand in his, knowing already what was coming. He used a small knife to slice through my palm, then walked me around the circle, dripping blood on the stones. Each one caused another blast of that power, sounding almost like a gunshot. When we reached the start, when the entire circle had been exposed to my blood, the portal shifted from black to gray, to a bottomless void that beckoned me, as if it knew me.

I took a step, called by it.

Grant caught me. "Not so fast," he said above the howling wind. He took a small vial from his pocket, then dipped his finger into the blood of my palm, collected the ash from the vial, and smeared it onto my forehead.

He whispered more words, a focused, almost pained expression on his face. He repeated the process on Hunter, Troy, Kase then himself, leaving a bloody, ashy thumbprint on each of our foreheads. "The air is toxic," he yelled. "Remember Hunter nearly dying? It'll be worse in our physical forms, so do *not* let that mark rub off. If it does, don't breathe until I reapply it. One lungful of that mist will kill you if you don't have protection."

"What are you doing?" The screaming voice drew my attention back toward the stairs, where Jameson stood, his hair not so pristine now that that the wind had messed it. "This is reckless and dangerous. A portal like this can't be contained, even by you."

"This has to be done," Grant answered.

"You'll kill everyone!"

"They're dead if we don't do something anyway."

Jameson took a step forward, his hand out in warning. "You're too damaged to know what's safe and what isn't. You shouldn't even be able to *open* that portal! You're a mistake that should have been put down when you were created."

As Jameson spoke, other mages came to the top behind him, all of them with wide, terrified eyes. The violence was thick, as if amplified by our proximity to the portal.

The point was clear…they weren't going to let us go.

As much as I trusted Grant and the others, no matter how powerful and dangerous I knew they were, more and more mages poured to the roof, until I saw no way it would be possible to win…

And I somehow doubted that losing was an option that would let us keep our lives.

Grant took a step forward and jammed a finger at Jameson. "*You* made me what I am!"

"I wasn't even on the council then," Jameson argued.

"But it was your type — men who want nothing more than power. You don't get to make monsters, then get upset when we use what *you* turned us into!"

Grant calling himself a monster chafed, but I got the feeling it was true. The looks of horror on the mage's faces, the way Jameson looked at Grant — it all said the same.

He wasn't just some mage. While I didn't understand the details, while I still had no true grasp on what was different about Grant, it was obvious they all knew.

"Close the portal," Jameson yelled, "and I'll let the girl live. She'll get to walk away from here."

Boy was *that* a lie. It was in the way he said it, the slight sneer.

Not that I would have let Grant take that option, since I was pretty sure even the fake mercy toward me didn't extend to any of the others. There wasn't a chance I'd walk out on them.

Grant stood tall. "Not a chance. You want to stick your head in the sand, fine. *I* will do what is needed. Even if I did what you said, even if you let her go, if we don't deal with Lilith, she won't live long anyway."

Jameson curled his lips into an ugly smirk, as if Grant's refusal was exactly what he'd hoped for.

Then again, Grant had explained how one took power in their world. No doubt Jameson saw this as his chance to do away with Grant and seize the Magistrate position on his own.

Jameson lifted his hand, and a flash of white left his palm like a streak of lightning.

Before I could shout in warning, before I could do anything, Grant lifted his hand. The lightning dissipated, fizzling out to nothing.

Fury covered Jameson's features, as if Grant should apologize for daring to still be alive.

Grant didn't stop though. His gaze locked on Jameson. "You've been plotting my death for years."

"You shouldn't rule," Jameson said. "You have no right."

"I have every right!"

"You are an abomination."

"Because the council thought it fit to rip the magic out of orphans? They *couldn't* rip mine away though, could they?"

"A fluke," Jameson answered. "You were just a mistake that never should have happened. If your father had any sense, he'd have killed you the second he realized what you were."

Grant let out a hollow laugh. "No argument here. I am a mistake, but maybe I'm also a consequence, a lesson to you all that you can't do whatever you want without repercussions. The council made me what I am."

Jameson shot his hand out again, with no more luck than the first time. "I'm going to kill you," he assured him. "And I'm going to kill everything you've touched, scorch it from the earth like an infection."

Grant narrowed his eyes, then spoke, his voice soft. "Ava, you and the others should go through the portal."

"I'm not leaving you," I told him.

"I've got long-overdue business here to deal with. You're the one who needs to get to Lilith, not me." He tossed the vial of ash to Kase. "Use this just like I did if it gets wiped off anyone. Go."

Kase exchanged looks with Troy and Hunter, but there wasn't much of a choice.

Grant was the only thing keeping the mages from killing us, and we didn't have a shot against that many in a real fight.

Hunter nodded and went through the portal. Kase and Troy looked back and forth, as if deciding who had to deal with me. It seemed Troy drew the short straw, because Kase stepped through next.

"Come on, Ava," Troy said as he wrapped a hand around my arm.

I pulled, but my strength was nothing compared to his. "I'm not leaving Grant."

"We have to go," Troy said. "Or this will all have been for nothing."

But if I lost Grant, it would be for nothing. The promise I'd made came back to me, when I'd sworn that I'd protect them all as they had me.

I'd lost Gran already. I wasn't going to lose anyone else.

When we neared the portal, I twisted and tried to bring my forearms together, to hit Troy with a blast of power. I'd tossed him before with it.

He must have expected it, because he caught my arms before I managed it, a pointed look on his face saying he didn't appreciate it.

Too bad.

I wasn't a one-trick-pony anymore. I let go of my corporeal form, causing his hands to slide through my arms, for him to lose his grasp. As soon as I became whole again, the action smoother and more practiced than it had been before, I brought my forearms together.

He gave one snarl before the blast hit him and sent him tumbling backward through the portal.

If Grant saw any of it, he showed no sign. He kept his gaze locked on the mages as if the rest of the world had disappeared. It was just him, them and a lot of ugly history.

When Jameson took another step forward, Grant raised both of his hands and a column of fire consumed the mage. It happened so fast, the heat terrifying even as far away as we were.

The wind that had blown the whole time strengthened, enlivened by Grant's magic, by his actions.

Screams erupted from the other mages, full of fear and confusion.

"You think I'm a monster?" Grant screamed into the wind, into the crowd. He held out his hands to his sides, but it wasn't flames that escaped this time. Instead, it was as if he drew something into him, as if he yanked something away.

The wind increased until I struggled to stay on my feet.

Those screams stopped, and that was *worse*. The mages around arched forward, feet rooting in place and bent at unnatural angles.

It was just like the tattoo he'd shown me, as if he'd been trying to tell me something without having to say it. I'd assumed it meant he'd hit them with some sort of magic, but now I realized it depicted him pulling something *from* them.

He was draining them, stealing something from them. Even as the stench of burning flesh from Jameson filled the space, all I could see was the horror and pain on their faces.

They had been planning on killing us all, but still, I couldn't ignore it.

I fought against the wind, even when I was thrown to the ground, when I had to crawl to move forward, my fingers gripping the stones of the floor.

I grabbed his jean jacket to get me to my feet in front of him. His eyes weren't the green I was used to but a bright, almost neon shade. They were empty, too.

Just hunger and anger and pain. Nothing of the jokester I knew, of the passionate man who smirked at me, who had kissed me just hours before.

"Let them go," I screamed.

He lowered his gaze to mine, but I still felt as if I didn't know this person. Was this the real man? The one he'd hidden from me? The part of him that that had peeked through before, but he'd always kept a leash on? Or was it just whatever he was doing? "They were going to kill you," he said as if that explained it all. "They squander the power they have, the power they *stole*, so why should they have it at all?"

I didn't have an answer to that, but it wasn't about *them*. It was about that look in his eyes, about not wanting him to do something that would make him hate himself all the more. I recalled the tattoo, the way he called himself a monster. Doing this would only be him proving to himself that he was nothing else.

I set my hands on his cheeks, forcing him to bring his attention back to me. "Let them go. This isn't you."

"Isn't it?"

I went to my tiptoes and brushed my lips to his. "No, it isn't."

He relaxed just the barest amount, as if giving in, and the collapse of the mages around us signaled that he'd listened.

Not that I planned to wait around for round two. Grant had shown his hand, but people did stupid things when they felt backed into the corner, and I wasn't sure I could talk him down a second time. Instead, I braced my weight and shoved, sending us both sailing backward and into the portal.

And I was reminded…

I really hated portals.

Chapter Fourteen

Darkness crushed me, and I understood what Grant had meant about us not being made to cross the barrier. It felt as if I were attempting to pass through a brick wall, as if existence itself didn't want me to enter.

Still, I pressed forward. I'd come this far — I'd risked and lost so much.

Some stupid barrier wouldn't stop me, not this close to the end.

It seemed like forever before I broke through, before the weight eased off me, but I didn't find myself in some mist-filled horror like my dreams.

Instead, I was trapped in total darkness.

Was this the between Grant had mentioned? The space that separated life and purgatory? The abyss and the void I'd fallen into before?

Not that me being stuck shocked me. I wasn't exactly an all-in sort of girl, the type who knew what I wanted and went after it. My history had been more about being pulled — kicking and screaming, usually — into what I needed.

I'd ignored my real power for as long as possible, until Lucifer himself had forced me into accepting it.

So the fact that I might have a few unresolved feelings that would keep me trapped wasn't exactly new information.

Which meant I needed some sort of great revelation in order to move forward.

So what was it going to be for me? My abandonment issues, my paranoia, my need to use humor to mask my massive insecurities?

It felt like a shitty gameshow with only horrible prizes.

The blackness shifted, taking form into a scene before me. I had to let out a soft laugh when it came into focus, when the memory it showed became clear. It wasn't funny, but damn, it figured.

There I was as child, huddled in that bed, with the man who had abused me walking down the hallway. He had that slow walk, his steps soft and careful and so quiet.

I wasn't the girl in the bed, but that same fear consumed me.

That inability to breathe, the way I'd tried to hold completely still, as if that would convince the man to just leave me alone, all swamped me.

And those damned *steps* wouldn't stop.

Back and forth, as if testing, as if seeing if anything would stop him.

I remembered how during the day, the house had felt so perfect. It was the family I'd wanted all my life, the picture-perfect Christmas-card sort of life.

And me? I'd stayed quiet. It hadn't been fear of him that had kept me silent, but fear of *losing* what I thought was my only chance at being happy.

I'd been willing to give anything for it, to endure anything if it meant getting the life I believed I was supposed to have.

I couldn't get off the track.

Funny, that even when I knew what I needed to do, when I knew this wasn't real, it could pull me in so fully.

It trapped me there, wouldn't let me free.

I could only feel that crushing terror at the steps that never stopped, that neared closer but never arrived, at the shame that I'd been willing to accept anything to just feel loved and wanted and accepted.

A hollow place inside me sank, collapsing in on itself. All the things I'd felt, the ones I'd tried to shove down or ignore, rushed over me.

I'd always be alone, always be that little girl struggling so hard to fit in, to be wanted, willing to do anything if it meant a speck of affection.

No wonder I couldn't find what I wanted...I wasn't worthy of it.

All the times I'd been pushed aside, the times I'd been underestimated and cast out came back to me. Even my own parents hadn't wanted me—they'd thrown me away.

My father was a reaper, as far as I could tell, and my mother was that woman from the vision, one who had dropped me off at a fire station because she couldn't deal with me anymore.

I wasn't supposed to exist, and maybe that was the point—the world couldn't get rid of me, but it could ignore me.

I had *no one*—even Gran had left me. When she could have chosen to fight harder, to stay, she'd given up, too.

The emptiness grew inside me, consuming everything, dragging me down until I saw nothing except the gaping void between me and anyone else.

I was completely and utterly *alone* and always would be—

Hands wrapped around my arms and shook. "Ava!"

I twisted to find whiskey-colored eyes drawing me in.

Hunter.

Just seeing him helped me find the ground beneath my feet.

"I'm alone," I told him, the words empty and full of the fears that had plagued me my entire life.

"You aren't alone, shadow-girl." He captured the nape of my neck.

"I am. I've always been alone, and it's never going to change. I'm not good, and everyone knows it. I'm not supposed to *be* here."

"Course you are."

"There hasn't been anything like me before because I'm wrong."

"Being unique isn't the same thing as being *wrong*. I'm the only hellhound who isn't out there murdering people for fun. Kase is the only vampire as old as he is who isn't sadistic. Grant has power no mage has had before. Troy is annoyingly boring in a way no mortal or immortal has *ever* managed. We're all unique."

His words sank in and reminded me of what I'd somehow forgotten.

Kase. Grant. Troy. Hunter.

I wasn't alone. Somehow, in this place, I'd forgotten that. I'd forgotten *them*. I had people in my life, people who loved me, who had followed me into hell, people who knew exactly what I was and hadn't turned away.

Hunter's lips curled into a smile. "You're getting it, aren't you? You've literally got four possessive and stubborn men who won't leave you be for more than a few hours at a time, so how are you going to stand here and say you're alone?"

I swallowed, trying to push away the sound of those steps.

Something shifted, the scene changing. The bed was gone, a new scene taking its place. It was the day that asshole had died, the day I'd watched him fall down the stairs and break his neck.

Except...

This time something was different. The first time, when I'd lived it, I'd seen it through the eyes of a traumatized child, someone who wanted to see the world in the safest way.

I wasn't that kid anymore. I was an adult, and even if it was hard, I saw the truth now.

Age allowed me to catch what I'd missed before.

A shadow stood beside him, floating, menacing.

A reaper.

The man's eyes widened, just as I remembered, but he didn't fall out of nowhere like I had always thought.

The reaper reached out, curling his fingers into the man's chest, and ripped his spirit free. The man's body collapsed backward, his neck snapping, but his spirit was in the reaper's grasp.

As quickly as it happened, the scene faded away.

Hunter made a soft sound in his throat. "Well, shadow-girl, looks like you weren't quite alone, even then."

Seems that way... Everything twisted around me. The darkness stretched, like a picture bent and folded, and I couldn't find ground beneath my feet. I reached, clutching for something, anything, to hold on to, but found nothing.

It seemed Hunter had unstuck me, had given me what I needed to yank free from the hold. Still, I couldn't find him anywhere, as if he hadn't come with me any farther. Did that mean he'd made it through? I had to hope.

Across the way, a hazy image appeared.

Kase?

He knelt, with the space around him colorless but there. I went toward him, unsure how I even moved when I couldn't find ground.

"Kase?" I shouted but with no luck.

Was this Kase's memory? The part of him that tied him to purgatory, the piece of him that he couldn't seem to move past?

He looked like he always had to me yet...different.

He didn't wear a suit, but rather a simple tunic, one that opened in the center, just below the neck, and had two hanging strings. Dark pants covered his legs, simple and seemingly made of hide.

"Kase?" The smooth voice of another came from the darkness, from the space I couldn't see into.

Kase turned, and I'd never seen an expression like that on his face before.

Fear.

It was all-consuming, an absolute terror that didn't fit at all with the man I knew.

Still, Kase swallowed, his Adam's apple bobbing before he rose to his feet. "Yes, Master, I am here."

Master? Was this the vampire who had made him, the one who had abused and tortured him?

My hands tingled as if I could rip him apart myself.

But he wasn't here. This was only a memory, only a place in Kase's mind where he trapped himself with doubts and regrets and fear.

I tried to follow as Kase walked out of the light, following the one who had made him, but I couldn't. Screams came from the darkness, sickening ones that chilled me to the core. They were Kase's, and they were full of agony, of helplessness.

I rushed blindly through the darkness, trying to find him, needing to intervene even if it was in something that had happened so long ago.

The screams faded away before another sight took its place.

A figure I didn't recognize—a man—walked away from Kase had been. He held his hands out, as if studying them, and they were covered in the dark blood I recognized as vampire. It dripped from his fingers, some running down his forearms.

"He's rather soft," a different voice said.

"Yes, he is," the man with the bloodied hands answered. "But there are some benefits to that."

"If he survives long, I suppose. Still, there's something there, in his eyes sometimes—a fire. I would watch him carefully."

The man with the blood turned, as if planning to return to the room where he'd come from. "You'll see—Kase will be the most interesting of my children."

Everything shifted again, but this time Kase stood there as the man I knew. He wore a suit, one that fit him as I was used to, that showed power and self-control. His hair was perfect, his face without any hint of hesitation.

Even with his screams still echoing in my ears, a sound I wasn't sure I'd ever shake, there was no denying that *this* Kase was the one I knew. This was the man I'd fallen for.

A man knelt, shoulders slumped forward, trembling. "I'm sorry," he babbled around tears.

Kase's expression didn't soften. "You knew the rules. You knew the consequences. You chose to break them and force my hand. Apologies and pleading have no place here."

The man on his knees bent forward, into almost a bow, his head to the floor, his words jumbled. "I wasn't thinking. It was just instinct, nothing more."

Kase gazed down impassively, as if the pleading meant nothing to him. "We vampires are bound by very few rules. Those that we do hold to are without grey area or exception. Do you deny that you turned a human? That you left that fledgling vampire to fend for themselves? That because of that, your fledgling killed humans and threatened the safety and secrecy of the entire coven?"

"It was harder than I realized," the bowed man said. "I thought creating a vampire would be different, that it would be fun. He wouldn't listen, was always complaining, demanded all my time."

Kase's eyes flashed, the only sign of anger he'd shown. "You made a choice—a bad choice—and the fledgling's actions and death are on your head."

The man babbled, but Kase showed no other reaction. He crouched, as if to comfort the vampire, but instead wrapped his hand around the man's throat. He shifted, such a quick motion it had me stumbling backward. Kase dropped the man's bloody throat to the ground as if it were trash, then stood.

The efficiency he showed in killing was terrifying.

I expected the scene to fade, but it didn't. Kase left the body there, the sound of others on the periphery making me suspect he hadn't been alone, that others had dealt with the body.

Once alone, Kase stared down at his hands, at the deep red that covered them, then froze.

He looked so much like his maker had after those horrendous screams…

The world shifted once more, and it was Kase on the ground again, just like it had started.

It looped, over and over — his torture, then his killing of that vampire. Time and time again, it showed the two scenes, and no matter how much I screamed, what I did, it never seemed to change. He was trapped there, between his own monster and his fear that he had become what he'd hated.

A sigh had me turning to find yet another version of Kase sitting in the driver seat of a car.

Everything else was so weird, I didn't question it before opening the passenger door and sliding in.

Across the street was Gran's shop, and through the window?

Me.

"It never changes," he said.

I looked around as if he'd spoken to someone else. The other versions hadn't noticed me, hadn't heard me.

No one else was there, though.

"You aren't your maker," I told him when I decided he must have spoken to me.

"No—I'm worse. He did what he did out of pleasure. He *enjoyed* inflicting pain, was driven by it."

"How does that make him better?

"Because he didn't know better. He was like an animal, reacting because it was all he knew. Me?" Kase shook his head. "I know better, but still I end lives. I do the same monstrous things he did, but pretend they aren't as bad."

"That's not true," I assured him.

He made a soft sound, one that said he didn't believe me. Even as we sat there, the sounds from the loops continued somewhere behind me. Kase's horrible screams, the babbling of the man, the sickening crunch as Kase tore his throat free.

"What are you doing here?" I asked him instead. This scene had to mean something if he saw it.

He nodded across the way, at the other me, who seemed so much sadder than I realized. Was that really how I'd looked before? "She's mine."

I ignored the flutter at the statement, because in *this* context, it was less sweet and more extremely creepy. While I wasn't sure when this was, staring at women through windows from dark cars wasn't the sign of a well-adjusted person.

"Pretty sure she isn't."

He didn't take his eyes from the other me, as if he couldn't. "She is. I knew it the first time I saw her, *felt* it. I haven't felt anything in so long."

"Are you sure it wasn't just that you ate someone bad?"

"I was told a long time ago that if I held on, I'd meet the one I was waiting for, the one it would be worth it for. It's her."

That was oddly sweet, even if it was still creepy. I supposed it might be an old-dog-new-trick situation. Kase came from a time when just declaring ownership over a woman made it true.

"So why don't you talk to her?"

"Because I have nothing to say to her." He stared down at his hands, and despite them being clean, I had no doubt he saw the blood from before. "What if I'm nothing more than *this*? What is the point in meeting her, in speaking to her, if I have nothing else to offer?" He dropped his hands to his lap. "Just knowing she exists, maybe that's enough."

It isn't enough for me. I tried to imagine what would have happened if he'd left it like that, if he'd never hired me that first night, if I didn't know him as I did now.

Empty.

It felt like the abyss, like that blackness outside the image of him.

He blew out a breath before shifting and looking at me. How he didn't recognize me, I wasn't sure, but he didn't seem to. "Do you ever feel trapped? As if everything in your life is headed one way and nothing you can do will change it?"

I thought back to before I'd met him, to when each day had felt like a repeat of the one before. "Yeah. It feels like you're on this track and nothing matters. You're always going to end up in the same place whether you like it or not."

He nodded. "Exactly. I think I learned early where I was headed, and no matter what, that's where I am always going to go. I've tried to change, to shift my direction, but I just feel closer and closer to that same place." In his eyes, I saw where his endpoint was, at least the one he thought of.

"You aren't your maker. You won't ever be him."

He tilted his head, as if the comment was unexpected. "Maybe."

His phone rang and he frowned at it. He answered, and after a moment, he hung up. "Maybe," he said softly, again. "Maybe fate has a few more twists left." After that, he made one more call. Inside, Gran looked at her phone, then answered. She stepped aside, out of earshot of the other me.

"It seems I need to hire that mortal acquaintance of yours," he said.

Gran's laughter was like a whiff of apple pie—something that took me straight back home, to a feeling of safety and happiness. "Finally sick of pretending that it isn't *her*?"

He made a soft sound full of annoyance. "It isn't like that. I simply need her for a job. We have a missing vampire, named Olin, and I require her skills to find him."

The name hit me, let me place the time. This had to be the night before Kase had shown up at my house for help...

When he hung up, after Gran gave him my address—the meddling woman—Kase looked at me. "Nothing really changes. I don't know why I thought she would make it all different."

I reached out and grabbed his arm, surprised when I could, when I didn't pass through him. Was this the *real* him? Or just a stronger, fractured part of him? "It does change. It *did* change. You aren't the person you're afraid of."

"How do you know?"

"Because I know you. I've seen you."

"I've killed people."

"So? In my world now, anyone who hasn't killed people is suspicious. You don't enjoy killing, and you don't do it for no reason."

"What if I end up hurting her? What if after all that waiting, I didn't learn enough, I'm not good enough, and I lose her because I hurt her? Or because she realizes what I am?"

"That won't happen. Kase, I know exactly who and what you are."

"And what is that?" He didn't ask it like a challenge, but rather like a real question, as if he desperately needed that answer but didn't know what it was.

And there was only one answer that would work. "You're *mine*," I told him. "You're the person who dragged me kicking and screaming into this world, who changed where I was headed when I didn't think anything could."

He blinked slowly, then, after a moment, frowned. "Ava?"

I leaned in to kiss him, wanting to prove it was me, but when I did, I tumbled forward into the empty darkness.

Was that a good sign? Did that mean he'd traversed the abyss around limbo? That he'd broken through and reached the other side?

I wanted to know, but I had no time to worry.

Instead, a roar I recognized echoed through the darkness, so loud I pressed my hands over my ears to try and block it out.

And in front of me?

A scene somehow even worse than Kase, perhaps because I hadn't been forced to witness Kase's pain, but only to hear it.

Troy was on the ground, blood covering him, a body clutched in his arms, his body shifted and crazed.

Troy cradled the body of his murdered mate.

Chapter Fifteen

The woman was beautiful, or at least she had been before someone had torn her apart. She'd had long blonde hair that now had splotches of red, and tan skin that made her look like she'd lived by the beach her whole life.

It was strange to see Troy there, broken and clutching her lifeless form.

Troy was my neighbor — well, he was a lot more than that now — but to think of him having had a mate before? Of him being romantic, of him having a strange domestic life?

It felt odd.

And voyeuristic in a not-fun-and-sexy way.

Troy had never talked about his mate beyond telling me how she had died. I hadn't ever pushed because it wasn't my place.

Seeing him there, though, it made it clear that perhaps I should have asked. Maybe I should have made an effort to understand that part of his life.

I'd always been the sort to move on, to not dwell in the past, but maybe he needed that.

Then I thought about Gran, about how I didn't want to let her fade to nothing, and I guessed that before her, I'd never had anyone I wanted to remember.

Just because she wasn't living didn't mean she was gone from him, and if anyone understood that, it should have been me...

I dropped to my knees beside him. He had his face buried against her neck, his shoulders trembling.

"Hey," I said, voice soft.

He ignored me. Would this be like it had been with Kase? Would I eventually find a version of him that wasn't locked in the past?

He sobbed, broken, not fully human noises, as if both he and his wolf mourned together.

"She was beautiful." Troy's voice from behind me made me twist to find him dressed as he had been before, watching the other him hold their dead mate.

I didn't rise, but nodded. "She was."

He let out a long sigh. "I should have never thought I could keep her safe. Humans are *so* fragile."

Boy, wasn't that the truth? It seemed anything could take them out, as if the world were just waiting to off a few more.

I thought about falling in love with one and shuddered. Maybe there was a benefit to falling for immortals. Sure, the ones I had chosen were exceptionally frustrating, but even with how strong they were, I worried constantly about something happening to them.

How would it work if they were as easily damaged as mortals?

"You tried your best," I said, not sure what else to say.

"I did, and it wasn't good enough. She only had the enemies I made, and I still couldn't keep her safe."

It was then I realized how poorly I'd chosen my pep talk.

Troy wasn't blaming himself because he thought he could have done something different. He was blaming himself because he knew he'd done everything and had *still* failed.

That was far worse.

If I played a game and kicked a soccer ball, missing the goal, I could train and hope to do better. If I tried to play the game against Troy, who was faster and stronger than I'd ever be, well, that was the time to throw in the towel all together.

Which suddenly made sense of his reluctance.

"I thought we got over this," I said, frustration eating at me, a fear that we never would fully move past this fear of his.

"Clearly not."

Right. If he was trapped here, before making it into limbo, then he hadn't let go of that. It was a tether that held him between the two realms.

The Troy who held his mate made that awful sound again, something from the depths of his soul, as if being torn apart himself. It wasn't looped like Kase was, but rather a seemingly never-ending moment, trapped between one second and the next with nothing but that anguish to fill it.

"It almost killed me," the other Troy said, voice calm. "After she died, when I moved away from the pack, I didn't eat for days. Maybe weeks? I was just a skeleton then, just waiting for something to take me."

I wanted to grab him, to shake him in anger at trying to let go. However, that wouldn't help. My anger wouldn't unstick him any faster, so I tried to stay focused.

"But you didn't die," I said.

"I didn't." His shoulders sank as if that were a failing of his. "A woman I didn't know at the time took me to a meeting for people who had lost their spouses."

"At the time?" A suspicion crept in.

He nodded. "Gran had her influence everywhere. She dragged me from the house and to that meeting."

I thought back to when I'd been house hunting, to how she'd all but thrown me into the car and given the real estate agent the address to the house I'd ended up falling in love with and buying.

It made me let out a soft laugh at the way she seemed to have a handle on it all so long before I'd even understood there was something to know.

Of course, it also dug in that sorrow a bit more, because I no longer had her looking out for me. I didn't have her hand there, guiding the pieces together, keeping things moving the right way.

Now I was on my own.

I thought back to the tunnel and shook my head. I was *not* alone.

"And the group fixed you?"

"No. There isn't any fixing a pain that deep."

"So what changed?"

"I listened to a man who talked about how his wife's killer hadn't been caught. It made me think about how horrible that had to be. You see, I dealt with Sasha's killer. I went to bed knowing he wasn't breathing, that he didn't get to go on while she didn't. That meeting made me realize that while I couldn't bring Sasha back,

I *could* give that peace of mind to others by dealing with criminals."

"And that's why you became a cop?"

He nodded. "I was able to get the right documents for an identification, easily passed the tests and went through all the training. It's what saved me, or at least what let me hang on." He stared over at her lifeless body. "She would have been proud of what I'm doing. She always wanted to do something good, was the type of woman who put bird seed out every morning because she didn't want them to ever go hungry, you know?"

That figured. Troy would have fit with a woman like that. Two noble, honestly good people.

It made me wonder how I was supposed to fit with him. He'd gone from some sunshine woman who fed the birds to a reaper who took out a bush in the front yard because the birds would sit on it and chirp and wake her — *me* — up.

However, this wasn't *my* mental breakdown — it was Troy's. I needed to focus on him and his problems, because only one person could lose their shit at a time and this was his turn.

"She would be proud," I said, unsure what else to add. I knew what held him back was due to his mate, but what exactly was I supposed to do? He seemed okay, seemed to accept that he couldn't have changed the outcome, had even found a way to try and carry on her memory, so what else was stopping him from crossing over?

I frowned as I turned back to the other Troy to find something changed.

He crouched over a body, shifted and looking monstrous, but it wasn't his mate.

It was…*me*?

It took a moment to realize that it wasn't a random image. It wasn't a fantasy. This had to have been after I passed out, when I'd pushed Lilith's presence from him.

He trembled as he had before, nuzzling me as if that would bring me to life again.

And that was when I understood. He had let go of his old mate, but he hadn't let go of the fear that it would happen again, that he wouldn't survive it a second time, that he might be the cause once again.

Which was why *this* scene mattered so much to him. He hadn't known if I'd live or not, only knowing that he'd nearly killed me, and that I might have been hurt or worse trying to save him.

What tethered him was the fear of going through it a second time…

"What would life be like if you'd never met her?" I asked.

A frown touched his features. "Empty, but less painful."

"You say that because you don't understand what it's like to be alone." I stared at the other him, at the broken man who seemed to clutch to his mate as if by holding her, he could change what was. "I spent my entire life alone, wanting nothing more than to have someone there. I went to sleep at night knowing that if I slid out through the window and disappeared, no one would care. No one would shed a tear or miss me."

"I saw you after Gran died. Do you really think *that* is better? That pain?"

I considered how it felt when I'd met Gran, when I'd had *someone* who cared about me, someone I cared about. Even with the pain from her loss, the answer was easy. "It was completely worth it."

He shook his head. "A mate is different. How would you feel if you lost *me*?"

And *that* hit differently. He was right…

My lungs froze at the question, at all the *fuck that* which rushed through me.

But he'd made his point.

Losing Gran had felt like a shaking of my foundation, but to lose Troy? I thought back to when the reaper had charged them, to the fear that had swamped me as I'd watched them fight a losing battle.

What if the worst had happened? What if Troy had fallen—if they'd *all* fallen and I hadn't been able to save them?

Still, even with how deep that hit me, with how terrifying the idea was, it didn't change anything.

I rose to my feet and faced Troy. "I almost lost you more than once so far, but I'm still *here*, aren't I? Every time we do any of this together, I know something could happen to you, but I'm still not giving you up."

"How do you do that?"

"Because I've been without. I've lived alone, and there isn't anything worse than that."

He let out a sigh. "What does it matter, anyway? It isn't as if I could let you go. I've shown that, haven't I?"

"If you knew it for sure, you wouldn't be stuck *here*. If you're here, then there is some part of you that can't let it go."

"So how do I let it go?"

I thought back to when I was trapped, to my own little piece of the abyss, to how I'd forgotten everything that mattered and focused only on that fear. "You look at me and you make the choice. Stop reacting, stop pretending this is all preordained. We might be mates, but you have to choose that."

He took a deep breath, as if steeling himself, before he lifted his gaze to mine. I hadn't realized how much I'd missed his silver eyes, the slightest hint of blue there. It hadn't been that long since I'd seen him, but somehow this was different.

It took me back to our date, to his hesitation, to it all. He'd tried to accept me, to accept our connection, the uncertainty of it all, but some part of him hadn't. Some piece of him had wanted the date to prove something, to show we could be normal, that we didn't have to succumb to what he'd been through before.

And it all came down to a similar fear, at its core.

His wolf. That shine that happened in his eyes, when his body twisted, when he became something else. It wasn't just that he was afraid of hurting me, but that he was afraid of his wolf. He blamed his wolf for his mate's death, for dragging her into a world that had killed her and not being strong enough to stop it. He blamed the wolf for the fears about me, for everything wrong in his life.

I glanced to the side and saw it—a shadow there, a darkness in a form I recognized. His wolf didn't frighten me. It never really had.

I rose to go there, but Troy grabbed my hand. His eyes were wide, pleading in them. "Don't," he whispered.

"I'm not afraid of it."

"You should be. If I'd been normal, if I'd been human, she wouldn't have died. You wouldn't have almost died."

I tugged my hand away from him, then crossed the darkness until I stood before the creature. It looked more massive than before, the claws longer, the body more misshapen. This was every bit the monster Troy saw it as, as if his human form forced it to normalize somewhat.

It stood almost two feet taller than I was, making me to crane my neck up. "Is this what you really look like?"

It chuffed, a soft sound that reminded me I wouldn't be having any big verbal heart-to-hearts with it.

I reached, but Troy called from me behind me. "Don't touch it!"

I twisted to stare at him, to see the agony on his face, the fear. His voice came out like a desperate plea. "If I didn't have that, I could have had a happy life. Don't you get that? It's all its fault, everything. Sasha wouldn't have died because I wouldn't have been in that world. I could have settled down with her, I could have had children, had the life I wanted."

I had no idea if my next words would help or not, but what was there to lose at this point? I had to shake Troy loose of this or he wouldn't ever get out. "You wouldn't have me either. I'm *not* human, Troy. I'm not mortal. I'm not of that world. If you were, you wouldn't have been there to help me, to protect me, to fight with me."

He pressed his lips together as if he knew he couldn't argue. I wasn't trying to pit his old mate against me, as if it were one or the other. I was only trying to show that not everything from his wolf side was as horrible as he thought.

"You wouldn't have had Sasha either. She was your mate, bound to you because of your wolf. Your wolf picked her, in fact, from what you told me."

He swallowed hard, his throat moving, that same fear consuming his eyes. I turned from him, staring up at his wolf, at the eyes that were familiar yet different. They were brighter, like twin flashlights, but still held a hint of that silver color. It hadn't moved closer, hadn't done anything but stare.

The issue of losing Sasha or the fear of losing me wasn't the real thing that had him stuck, as it turned out. It was *this* battle. It was him against his wolf, unable to accept a huge part of himself. Perhaps he hadn't chosen it, hadn't wanted it, but that didn't change that his wolf was as much him as his human side, now. They were bound, and if Troy couldn't accept that, if he couldn't embrace his wolf, he'd never get out of the abyss.

But how was I supposed to get him to do that? He'd spent the decades since he'd been changed hating himself. It felt like someone trying to convince me that my ass was a benefit after I'd grown up looking in the mirror and trying on pants, cursing the damn thing.

I had to try, though. I reached out, slowly, before setting a hand on the wolf's furred chest. It reminded me just how large it was, how far up I had to reach. I wondered, if he ever really accepted this part of him, would he look like this? Or was this only the reality of his beast, and he'd always be a combination of the two, even when transformed?

The fur was thicker than when he shifted, and softer. The muscles beneath were hard and entirely still, as if he didn't move out of fear of losing the touch. Perhaps his wolf was as afraid as he was, sure I'd reject them both. Then again, while the wolf seemed to lack much language, I couldn't imagine it would be all that confident, given Troy's feelings.

Maybe what they really needed was couples therapy. I wasn't sure what sort of masochist would sit down to try and sort out their problems, but I'd pay good money to watch them untangle all the doubt and bullshit between these two.

The wolf rumbled — not a growl, but almost a whine. It was the sound a dog made when wanting to tempt someone closer.

"I'm not afraid of you," I said, surprised by just how much I meant it. Yes, the beast was terrifying. It was huge, with claws that could disembowel me with ease and teeth that would give a saber-tooth tiger some fears of inadequacy, but that didn't matter. Then again, Troy had accepted my reaper side, so maybe we had a deeper trust than either of us had realized.

Besides, I knew his wolf. I recalled the times I'd slept with Troy, when near the end those bright eyes would look out at me, when his claws would lengthen, when I'd feel fur against my back. It was never to this extent, and he always tried to hide the slight signs of change, but I still knew I'd been with his wolf this whole time, and it had never hurt me.

I moved in closer, rewarded with its crouching so it was nearer my height. Of course, that brought those massive fangs inches from my face, but I didn't recoil. Instead, I took my hand and traced the features.

The muzzle, that didn't appear human at all, the snout, the large, glowing eyes. It looked much more canine, but not entirely. I saw the wolf resemblance far more in this way, the ears that stood tall, the whiskers over the muzzle. When I let go of all my preconceived notions, I had to admit — it was beautiful.

Yes, it was lethal, and monstrous, and not at all human. The arms were longer, the hands much larger, the claws that tipped the fingers sharp and so deep black that they shone. It was everything Troy feared, but that didn't change that the wolf was as much my mate as the man.

"Did you ever show Sasha this? Did you ever really let her see your wolf?"

Troy, from behind me, spoke softly. "No. I fought it, every step of the way. I left during full moons, kept the lights dark if we were intimate."

I grinned at his phrasing but let it be. Troy was an old-school gentleman at heart, and even though I'd had sex with him and a vampire at the same time, it seemed we were going to use the term 'intimate' when discussing such things.

No jealousy happened, though. How could I be jealous? Him having loved another woman before didn't change what I had with him.

The wolf made another soft sound, one that screamed exhaustion. Then again, who wouldn't be tired? It had picked two mates, and both times Troy had done everything he could to keep the wolf from them, to lock it away.

The date made sense, again, and his reaction when I'd suggested we didn't need it. He'd been trying to put me into the same box he'd done with his old mate, trying to fit us into this perfect mold where we were normal humans, and his wolf could have no part of it.

Which simply wasn't the truth.

I stepped closer, until I was nearly enveloped by the wolf's large body, its heat warming me. It smelled of the forest, the things I had smelled from Troy, but stronger. It made a soft noise deep in its chest, as if reassuring me.

Which I understood. I was closing in on something that could kill me in moments, something used to everything being terrified of it, and it wanted to make me feel safe.

I slid both my hands over its shoulders, over the massive expanse of its chest, up its neck, taking in the entirely foreign shape of its body. *This* was my mate.

It was as instinctual as when Troy had bitten me, a connection that went so much deeper than I knew existed. Troy might see himself and his wolf as different — and clearly they were — but they were also part of the same being and they were both my mate. I couldn't separate them, couldn't love or want one without the other.

I dug my fingers into it and crossed the last scant inches of distance, burying my face against its neck, breathing it in, nuzzling against the softness of its fur. The noise it made was full of contentment, and those long arms came back around me, possessive and hungry, as if it had been waiting for this the entire time.

It was a surrender, an acknowledgment that I wanted it as much as I wanted Troy. I got that, didn't I? The feeling of being unwanted sucked, and Troy's wolf had suffered through that the entire time Troy had been a werewolf. Always shoved aside, always hated.

The wolf ran its snout against my cheek, its warm breath tickling as it nuzzled back, moving over my throat, my collarbone, between my breasts. It almost seemed like this was a claiming of its own. It returned to the crook of my neck, where Troy had bitten — or had it been the wolf? — and licked there, the action sending a wave of pleasure through me.

Which was one hell of a thing. Fucking Troy partially shifted was one thing, but taking the wolf like this would be an entirely different level of kink.

Was I ready for that?

Jayce Carter

I wanted to say no, as in *of course* that was too far, but the way I clutched him tighter said the answer wasn't so cut-and-dried.

Not that I needed to come to terms with my feelings on it right then, since Troy set a hand on my back — the human Troy, not his wolf.

A Troy-wolf sandwich didn't sound half bad, either…

I twisted just enough to see his face, some of the lines of tension gone. He pressed a soft kiss to my lips at the same moment his wolf nipped the bite mark.

It was a moment of surrender for us *all*. Me, into being the mate to both, Troy from his fears or need to distance himself from his wolf and the beast for being accepted.

As much as I would have loved to see just what that could mean for the three of us, everything dissolved around me, Troy and the wolf turning to dust, as I was cast into yet another scene.

And I had a feeling the next wouldn't get me any closer to a kinky threesome.

Chapter Sixteen

This had to be the last stop. I'd seen Kase and Troy, waded through their problems and faced down my own. Hunter had appeared in mine, making me suspect that he wasn't stuck himself. It meant that when the darkness took shape once more, I wasn't surprised to find Grant.

He sat on a ledge, looking as casual as ever, as if the craziness of the world couldn't reach him. In fact, he almost seemed at ease in it.

I waited for something horrible to happen, something that would keep me up at night after having to relive it with him.

Instead, Grant patted the seat next to him. "Come on, Ava. Show's about to start."

That made me pause. The others hadn't recognized me at first.

Grant gave me a tired smile. "I'm a mage, Ava. I sure as hell know how to deal with a bit of mind-fuckery like this. I've spent a lot of time in altered states, so I'm pretty good at identifying and staying in control when it happens."

I went over and sat on the ledge beside Grant, a little surprised it remained solid. I'd partly expected to end up on my ass when the ledge turned out to not really be there. The rules of the abyss didn't make a lot of sense to me.

"So, did everyone else make it?"

I nodded. "Wasn't easy—everyone but Hunter got stuck."

"Hunter's too stupid to get trapped. You need a lot more brain cells that he has to be conflicted enough to get stuck." His snarky comment had me elbowing him. He offered a half-hearted smile. "He wasn't ever mortal, so I'd guess that's why he can't get stuck. I'm glad they're safe, though. You, too."

The moment was oddly quiet—almost peaceful. It lacked the fear of the others, the loudness and busyness of them. Then again, both of us knew what would happen, how this worked. Maybe because we expected some horrible revelation, there was no reason to stress.

I was about to ask him what was supposed to happen when something skirted across me like a wave of electricity.

"Looks like it's the matinee show," Grant said on a sigh.

In front of us, the picture came to life. A scrawny kid appeared, and those green eyes gave Grant away, even if I hadn't recognized him from the painting.

He was skinny and on edge, reminding me of a feral cat. He had the wariness of a person used to being kicked, of someone watching for it.

It was the same spark I knew from him, though. Grant was tenacious, someone used to fighting as hard as he had to in order to survive.

The kid walked, glancing from side to side. He was clean, but the scratches and bruises on his skin suggested the washing was a new thing.

"What's your name?" a man asked, and when he came into view, I recognized him. The man from the painting — the Magistrate and Grant's 'father'.

"Grant," the kid said, pulling his shoulders back, his chin lifted.

"What's this?" I asked.

"I told you how mages could get power, didn't I?"

I thought back to when I'd asked him about it, to what he'd told me about the forbidden method.

Unease filled me. "They steal it from kids."

He nodded. "They got us off the streets from a bunch of different cities like some big sweep. There were at least thirty of us, all thinking we'd won the lottery by being picked. We'd been living in nothing, scraping by, and here we were — food, clean clothing, finally thinking we'd found a place."

I knew that feeling, and how crushing it was when it didn't turn out to be true...

"You're special," the Magistrate said, and when Grant didn't answer, he offered a cruel smile. "You know that, don't you? You can do things others can't."

The kid narrowed his eyes at the Magistrate.

"I knew he was bad," Grant said. "I lived with nothing, so I damn well knew how to tell when a person was bullshitting me. You learned that on the streets, knew who was offering things just because they had bad things planned. He was the most dangerous type of dog. See, the ones that snarl and bark, they're not so bad. It's the quiet ones you have to watch out for, the ones who don't give you any warning before they tear your arm off."

Even as Grant talked to me, the image still moved. The Magistrate spoke and young Grant watched him with suspicion. The Magistrate came forward and set a hand on the boy's chest.

"They sucked the magic out of each of the kids who walked in before me and tossed the bodies into a firepit out back, like trash they no longer needed."

The boy arched backward, reminding me of what I'd seen from Grant on that roof.

Except, where they'd been unable to fight back, young Grant closed his hands into fists and jerked away. The bond between him and the Magistrate broke, and the Magistrate fell, eyes wide.

"What was that?" I asked.

"Do you know why I survived on the streets when so few kids did? Because I'm stubborn. Because I used everything I had to keep on living, to scrape by, no matter what was thrown at me. Often, it was my magic that gave me that edge. When I realized that the Magistrate was trying to steal it, I was furious. That was *mine*. It was all I had to my name, all that was mine and mine alone, and I lost my temper when he tried to take it."

"What does that mean? Is that why you're different?"

He nodded. "When the Magistrate tried to steal my magic, he left a wound. It was as if the space where my magic fits against me was torn. When I refused to let him have it—which no other mage has ever done—the wound healed with..." He sighed, as if trying to figure out how to phrase it. "Think of it like thick scar tissue.

It adhered the power to my soul, made my grasp on my magic stronger than it should be."

"And that made you more powerful?"

"No," he said softly. "The power came later. I knew what the Magistrate was, what the whole council was. They drained those kids and so many before them and split the power among themselves to help them stay in power. He kept me, like a pet, because I intrigued him. I was different, and he thought he could use me, make me his heir and turn me into his perfect little puppet. The Magistrate swore he'd stopped the practice of stealing magic after me, but I found out that wasn't true. I think maybe I always knew it, but it wasn't until I found one of the rejects that I knew for sure. See, most kids die in the process, but a few unlucky ones survive it as a shell of their old self. That's what I found, this girl, no older than seven, who just sat there in a hidden area of the guild, rocking back and forth, fingers shifting in the motion to make a ward but without the magic to do it. I realized he'd never stopped, that he never would, that he'd always steal from others and it wouldn't ever end unless I ended it."

The image shifted to an adult Grant. He had no tattoos, telling me this had happened a long time ago. His steps were hard, striking the stones I recognized. *The Jade Room.*

So much anger rested in his green eyes despite his face showing none of it. Then again, Grant had always been good at hiding what he thought. It was probably a lesson he'd learned young. Keeping things to himself was safer.

"Grant," the Magistrate said, the council room coming into sight with the others seated at those tables and benches. "I wasn't expecting you. Is there a problem?"

Grant walked up the center of the room until he stood before the Magistrate, who sat on that stone seat. "You didn't stop," Grant said. "You said you would, but you didn't."

"What do you mean?"

"I *found* her."

They stared at one another for a moment, a tense silence as if no one wanted to interrupt the exchange, to break first.

Finally, the Magistrate smiled without a speck of regret on his face. "Of course we didn't. Why would we stop doing something that makes us more powerful?" He offered such a condescending look, one that said Grant was still a child who needed to grow up and understand the world. "You understand what power does for people—it's why you spend every day nose-deep in old books. The difference is that you're trying to make use of a limited pool, whereas I'm willing to do what it takes to gain actual power."

"At the cost of innocent lives?"

"There are no innocent lives. There are people who haven't betrayed you *yet*. That is all. If those mages gain immortality, if we allow them to learn and grow, then they'll reach the point where they become a risk to you. That's how life works. Better to put them down early and take what you need to protect yourself."

Grant didn't move, staring at the Magistrate as if everything were sliding together, some puzzle he hadn't fully understood.

The real Grant spoke with a soft voice beside me. "I knew I'd end up killing him, even from that first day I met him. I never loved him, never cared for him. He was useful, taught me a lot, but at the most, I respected him for what he knew. Still, I never doubted I'd end up killing him for what he did to those others, for what he did to me." Grant rubbed his chest with the heel of his palm. "I can *feel* that scar tissue inside me. It's twisted, and it hurts when I use magic, and *he* did that to me. Magic is supposed to be a part of a mage, something inside us that is easy. He changed that in me, broke me. He kept me around because he had no idea what it would mean for me, what I'd be capable of. If he'd known what it would turn me into, I bet he would have killed me on the spot."

"What did it turn you into?"

"Most people can't steal the magic of an adult mage, especially an immortal, because it's entrenched too deeply, connected too strongly to the mage. If someone tried to pull it free, they'd damage themselves and their own magic." He dug his palm against his chest harder. "But that scar tissue adhered my magic to me in a different way, in a way that won't break."

"Which is how you could do that on the roof?"

He nodded. "I had no idea I *could* do it until I was there, in front of the Magistrate. I remembered how it felt when he'd tried to take my magic, and I just did it back. It was automatic."

In front of us, the same thing I'd seen on the roof happened again. That horror on the mages' faces, a realization that something they didn't think possible could happen.

"They lived their entire lives in power, given everything by the ones who came before, so sure they'd always have their precious status. They crushed others beneath them just to keep it, and that was the *first* time any of them felt helpless. I wanted them to feel what those kids felt—I wanted to take from them what they stole. They didn't deserve to keep it. I would have given it back if I could, but even the kids who'd survived could never have the magic returned."

The scene was horrific. Whereas I had stopped him on the roof, I could do nothing but watch this time, watch as Grant tore the mages' magic away.

It was hideous. The fact that the mages were monsters didn't faze me, and even them dying wasn't any sort of hang-up for me. Instead, it was watching Grant do it. It was knowing he would carry those scars with him, worse than the one left on his magic.

This was the moment he'd decided he was a monster, that he was damaged, that he was some abomination who didn't deserve to exist.

It hit me how well we matched in that belief.

I recalled Hunter's words to me when I'd been deep within that pit, when I'd struggled because I felt that, at my core, I was *wrong*.

Here was Grant's moment when he had told himself the same.

"They needed to die," I said, even though I wasn't sure I fully believed it. It was easy to say people should be dead but harder to watch it, to see them killed not in self-defense but as retribution.

"Yeah," he said with a nod. "I know it. If I hadn't ended them all, they'd have kept doing it. They'd have killed countless other kids, used that power to hurt more mages. It was the right thing to do."

"So why is it trapping you here?"

"Because I didn't do it by turning them to ash. If I'd done it the good old-fashioned way, with normal magic, it would have been part of life. I killed them by doing something that shouldn't be possible, though."

The mages fell, one by one, until only the Magistrate remained on his feet. The bodies were limp, clearly dead, all except his father.

"I could have let him go," Grant said. "I'd made my point. I'd stolen enough of his magic that he wouldn't have been a danger to anyone ever again. I could have just stopped right there."

"But you couldn't because of that girl?" I guessed, recalling how he'd talked about that young girl he'd found.

"Would it make it better if I said it was because of her? Because it wasn't. It was because of me. I thought about how things could have been different. They could have taken in those children, given us homes and training and lives. I got it all after they'd already screwed me up, but what if they hadn't done that? What if they actually took care of those kids? We'd have more numbers, better adjusted members, and we'd take care of our own. I stood there thinking about everything he'd stolen from me."

"What-ifs are the worst," I acknowledged. "The world always seems better when you think about what could have happened. I used to think about that, how if I were just normal, how different things would have been. My mom wouldn't have abandoned me, I wouldn't have been ostracized—I'd have had friends, family."

Grant nodded. "If I hadn't been broken as a kid, I would have become a healer, I think. I always wanted to learn healing magic, to do something good. I would have focused on trying to fix the system, on helping those who needed it."

"Why don't you do that now?"

He turned to cast me a look, eyebrow raised. "Turns out healing isn't my thing. I'm pretty much set in destruction magic."

"You can set wards. That's protection, at least."

He snorted softly. "You're pretty good at finding the silver lining, aren't you?"

"I'm serious," I said. "Just because you're better at one thing doesn't mean it's what you have to do."

"We're all stuck with what we're born into," he said.

"No, we aren't. I'm a reaper, right? Last I checked, I'm not ripping spirits from bodies and escorting them to the afterworld."

He snorted softly as the scene replayed with him a child again, caught in that loop. "I don't even know what it would mean for me to do something different."

"Well, think about it. If you could do anything, what would it be?" He opened his mouth, and I knew it would be to say something dismissive, so I shouldered him. "I'm serious. We get back home tomorrow—what would you do?"

"I don't want to be Magistrate. I don't want to deal with the politics or the bullshit." He leaned forward, his elbows on his knees. "I'd open a school for mages, for the kids who don't have anywhere else. I'd create a better system for finding foster parents for them. I'd turn it into what it *should* be, taking care of the young mages and giving them what I never got."

"So why not do it?"

"Because it isn't my place in life. You don't get to be normal, and I don't get to just go help kids."

I shook my head. "I realized what I wanted wasn't ever to be normal, but to have a place. I've found that place where I belong despite all the bullshit, so why couldn't you set up a school?"

"You're only saying that because you want to play professor and naughty student with me." He threw his arm around my shoulder and pulled me against his side, his gaze taking in the darkness as if he could figure something out from it. "You know, I've never had a single person in my life who told me I could do anything, someone who cared what I wanted. Not sure I've ever even thought about it, because it never mattered before."

I wanted to press, to say something that could seal the deal and make him understand, but sometimes it was better to stay quiet and let someone work it out themselves.

He blew out a slow breath, his voice quiet as if he were talking more to himself. "Quit the guild, open a school" — he gave me a salacious grin — "screw the girl of my dreams in every free moment in between. Maybe that's not such a bad idea."

Yeah, I have no complaints with that plan.

It was weird to look at him like that, to feel him staring back and for the first time *really* see him. Not the person he liked to pretend to be, not the monster he feared he was, but him. No worries, no doubts, no stupid jokes in the middle to keep me off balance.

Just Grant, a man tormented by what he was and what he'd done and what he never thought he'd have. A man I loved without reserve.

"You know..." His smile slipped away, as if what he had to say meant everything. I leaned toward him, drawn to hear, needing the glimpse into whatever it was he'd figured out. Before he could tell me, however, that sinking blackness swallowed me again.

No, not yet! I wanted to scream at how unfair it was. Grant, the man who was at least half impenetrable safe, had been *this* close to opening up! I tried to hold on to him, to that moment, need to hear what it was he needed to tell me, but everything dissolved around me like sand pouring through my fingers.

Chapter Seventeen

The other times, when the visions changed, I'd seemed to be adrift. This time, I missed that floating sensation when I hit the ground hard enough to shove the air from my lungs.

Waiting around and whining wasn't in the cards for me, though. The memories of the men as they'd suffered, as they'd faced the worst in their own heads, had me shoving to my feet. They'd all gotten unstuck as far as I knew, but what if something had gone wrong?

I mean, we were in purgatory...I had a feeling that things didn't generally go according to plan here. I needed to see them to know we'd made all made it together.

Soft grumbling from a certain silver fox let me breathe. If Troy had made it, if he'd been able to move past his hang-ups, the others had to be close by.

From the thick mist came a dark figure, and as it neared, I recognized Hunter. He strolled as if walking on some lovely hiking trail rather than through purgatory. He paused, then stuck his hand down into the mist. When he rose, he pulled Grant to his feet.

Each person loosened my chest further. Sure, we were in the one place nothing was supposed to be, and arguably one of the most dangerous places anywhere, but I didn't want to lose anyone on the trip there. I mean, I didn't want to lose anyone facing Lilith, either, but someone dying before we'd even gotten *here* would be a serious insult.

I hadn't found Kase yet, though. I turned, a chill in me as I recalled the horrific sounds he'd made in the memory I saw. What if he was *still* stuck? What if something had happened, and he hadn't made it? What if he was trapped in that horrible loop?

"Kase," I called out, cupping my hands in front of my mouth to let my voice carry as far as possible.

"You called?"

I twisted to find him standing behind me, and I had a moment of wanting to wrap my arms around him. It was from the fear of him missing, from the memory of his I'd experienced.

I took a step forward before pausing. *Right.* Kase wasn't a fan of affection like that. I dropped my arms.

A crease appeared in his cheek, as if he were charmed, before he held out a hand and beckoned me forward.

And I wasn't about to second guess that offer. I crossed the few feet and slid my arms around him, needing to feel how solid he was, that he wasn't the same broken man I'd heard scream.

He pressed his lips to my head and tightened his grip around me, as if maybe he needed the same reassurance.

The hug helped. He *was* the same man I'd heard, but he'd grown since then. When what he'd suffered could have made him cold, when he could have ended up just like his maker, he'd fought it. Instead, he cared — even if it wasn't easy to tell all the time, even if it wasn't in the same way as others, it was still there.

Too soon, I pulled away, glancing up to meet his dark eyes.

He stared back, a quiet moment as if trying to decide whether he'd really seen me in his memories, as if he weren't sure it wasn't just all a dream.

He seemed to come to a decision, because he pressed his lips into a tight line.

He didn't like his secrets out in the open?

Too fucking bad.

I turned to take in my surroundings, the mist that was heavy despite being thick enough to rise as high as I could see. Unlike hell, where there was an actual landscape, there was nothing around us but the mist. It twisted, moving as if there was a breeze despite there not being one.

My forehead itched from the mark Grant had put there, but I was too smart to wipe it off. The chill as the mist brushed my skin reminded me of when I'd choked on the mist in my sleep, of what I'd felt inside me when I'd ventured into the abyss.

I didn't need any imagination to know how it would feel if that mark came off, and I was in no hurry to experience it in real life.

"We all made it," I said, finally letting out a big breath.

"Seems that way," Hunter answered as he slid an arm around my shoulders. "Good job, shadow-girl. When we get back, you might just want to consider looking at a job as an immortal therapist. Could make a killing helping stupid men past their hang ups."

"Thanks, but I'm pretty sure that was the extent of my advice-giving skills. I much prefer being the one fucked up rather than the one fixing other people."

"I like you being the one fucked as well," Hunter offered with a salacious grin.

Even here, in the middle of all this, he could make me laugh.

Troy peered into the mist. "So, where to now?"

Grant looked in the opposite direction, as if they could see anything. "You think we could find one of those information kiosks, like at malls? What we need is a big 'you are here' star."

I frowned, something nagging at me that I'd ignored as I'd dealt with my fear for the men. Now, with them safe, I could focus on it.

It was a pull, as if a waterfall pulled all the streams in that direction. I pointed toward where it came from. "She's that way."

"How can you tell?" Kase asked.

"I can *feel* it, like something wrong that's drawing everything that way."

The walk was different from how hell had been, and not just because there were no weird trees, no brimstone scent or things trying to kill us at each step.

Those were all true, but what really hit me was how *quiet* it was. Hell hadn't felt empty. No matter how open an area had been, it had had edges, movement and life—or, well, afterlife…

In purgatory, there was nothing. It felt like walking on a treadmill covered in mist, so no matter how far we went, nothing changed, nothing appeared, nothing *happened*.

Even with that, I kept panic at bay because I knew damn well that we *were* getting closer. Some deep part of me had a connection with this place and sensed it. It was the same thing that told me no matter how I fought it, this place was home to at least something inside me.

"I thought there were *things* here," I said when the silence became too heavy. "I've seen this place in my dreams, and there were creatures in the mist."

Hunter had his hands in his pockets, a sure sign he didn't plan on getting attacked. "There aren't monsters here, at least not the kind you're thinking of."

"So what did I see?"

"Memories."

I stopped, forcing him to pause and turn so he could look at me. "What do you mean, memories?"

"What we went through to get here happened in the abyss because we're still alive. Normally, that's what the trapped spirits go through here."

"What are the monsters, then?"

"They're part of the spirits loop, of what keeps them here."

"Can the spirits ever escape it?"

"Not really," Hunter said, voice slowing as if he knew I wouldn't like the answer but refused to hide it from me. "People get stuck because they can't move past something on their own, and because they're trapped alone, they never have what they need to get there. The longer they spend there, the more of them drifts away. Before long, they're just echoes driven by whatever trapped them. Spirits have gotten trapped here from the start, and I've never heard of one getting out."

That idea plagued me. Sure, I'd known when dealing with spirits that purgatory wasn't exactly the place anyone wanted to end up, but I hadn't realized it was so…permanent. The idea of them getting stuck here and never being able to move forward, never managing to get past whatever plagued them, forced me to recall each spirit I'd written off as unimportant.

A moment of regret hit me. Maybe I should have signed myself up for that ghost concierge position I'd joked about before. Maybe I should have worked harder — or at all — at helping them come to terms with their past?

"Where are they?" I asked. At his look, I clarified. "If they're here, where are they? Why haven't we seen any?"

"Because the mist hides them. Clear it away, and you'll see."

I was ready to roll my eyes until his expression said he wasn't kidding.

Right. Control the mist. It sounded so easy when he said it, as if it were something anyone could do.

"It's like riding a bike," Hunter added.

"I didn't have parents, remember? No one taught me to ride a bike," I snapped.

"Well, you ride me well enough — pretty sure you can figure it out."

I didn't glare at him. What was the point? He never learned his lesson about inappropriate humor.

Instead, I closed my eyes and shifted my hands around, trying to mimic what I'd seen Grant do so many times. I mean, he understood how to do this sort of magic stuff, so just doing what he did should make it work, right?

A soft snort had me opening one eye to find Grant with his hand over his mouth as if to muffle his laughter at my shoddy attempt.

Asshole.

I should have left him in the abyss.

He had a point, though. *He* wasn't doing this because he couldn't. Because it wasn't his sort of magic — it was mine.

So I stopped trying to copy anyone and focused only on my own feelings. Just like I was drawn toward the disturbance, to where I was pretty sure Lilith was, I could also *feel* the mist.

I used powers that felt rusty and awkward but were still *there* to push that mist away, and when I opened my eyes?

It was gone...

Well, at least scattered in the area directly around us.

And I wished for a long moment that I hadn't figured out how to do it. Spirits sat there, faded versions of what I saw on earth, and they were *all* horrible.

A man stood in front of a pool where a small body floated, a woman cowered, her back against a door someone banged again, a man held someone else at gunpoint. The memories all moved at once, like a hundred movies playing, and the sound of it all hit me in a wave.

The mist must have deadened it, insulated it, and now I was struck by the reality of this place.

It drove me to my knees, and I couldn't block it out. I couldn't ignore it. Even when I put my hands over my ears, it didn't help. The sound wasn't physical and bypassed my hands.

The mist floated in quickly, as if without me actively holding it back, it moved in to refill the space.

Not that I planned to clear it out again — ever.

The experience haunted me, and I was reminded of the lesson hell should have taught me.

Sometimes I really was better off not knowing.

When I opened my eyes, I found Grant before me. He didn't touch me, staring at me as if he didn't understand.

"Couldn't you hear them?"

He shook his head. "I could hardly see anything, just a shimmer." He pressed his lips together. "You could see the trapped spirits, couldn't you?"

"And hear them," I whispered. "There are *so many* of them here, just stuck in their own hell."

Hunter walked up. "Not hell. Even hell has an end when spirits die. Here, though? Everything loops. Just over and over again."

"Can you see them?"

"Better than Grant, not as good as you, I'm sure."

"Can we do anything?"

"Not really. Even if they could have been saved before, now? It's too late. They aren't really even here anymore, just echoes of who they were, like a video tape that was left playing."

That made me feel better, then worse as I realized it meant they were gone. I was glad they weren't necessarily suffering and aware, but saddened that there wasn't a way to save them.

This entire place felt like an option for suffering, just a torture room large enough to fit countless victims.

"Why is this here?" I finally asked, frustration eating away at me. "Why is this place a thing? I don't pretend to have all the answers, or to need them, but damn it, *why*?"

Kase crossed his arms, standing beside Troy as if to let the other two handle this. It was a good idea, since life and death metaphysical questions weren't exactly his area of expertise.

Hunter shrugged. "There's always balance. There's life and death, two sides of the same coin. Mortality and immortality."

"So where does *this* fit in? Because it doesn't make any sense. It isn't balancing anything. Life is temporary and the afterlife still allows for movement, for change. This is forever—it doesn't fit."

"I didn't make this all," Hunter answered. "No one asked me how to set it up. My best guess is that purgatory happened when people couldn't move forward, when that fight inside them was strong enough that they couldn't break free. Universe needed somewhere to put them, and that somewhere ended up here. The universe isn't doing this—the spirits trapped themselves here."

The answer was highly unsatisfactory. It didn't explain why the reapers were here, or how it all fit together. It felt like a huge 'screw you' from the universe to create a place like this where people could *never* escape.

I wanted to walk over, to grab one of the trapped souls, to see if I could do something. Could I wake them as I had with the men? Could I free them from this place? Grab a hold of their soul as I'd seen reapers do and just haul them out of purgatory? Hunter had said it wasn't possible, though.

So the loops sat like some sick monument to them and their pain.

I leaned forward, breathing slowly, trying to tell myself it was okay.

It wasn't, but what else was I supposed to do? It felt like the damn plants in hell again. The situation sucked, but I couldn't stop it, couldn't fix it. I had to focus on what I could do.

So I shoved myself to my feet as the mist closed all the way in on us, forcing myself to move forward, toward Lilith, no matter how hard it was.

How long we had walked, I had no idea. I wasn't sure it really mattered. If hell was strange, it was nothing compared to purgatory. Everything around us screamed that we weren't meant to be here, that this place obeyed none of the rules I had come to understand.

Still, we were so close. The hair on my arms stood, a never-ceasing charge that ran along the mist and told me she was close.

She *didn't* belong. It was clear as anything. She altered the entire realm by her presence, like a poison leeching away what it was supposed to be.

The path went up, as if we were climbing a hill, but because I couldn't see far in front of me, I couldn't tell visually. The soft sand beneath me, however, shifted to a firm surface.

I paused, dragging my foot over to find stone. That was a good sign, right? Any change had to be something good at this point.

A sound from ahead of us made my steps slow, something low that I felt more than heard. It reminded me of bass turned low on a car, when the deep sounds vibrated through me. I couldn't identify it, but I *knew* it was her. It was like a sound that grated, something that I damn well knew shouldn't be there, as if it were on a frequency that wasn't right.

"She's up here," I said, whispering it even though the mist had seemed to create a sound barrier.

"Yeah," Grant answered. "I feel something, too."

If it was strong enough for him to catch, it meant we were close. I was sensitive enough to feel it from far away, but this near? Even the men could feel the way the air was disjointed.

"You know," Hunter said with a serious tone. "I think we'll be fine."

"Oh really?" Troy asked. "And what is it about any of this that makes you think that?"

"Lilith once screwed a hellhound I knew. He said she could only come once, so, you know, not a lot of stamina there from her."

The words were the last thing I expected, which was probably why the joke didn't land very fast and I just frowned in return.

"Maybe it wasn't her, but your friend who was the problem," Grant added.

"What else would you expect from a hellhound?" Troy said.

Hunter set a hand over his chest, his mouth open as if he'd never heard a more offensive thing in his life. "You know, not all of us can impress partners with a knot."

Kase snorted. "Werewolves evolved a knot because they know any smart female would take off running afterward. Their only chance is to trap one."

That stopped me. I turned around to find Kase, his lip curled into the barest hint of a smile, his snarky response dry enough for me to wonder if he'd meant it as a joke at all.

Then it hit me—the joke, and just how absurd it was to *make* that joke here of all places. I laughed because I needed it. In the middle of purgatory, with shit odds of succeeding, here we were making jokes.

Not even *good* jokes, but maybe that was the point.

The men joined in, even Kase letting out a soft chuckle.

It eased the tension, helped remind me that even with all this craziness, with all the unknown, I still had them. They made sense, at least to me, when nothing else did.

The mist shifted around us, and even with the laughter, the movement caught my attention.

It settled, having created a path with a figure at the end. There, in front of us, stood Lilith.

So much for our happy little reprieve… Leave it to Lilith to fuck up a good thing.

Chapter Eighteen

Lilith didn't appear all that amused with our jokes, and our laughter dried up.

Somehow, she was scarier than she had before. I think that was because I'd had the chance to see what she was capable of. In hell, she'd been an interesting mystery. She'd been a story I'd heard, a frighteningly beautiful woman with a past I didn't like thinking about.

The memory of Gran falling hit me, of Lilith stealing from me the one person who had watched out for me for years. Lilith had proven she was *far* more than I'd realized at the start.

I tightened my hands into fists before forcing myself forward, one step at a time. I'd come this far — I'd damn well face her.

She didn't move, didn't retreat or show any fear. Then again, look who she was.

She was Lilith, the first woman, a child of Lucifer himself. She'd bested Gran, who was by all accounts one of the most powerful beings there was, and was here in a place where few could venture.

And what was I?

Pissed off.

"So, you found your way here?" She moved her hand out to examine the pointed nails at the ends of her fingers. "I had started to doubt you'd manage it. It took so long that I'd thought my worry might have been unfounded."

As I walked up the rest of the small hill, the mist cleared to reveal the altar I'd seen when I'd pulled Hunter back—the same stone floor, the mist on the edge.

"You have to stop." I stepped onto the main stone floor and came face to face with Lilith. "You're going to destroy everything."

"I know," she said with a shrug. "That's the whole point. This all?" She waved her hand. "It was all built wrong. Why not tear it apart?"

"Because this is better than the alternative," I said. "Life is better than just not existing."

"Something will exist—you should know that by now. This place is proof of that. Even when nothing should be, something always is. The universe won't abide a vacuum. So the barrier between the living and dead realms will fall, and yes, it'll destroy a lot, but maybe what comes after will be better."

"You're betting a lot on *maybe*."

She gave me a smile dripping with condescension. "Experience all I have, see all I have, and you realize that maybe is good enough."

"So because you had something shitty happen to you, we all have to pay the price?"

"It isn't about *paying* a price." She shifted, as if she wanted to pace but didn't dare turn her back on me. "I'm not punishing the world."

"Sure sounds like it. Seems like you're mad things didn't go your way, so you're flipping the table and going home."

She narrowed her dark eyes. "You know so little, have lived and seen so little. You find out you're some sort of supernatural abomination and assume you can stand toe-to-toe with those of us who have been here from the *start*?" Flames danced in her eyes, reminding me so much of Lucifer. "What happened to me was just one example of this world's failings. Come on, you must see it!"

"I don't blame other people just because my life isn't going swimmingly."

She stared at me, and everything slipped away. It was horrible and wonderful at once, like sliding into a hot tub that was a few degrees too hot. The heat burned me but also eased me.

Her voice floated through my mind, deep and terrible. "I have a gift, an ability to see how people were wronged, to see the things that broke them. It's what has always made me crave freedom. I saw it in Adam, that pompous man who thought to own me, twisted by the expectations and praise heaped upon him by the one who made him. I saw it in Lucifer, who wanted nothing more than recognition for who he was rather than *what* he was, all because he was made damned and vilified from the start. And, Ava Harlin, I see those cracked edges in you. The little girl who was unwanted from the start, who was alone from the beginning, who has twisted herself into a parody of a person just to try to find a place to belong. It wasn't your fault your parents created something that never should have been, or that the world *knows* you're wrong, yet you suffer the burden. You carry the shame for things that aren't your fault."

I tried to block her out, but I couldn't. Her words were there, in my head, and the splinter of her influence dug deeper into me. That piece of her tore away my resolve as it took over.

"That's not true," I whispered back weakly.

"Of course it is. You've never done what you wanted, never been truly free, because you're too busy trying to fit in." A soft *tsk* in her voice said she didn't approve. "Me? I was rejected for not fitting into the role I'd been cast for, and I've always resented that. I had no idea how much worse it could be."

"Worse?"

"You gave it everything you had to fit in, and you failed. How much more devastating that must be, to try so hard and still fall so short."

And…she was right. I thought back to every time I'd tried so damned hard. Each stupid conversation I'd gotten into when I'd plastered on a fake smile, when I'd mimicked what I'd seen from happy, normal people. I recalled each time I'd gone to a new school and sworn I'd reinvent myself and *this* time I'd be happy, this time I'd find the magical way of behaving that would change everything.

It had been exhausting and, in the end, pointless, because no matter what, it was as if people could see how damaged I was right from the start.

"Hush, child," she whispered like a lover, like some smooth playboy coaxing me into bed. "It's not your fault. That's what I want to change, though, the rules others put in place that keep people like us from being truly free. We are either forced to play a game we are destined to lose, or we have no place in this world. *Help me* to build a better one."

"How?" I didn't even mean to ask that, but something in her voice pried away all my worries, all my doubts. It left me ready to believe every word she said.

"Let go. I'll take away those rules, those fears, and make your *truly* free. I know you want it. You want to embrace the power you've found, you want to do what is natural to you instead of what you're *told* you should. That's what I did to the others — I *helped* them. I took away those rules, those fears and I let them be what they truly were without worry."

That splinter dug in deeper, her essence sliding through me, stealing away my objections.

Was this what it felt like to come under her power? There was something inescapably tempting about it. It was like each fear I had, each part of me that wanted so badly to change how the world was, to change *me*, went away. I didn't care if people liked me, if I belonged anywhere.

I was *me*. I was powerful and beautiful and terrifying on a level they couldn't comprehend. I wanted to tear the souls from bodies as I saw fit. I wanted to ruin anyone who had dared cross me in my life. I wanted to bask in that darkness just because I could.

Something pressed to my lips — warm and soft and familiar.

I returned the kiss without thought, as if driven by an instinct inside me, something calling me back from the brink of madness. It wrapped inside me, a presence even deeper than Lilith's influence, than the part of herself that whispered to me.

When my gaze cleared, I found Troy there. He broke the kiss and moved back so I could see into his bright silver eyes, a mixture of him and his wolf.

It was the mate bond. If I'd ever doubted the truth of it before, *here* was the proof.

I had ripped Lilith's presence from him with my powers, but he'd managed to coax me back from the edge of madness with just that kiss, with just a gentle tug upon the bond we shared. It was a trail of crumbs I could follow.

He was inside me deeper than Lilith could ever get.

Which was when the reality hit me. She was a liar, whispering things to me that helped her — not the truth.

Yes, I'd had a horrible life in a lot of ways, but she'd forgotten the *good*. She'd left out Gran, who had stayed up late with me, trying to teach me to read tarot cards because she'd known how lonely I was. She'd missed the way Grant always warded a place before leaving me, even when he knew damned well I could handle myself, just because he cared. She'd missed how Hunter would stare at my ass openly, even in public, and how much I liked it despite the glare I'd give him. She'd left out the way Kase would pull me against his chest while I slept, as if he couldn't get me close enough. She'd missed how Troy rumbled out a growled, *mine*, when he kissed me.

There were some horrible things in the world, but that didn't wash away the good.

A low sound to my left drew my attention to Kase. On the other, Grant stood, a glowing over his skin as if he couldn't fully contain the power inside him. Their eyes had gone black, telling me they'd lost the battle Troy had just helped me win.

Troy was fine—was it because I'd removed the influence once before? Maybe it was like a virus and once he'd gotten it, it couldn't happen again?—and Hunter hadn't changed.

Then again, he was a hellhound. He wasn't an immortal like the others, so maybe she didn't have power over him? The whys didn't matter at the moment, really.

Troy moved beside me, and Lilith's face showed the fury at having her plan thwarted. Then again, I doubted many others had stood against her like this.

"No matter," she said as if she wasn't fuming at her failure. "I offered you freedom, but you'll choose death instead. Fitting, really, to have your little friends here tear you limb from limb. Worse, with the barriers breaking down, I wonder if you'll have an afterlife at all. Even if you have a soul, I bet it will just drift to nothing like the mist here."

The thought of being trapped in purgatory forever was a pretty horrific one, but something to worry about later. Like if I lost.

Kase let out a chilling sound, one so much like Olin had but worse. Grant was deathly still, those black eyes of his calculating and terrifying.

I'd freed Troy before, had freed wolves since then, but it wasn't as if I had the same ability to do so here. Either man could tear me to pieces before I ever got close enough to do anything.

But...

I'd done it before, the only way I knew how. I wasn't as clueless as I had been then, fumbling blindly for something I didn't understand, something I refused to fully accept.

I shifted, letting myself fall into the now familiar reaper form just as Grant and Kase charged, as Troy and Hunter readied themselves to deal with the men who had become like brothers to them, to kill them, no doubt, if needed to protect me.

I used the power of this form, the shadows I was made of, and reached out at once in a hard shove. I targeted that now familiar presence, that splintered piece of Lilith she used to infect others. In this form, I could see it, like an ugly red infection inside each of them, something that throbbed poison through them. It was easy to find, to target and blast away.

It took only a split second, the mist at the edges of the platform moving away as well from the power.

The black faded from their eyes, that splinter of Lilith dissolving as my power forced it from them. All four collapsed to the stone. I had to trust that they were fine, that it was a side effect of what I'd done—the flames dancing along Lilith's arms said I had my own problems to deal with.

I let myself fall back to normal, the ground beneath my feet turning solid again. I could have remained reaper, but the form was hard to hold for long.

"You are playing with things you don't understand," Lilith screamed, that whole cool-and-collected façade dissipating against repeated failures.

I could hear it all in her voice.

She'd been created by one of the most powerful beings, to be *perfect* in his eyes, and yet she'd failed at every turn. She'd failed to be what Adam wanted, had created the vampires, who were flawed at best, had been bested time and time again by some girl who was little more than a mistake in the universe.

"I killed Gran. Do you really think you stand a chance against me?"

The reminder of what she'd done, of what she'd *stolen* from me, energized the fight in me. "You didn't kill Gran — she sacrificed herself."

"There's no difference."

"Of course there is. She could have killed you, but she didn't. She was trying to *save* you."

"I don't need saving, especially from that self-righteous fate." She lifted her hand and a blast of fire sparked from it.

And in that moment, I really wished Grant wasn't out cold. The lazy bastard would have been useful in a magic fight, but there he was, napping.

I lifted my hand out of instinct, and shadows left my fingertips, made of the same mist I used as a reaper. When her attack struck it, the fire died out as if the oxygen had been stolen from it.

Well, that's useful.

Lilith let out an indignant shout, the whole image of her being powerful slipping away. Or, rather, of her being controlled. No one could pretend she wasn't powerful, but whereas before she'd been the image of confidence, she was rattled now.

"You have powers no one should," she shouted as she fired again.

I countered each move, my shadows turning her hits to nothing. "I keep hearing the world needs balance. Maybe that's what I am, the balance to you," I yelled back at her before flinging all those shadows, using all the power I could muster, at *her*.

230

It knocked her backward, made her roll across the stone floor.

At the edges of the platform, shadows moved. Reapers stood there, watching. They were hazy, showing no desire to intervene, merely to watch the spectacle. Then again, they hadn't seemed to do anything so far, so why would I think it would change now?

I told myself that the audience didn't matter. I needed to keep my mind in the game, because I'd *seen* what those flames could do if I didn't move fast enough. Even with my hit, Lilith rose as if barely shaken.

That felt like the best I had, like the hardest thing I could do, and yet it hadn't done anything more than slow her down.

And worse? As a reaper, I couldn't see a soul inside her. Nothing I could grasp, nothing I could kill as a reaper would. She seemed...empty. Not even a spark as Hunter had.

So what was I supposed to do?

My distraction cost me. Searing pain filled my left shoulder, the scent of burning flesh enough to make me gag. It reminded me of what she'd done to my arm in my dream but so much worse. I guess having nerves endings in my real body would do that...

Still, even with the way it sizzled, with how the graze made the movement of air over it an agony, I tucked the arm to my front and countered the next blast.

"You are a foolish little girl," Lilith spat. "You're in over your head. Look around—you have four immortals with you who have *all* fallen. I've bested

Gran, escaped Lucifer and even the reapers here don't touch me. What exactly is it you think you can do?"

The blasts from her came faster, as if her monologue had energized her.

And worse? She had a point. The reapers gathered, but none touched her. Did they just not care? Was it that they couldn't? Was she somehow even more powerful than they were?

What chance did I have, then?

Heat passed me, singeing my hair when I couldn't fully reflect one of her hits. Exhaustion dragged on me.

She was overtaking me.

She didn't look any weaker, but *I* sure as hell felt it. She was running me down, and each deflection took more out of me. When I tried for an offensive, when I threw all I had into another blast her way, it didn't even topple her.

I'm going to lose.

It was becoming clear. The end of my power, the limit of what I could do, was approaching quickly, and yet Lilith showed no signs of slowing.

The men remained unmoving on the ground, and they'd suffer for my failure, just like everyone else. Lilith would win, and there would be no one to stop her, to keep her from destroying everything, and all because I wasn't strong enough.

Because despite Gran thinking I could stop this, that I was the only one, everyone had put their faith into the wrong person.

Another blast hit me, and while I kept it from burning, the force was enough to throw me backward. The stone slammed against me, hard, and I struggled to pull in breath. My vision wavered, every part of me beyond tired, as if I'd run miles and could barely stand.

Still, I rolled and forced myself to my knees.

"It never had to go this way," Lilith said, her victory showing all over her smug face.

Then again, was there a question anymore?

"You're like me," she said. "You're someone who doesn't fit into the world, but whereas I chose to change the world, you tried to change yourself. *Pathetic.*"

She lifted both hands, a sure sign that she was ready to end this.

Except, when fire sparked to life in her palms, when I tensed for the hit, everything quieted.

The mist shifting around us, the crackle of the flames, the fire in her eyes, it all slowed until it came to a stop, as if the entire world had paused between seconds.

I collapsed.

Chapter Nineteen

"You were not made to kneel." I didn't recognize the voice, but I wasn't sure I had the energy to care.

It took everything I had to not close my eyes and just give in.

I'd had the smallest moment of happiness when I'd accepted that Lilith had won. I didn't have to fight anymore, didn't have to try and fail and worry. There was something to be said for blessed nothingness.

"Up," the voice said again, something deep and dark and unmistakably masculine.

While collapsing sounded great, I had a feeling that whoever spoke wasn't going to let me, and there was no way I could rest with *that* voice bothering me.

I lifted my head and sat back on my heels to find a man before me.

He was tall—six and a half feet at least—with black hair and nearly white eyes. He wore a suit—black with pinstripes—but it looked like something from centuries ago.

I was sure I'd never seen him before. "What do you want?"

He approached and crouched before me, perfectly balanced as if he weighed nothing, as if gravity had no effect on him. "You are giving up."

"I'm accepting reality," I countered. "There's a difference."

"No, there isn't. I can't say I expected you to give up."

"Well, eventually everyone runs out of moves." I wanted to be annoyed at him, but I was too tired, too sore, too raw from a fight I was giving everything to and was losing.

He cocked his head, the action familiar, though I couldn't place where I'd seen it before. "When you were born — something that never had been, that never should have been possible — I would not have foreseen you giving up so easily."

"*Easily*?" I pointed at my shoulder, at the still smoldering flesh there. "This wasn't easy! Why don't you take a few shots and see how *you* manage!"

Maybe it was my injuries or my frustration, but it took longer than it should have to register his words, to think through them.

"*When you were born.*"

I lifted my gaze, my eyes wide. "Wait. You were there when I was born?"

He nodded, so still it was eerie.

"Does that mean you're..." I couldn't say it. It felt childish and stupid to say it out loud.

Still, he nodded again as if he knew the question. "Yes. Your father."

All the years I'd wanted so badly to understand where I'd come from, to know my parents, to have some idea of what I was, and *this* asshole had known it all along? He'd known about *me* and chosen to stay away?

I lifted my hand without thinking and a blast of that shadow escaped, rushing toward him.

He didn't divert it, instead simply shifting to the left to miss it by a breath of space, as if it didn't matter.

"You asshole," I whispered when words seemed like my only weapon. "All this time and you've known about me?" The idea that my father, at least, might have been unaware of me, that he hadn't left me on purpose, was ruined.

I hated him for that, for stealing at least the fantasy that I hadn't been purposely left by both my parents. I'd clung to ignorance over indifference.

He didn't react with shame, with *anything*. "Of course I have known about you. You are my only child, the only one I would ever have. I have watched you from your first breath."

"Well, then you know exactly what a shitty world you left me in."

"It was your world."

"I was *alone*."

He titled his head, as if the word meant little to him. "We are *all* alone. You were with mortals, though. That was important."

"Why? Why couldn't you at least *tell* me you were there? That you existed? That someone gave a damn about me?"

"Because I could not speak to you, not in the living world. You could not understand me there. Only here, in our realm, could you actually see me, could we speak, could you understand me."

"So you should have brought me here!"

He shook his head. "I couldn't bring you here—you had to make your own way when you were ready. We, here, are not like you. You are part of us, part reaper, but your other side would have withered and atrophied here."

"And my mother? Not that I want to have a sex-ed talk about reapers, but how the hell is it even possible?"

"I loved your mother. I watched her for a very long time, until I found a way to meet. A tiny tear in space and time, small enough for two, but the universe does not abide such things easily."

I frowned as I thought about that, about how a woman could fall for a reaper, about the sort of woman who would see one and decide to put out right then. "So it was a hit it and quit it deal?"

"It was something impossible to replicate."

"And where is she? My mom?" The old pain came back, when I asked something I knew better than to ask.

"I do not know. Watching her became too painful, to forever be on the sidelines, forever witness to a life I could never interact with." His voice held sorrow that surprised me, especially since looking at him, I wouldn't have thought he had much emotional depth.

I curled my hands into fists but kept from trying to hit him again. It hadn't gone well the first time. "So what is this? Some sort of fatherly pep talk? A little late, don't you think?"

"You haven't understood," he said.

"Understood what?"

"My lessons."

"Sorry, but absentee fathers don't get to talk about lessons."

He lifted his hand and in his palm, a bird made of mist flew.

The reaper in my dream...

I thought back to when I'd been there, when the shadow—what I knew now was a reaper—had shown me the visions of the bird and the fish, and how that *had* helped. "That was you?"

He nodded. "I have tried to give you what I could, to guide you when you needed it."

More hit me. The reaper who had brought Gran to me...the one who'd killed the man who had abused me. Was that him? Had he been trying, in his own fucked-up way, to help me?

I let out a soft laugh at how sad it was that even that made me feel wanted. No matter how much I tried to say I could stand on my own, I melted each time I thought I wasn't alone. "I did listen. It's what let me save Troy. It's why I've been able to do any of this."

"You've accepted your other side, but you are still trying to be something else."

"I don't have any idea what that means. If this is going to be the last conversation I get to have, could we *please* not play word games? Come on—I'm about to die. Tell me you're proud of me, something I can pretend means a damn thing."

He shifted again, the strange way he moved that told me this wasn't a form he used often. This was *not* someone who could have passed for human by any stretch of the imagination. "Do you know why Lilith hasn't been touched by the reapers here?"

"Because you are all lazy and rarely do *anything* that doesn't directly benefit you?"

"*Look* at her."

I sighed and turned my gaze to her. She was as she'd always been—beautiful in the way a spider was. Lethal and graceful and terrifying in way that made my skin crawl. The fire had moved more from her palm, but only a hair, as if time still passed, but too slowly to keep track of.

I went to tell him I didn't see anything when *something* caught my eye. It wasn't anything I could place at first, just a nagging feeling, but I stared at her and realized…

Something was wrong.

I spotted it when I looked at Troy, at Grant. With the others, I saw them as shells. Even Hunter and Kase, who had no souls as mortals did, still appeared to me as a casing. Inside Hunter I could see the twisting smoke and hellfire of his true form, and inside Kase — darkness.

Grant and Troy, who still retained spirits as I knew them, had a shimmering of their soul wrapped inside their outer form.

Lilith, though?

I pushed myself to my feet, forcing my body to move even when I didn't want to. I went closer to her, narrowing my eyes as I tried to figure out why she was different.

She had no shell.

The edges of her energy were soft, as if bleeding out, held together by something that wasn't a form like the others.

"What is she?"

My father didn't answer. He approached, circling around her. "Something unique, as you are."

I recalled Gran telling me the same, and it being about as useful.

Still, I studied her, seeing how her spirit — if it could be called that — was held in place by something that was not a body.

"So you can't do anything because of this?"

He nodded. "Reapers interact with spirits in the living and the dead realms. We are the ultimate control over spirits, the shepherds of them."

"So why not her?"

He didn't answer me. *Go figure.*

I again looked at her, then reached out to touch her. My fingers grazed her arm, the first time I'd touched her, and something *wrong* coursed through me.

It wasn't the sensation of a spirit, or even that horrible sharp feeling of a poltergeist, but something worse.

Something untethered and twisted and old.

I jerked backward and shook my hand as if I could fling the sensation off. "What is that?"

He let out a sigh—it seemed that parental disappointment was a universal constant. "You have so much to learn and so little time to do it in."

"Maybe you should have gifted me with a reaper how-to guidebook for my last birthday instead of, well, nothing."

He moved away from her and cast his hand out, parting the mist. "Look."

I followed him into the newly cleared space, suddenly surrounded by the spirits trapped there, repeating their misery.

The sounds still hit me, but something muted it. Maybe it was my father? Maybe it was wherever or however we were walking around, disconnected from the world?

He stopped before one, a man I recognized. The one who had abused me... He didn't see me in his loop, however. He saw himself, at the top of those stairs, and the reaper coming for him.

A deep anger inside me erupted at the reality that he was my horror, but I wasn't his. He might be stuck here, but he thought only of himself, nothing of what he'd done to others. He was as selfish in death as he'd been in life.

I wasn't sorry he'd ended up here.

I nodded at the man. "You did this, right?"

"Yes."

"Well, thanks. I'll sleep better knowing the bastard is here."

My father didn't smile, didn't show any reaction to the praise. Then again, maybe I just couldn't read reapers…

Instead, he gestured toward the man. "Look closer."

I forced myself to, even though that was the *last* face I wanted to see.

Then I realized…

He had no shell.

He was more translucent than Lilith, more faded, but he lacked the sharp edges just as she had.

He looped, over and over, but in all of it, I saw the same thing. Those bleeding edges, kept in place by whatever drove his echo to keep going.

"What does that mean?" I asked without looking at my father—he'd already proven that he didn't give direct information.

Instead, I came to my own conclusion, to my own answer. It was obvious even if I struggled to make sense of it.

"She is unique," my father repeated. "A spirit made by Lucifer himself, with a yearning for freedom that could not be trapped, even here."

It all came together.

The reason the reapers couldn't touch Lilith. The reason she could be here, in purgatory, when nothing else could. Lilith wasn't alive, not anymore. How she had died, I had no idea — maybe she didn't know either.

Lilith was a spirit stuck in purgatory, trapped in a loop of her own making, trapped by her own fears and regrets and anger, and that was one thing I had no idea how to fight...

"How can she talk to me, then? How could she have been in hell or interact with the living realm if she's dead? I thought the spirits here were trapped here."

"Lucifer created something powerful, something special. He gave her one thing above all others — a yearning for freedom. That yearning grew as she did, strengthened into resolve that allowed even the echo of her trapped here to crave it. She was the *first* to come here."

The first? She had been the first person created with Adam, right? It made sense she might have been the first spirit, the first to die. "So she ended up trapped because she had unresolved issues?"

"Yes. I heard you ask your companion *why* this place exists, but he did not understand enough to answer. This place was never intended to function as a prison, to hold spirits here forever."

I went to ask why it was happening, but before I got the question out, the answer became clear. *Lilith.* "She poisoned this place like she does to immortals, didn't she?"

He nodded. "She was never intended to be here, so she has twisted our realm. It was made to be a temporary stop, a place for spirits to rest before they pass on if they are not ready. Lilith's anger broke it, trapping all who came here in these loops. This place has become a monument to her pain."

I tried not to, but I couldn't help the pity that crept in.

I thought back to how Lucifer had spoken about her, reminded myself that she hadn't been given a fair hand in life. While Lucifer may have made her to the best of his abilities, he'd created someone destined to fail at the one thing she'd been created to do.

That pity didn't change anything, though. I *still* had to stop her somehow. It wasn't as if I could say, 'Oh, she's had a fucked-up life, guess I'll let her destroy everything.'

"It doesn't matter what she is," I said. "She's still stronger than I am. Knowing she's dead doesn't change that I can't beat her. I mean, *you're* a full reaper who knows exactly how to use your powers, and you can't do anything to her."

"Exactly."

I went still at his answer. *Exactly?* He sounded pompous, as if I'd just figured something out, which I hadn't.

"Exactly what? Exactly I'm screwed? Gee, thanks, *Dad*."

He shook his head. "I am a full reaper, so I can't do anything. You, however…"

"Aren't a full reaper." As I finished the statement, it felt like a key that I had no idea the lock it went to. Like an answer without a question. "So what? Doesn't that make me weaker?"

He held his hand out, but I waved mine to stop his little puppet show. "Enough with the fish-and-birds bullshit."

He paused, then shook his head. "I forget your communication is odd. Direct." The way he spoke said it was also not preferable. "There are times when things, on their own, are weaker than when combined. Some believe such things muddy the creation, that it dulls each, but that is not always the case. Some of the time, a mixture can be stronger *because* of that diversity within it. *You* are not wholly mortal nor wholly reaper. You are not bound by the constraints of either, but an amalgamation of both."

"Then why is my ass being handed to me out there?" I pointed back at the where Lilith still stood, frozen in time.

"Because you accept neither part of yourself fully. You see yourself as either mortal or reaper, but not both."

"What does that even mean?"

He pointed at my forehead, his eyebrow raised. The slight itch I'd ignored came back to me from where Grant had placed the mark, the spell, that protected me from the mist.

He can't be serious...

But what did I have to lose?

Other than dying a horrible choking death and the world ending because I fucked up?

At least the stakes weren't that high, right?

I sighed at my own stupid joke, especially because it really wasn't a very good one to go out on.

I closed my eyes and took a deep breath — what might be my last one if I was taking advice from a bad source. And really, my deadbeat reaper father was probably not the best person to put my faith in.

I walked back to my spot in front of Lilith, then reached up and used the palm of my hand to wipe off the ash, to do the one thing Grant had made me swear not to do.

The first of the mist that rushed into my lungs like frozen water made me regret the whole thing.

This was going to be an absolutely terrible way to die…

Chapter Twenty

I fell to the ground, the blast from Lilith sailing over me as the world moved again. I should have been grateful for that, but I was too focused on how the mist filled me, on how it made me cold and hollow.

I'd felt it before, that creeping sensation when I'd fallen into the abyss that first time, when I'd tried to find Rachel's spirit and Gran had removed it from me.

But where that had been the tiniest amount, this time I let it truly fill me. I choked, gasping, my body rebelling as it did in my dreams. I'd tried to hold my breath then, but I didn't now. I pulled in breath after breath, inhaling and exhaling as if it would fix it.

Was this how that first fish had felt when it had climbed onto land and tried to breathe, when it had realized what a monumentality shitty idea it was?

Maybe good old Dad wasn't too happy with my progress and had decided he didn't need me to fuck up the family line anymore.

Except there, above me, he stood. He was back to looking like a reaper, staring at me through the blackness of the shadows he was, as if waiting.

For what?

Oh, me dying.

Sorry, it's taking a minute, Dad.

Except then I sucked in a breath, and it didn't hurt quite so bad… One after another I took, each easing that choking sensation. It was like going out into a blizzard from a warm house, how the first steps were the worst, that shock before a body starts to adjust.

I rolled to my back, able to take easy breaths now, amazed by how much *better* I felt. The exhaustion had subsided, the soreness gone as if I'd been revitalized.

At least some part of me was *made* of this place, so maybe I needed this mist to recover. Maybe this was like blood to Kase, like hell to Hunter, like the moon to Troy.

I forced myself to my knees, then to my feet.

Lilith stood, mouth open as if she was as confused as I was.

It didn't last long before she threw another bolt at me, but this time? It passed right through me.

I looked down to realize I was neither fully reaper nor fully human. I existed in some middle ground between the two, drawing on the power of purgatory but not bound to it as my father was, as the other reapers were. What he'd said made sense as I stood between these two worlds.

Lilith took a step backward, as if thrown by how I didn't turn into a pile of ash as she'd expected I would.

I advanced, ignoring the way she repeated the action, frustration making her sloppy and erratic.

She was a memory, just an echo of who she had been in life, something trapped and twisted by fear and anger and a desire for revenge. She warped everything around her, including the immortals she influenced, and pulled in spirits to trap here.

This wasn't even really her, not the person she'd been before.

It made me wonder what she'd been before she'd turned into this. Did anyone else even know? What had happened to her?

"Why won't you just die?" she asked on a pant, a sure sign that she was at her end.

Echoes couldn't be wholly destroyed, so what was I supposed to *do* with one here? Hunter had said they couldn't be freed, they couldn't be killed, so what were the options?

I didn't have any answers, so I went with instinct, with trusting myself.

I reached out and set a hand on her cheek, staring into her eyes. When everything faded around us, though, it wasn't because she'd done it. She wasn't infecting me this time.

Instead, I followed her, deep into her mind, to the place that ultimately trapped her.

And there?

I saw Lilith, a woman who looked as she had when I'd known her, yet somehow different. Lighter, smiling, *happy*.

She stood in a home with stone walls and a dirt floor. She stared at a man who walked in with something I'd have never expected from her — *love*.

"Adam." She rushed forward to press a kiss to his lips.

A kiss he didn't return.

Instead, he moved away, his eyes narrowed and hard.

"What is it?" she asked.

"I'm tired of this," he answered.

"Of what?"

"Of you, of fighting, of *all* of this."

She took a step backward. "What are you talking about? We don't fight."

"Of course we do. I want to live here, you don't. I want to go there, you don't. Everything is an argument."

Lilith pulled her shoulders back, pressing her lips together. She might have loved him, but she was no wilting flower. "We settle together, compromise. What do you want? For me to blindly follow?"

"*Yes,*" he said, throwing his arms up. "That's exactly what I want! Why can you not just obey?"

"How can you love someone who simply obeys you? Who is less than you are?"

"How can I love someone who doesn't?" The venom in his voice made my stomach clench, reminded me of how often I'd craved acceptance and not found it.

There was no worse feeling.

Lilith drew her hands into fists, her chin lifted high. "Well, you'll have to get used to it. Till death do us part, remember?" She turned her back on him, but I suspected it was to hide the pain on her face.

"Exactly."

The sharpened tip of a wooden spear came through Lilith's chest, and she stared at it with the same shock I had.

Adam held the other end, having run her through when her back was turned, like a coward.

Lilith collapsed, blood running down the spear and coating Adam's hands. He didn't drop to his knees, didn't at least hold her, *something*. He let her bleed out in front of him, watching as if it didn't matter, not offering any comfort.

"Mankind needs a *good* start. That won't come from you, from disobedience."

"Our fathers—" Lilith said around a mouthful of blood.

"Have already accepted that this didn't work. My father will make me a new bride, a *proper* one, and yours will never know what happened. And you? Well, you'll be dead, so what does it matter?"

She shuddered, gasping, unable to speak any further.

The vision moved, showed Adam burning her body, before it came to an image of Lucifer walking into a room, one with Lilith in it. She sat on a bed, but there was something missing from her. She'd lost the spark I'd seen in the woman, as if Adam had extinguished it. But that was the point, wasn't it? This *wasn't* Lilith anymore—it was just an echo.

Lucifer stared at her for a long while, but did he see it? Could he tell that it wasn't her, that what was in front of him was the memory of her, the spirit left behind?

His lips pressed together into a tight line.

He has to know…

"My daughter," he said softly, his voice more gentle than I'd ever heard from him, before waiting as if to see if she'd look up.

She did, and his eyes widened.

It was proof enough that he'd known.

"Yes?"

"The wedding for Adam and Eve is today."

She nodded. "I won't attend."

"Of course. You should rest."

He left, and she sat there, alone, her gaze locked on the blanket.

And it all made sense... It was twisted, and yet I saw it all.

Lilith, who had been made perfect by someone else's standards, had been cast aside and killed because she'd been in the way of someone else. She had said she wanted freedom, but I knew better.

She'd wanted to belong. To Adam, to the world, but she'd wanted it to be as *herself*.

Instead, she'd been murdered for it.

The loop didn't stop right away or return to the start. Instead, it showed her witnessing the same thing, the same betrayals of the world that happened to others. Her pain ate away at me, and I felt every bit of it. Perhaps because I shared a similar pain, because I understood it, I suffered it along with her.

But it had to stop.

"You can't do this," I whispered.

She stopped, the scene she was in pausing as if she heard me. She turned toward me, now dressed in a slinky red dress in some night club a few decades ago. "I have to."

"Why?"

"Because *everyone* suffers. Look around at all these souls here, trapped because life doesn't work. I told you it was built on a broken premise, and now you've seen."

"Just because something grows out of shitty soil doesn't mean you should rip it out."

"Everything was spawned by one selfish man who murdered his wife because he couldn't bear to not control her. And what did he get for that? Punished? Cast out? *No.* His father rewarded him with a biddable wife, with children, with everything he'd ever wanted. *That's* why it should all be ripped out! It was all created from bad stock. A poisoned tree will give you nothing but poisoned apples."

I struggled to argue against that...

If I'd been her, if I'd watched all the world coming from someone who'd betrayed me, I couldn't imagine much love for any of it. Her eschewing the mortal world for the supernatural one made sense, too.

"I get it," I told her. "I get wanting to tear apart the system because it sucks. The problem is that you end up just as bad as everything else. If you do this, *you* end up taking everything from someone else, someone who doesn't deserve it."

"So?"

"So, you know what that's like. You've been there. How can you make someone else suffer like you did? Someone who doesn't deserve it."

She paused, frowning as the scene shifted to her on the ground, to when Lucifer had burst into the room after she'd killed Gran.

And there it was again to her. Another betrayal, and another person who was supposed to care for her tossing her aside.

Anger rushed back to the forefront, and I remembered what Hunter had told me.

"They're just echoes. You can't save them."

Lilith wasn't *her* anymore. She was just a memory, just a loop, and no matter if I got through to her for a split second, that loop would keep going and drag her under again.

She was as trapped as anyone else, just reliving the same anger and pain over and over again.

I wanted to save her, but I *couldn't*. Whatever she could have been, whoever she could have been, had died when she'd been killed, when Adam had shoved a spear through her back, and this was nothing but an echo in time.

It was the anger of someone wronged that lingered and festered and grew.

"You're just like me," she said, staring up at me as if she could force me to realize it.

"Almost," I admitted.

"You aren't supposed to be here, and you've been wronged and hurt and suffered because of it. We are exactly the same," she pressed.

I walked over and knelt beside her, ignoring Gran's body, ignoring the splintered wood from Lucifer's entrance. Those things didn't matter. They were the past, and *that* was one thing Lilith had taught me, something I had to understand.

I set my hand on her cheek, letting go of the anger I had — at her, at my parents, at the world for not accepting or wanting me. "We're different because I'm letting it go now. I'm not going to waste all my time being angry about what happened, because no one can change it." I dug deep, trying to unravel all that pain inside myself as well as her. I had to release my own anger to free her. "Life does suck some of the time. Things happen we can't control, and we get fucked over and we can't do anything about it. Guess what? Too bad. I can wallow in it, or I can move on. I can let it destroy me, or I can keep going. I can decide the entire world is bad because of it, or I can look for something good."

I thought about Kase, about Hunter and Grant and Troy and Gran and all the good things I'd found. They didn't cancel out the bad, but they sure made it worth sticking around for.

"You don't understand," she said.

"I do, finally. Maybe everything happens for a reason, maybe it doesn't, but I know nothing good happens if you stick your head in the sand and hide. You refused to move forward, and it stole so much from you. It destroyed you and hurt so many others. I refuse to make the same mistake." I used my power, the edge inside me honed by something between the living and dead, something not quite mortal or immortal, that place I existed which couldn't be quantified.

And that was what it was... I was accepting that I *wasn't* like anything else. Even now, even with my father watching, with me understanding what I came from, I finally sank into the acceptance that I didn't *need* to fit in. I didn't need to be reaper or human or anything else. I didn't need to be easily defined, digestible for other people to understand and categorize and accept for me to be okay with *me*.

She gasped, but I didn't stop. I used that power to sever the connection between her and purgatory, the one that kept her trapped. Hunter had told me this wasn't possible, but he meant it hadn't been possible for anyone else.

Before me.

Lilith shimmered, losing the sharpness of her form.

Once that tether was fully cut, when she was adrift and free, she started to fade.

I didn't move away, didn't leave her as Adam had. Instead, I remained, my hand on her cheek as she faded.

Where she went…I had no idea. She was an echo, or so I'd been told, but if I'd learned one thing, it was that we only knew what we knew. Maybe freeing her would release her, would let her go wherever the spirits of immortals went.

When she was gone, when her image drifted away and the picture of Gran's body, of Lucifer, disintegrated, I caught a glimpse for only a second.

Lilith stood there, in front of me, and beside her? Gran. The picture was just a flash, but the corners of Lilith's lips were tipped up in a smile, one that reminded me of the woman I'd seen before Adam had killed her.

Even better, though, was seeing Gran's withered face, her bright eyes. Despite it only being that tiny glimpse, I sure as hell saw pride in her expression.

It was gone as quickly as it happened, and the world rushed in on me again.

A racing sensation moved through the mist, returning to how the place should have been, the wrongness from Lilith gone. There was a lightness, an openness that took away the crushing heaviness from before. It was as if the poison from Lilith had slipped away when she had.

The reapers at the edge of the platform had left, except for one. I couldn't tell them apart, but that didn't stop me from knowing this one was my father.

I was going to respond—what I was going to say, I had no idea—but he moved, the shadows he was made of spreading out, surrounding me, consuming where the men lay, still unconscious, and the world around me shorted out, as if blinking from existence for a second.

When I opened my eyes, we were back, as if it had never happened at all, in the back room of Gran's shop.

Is it really over?

Chapter Twenty-One

"I never figured the devil would stop by for tea." I set a cup in front of Lucifer. I'd picked one of Gran's favorite teas, with angels across the box—something called 'good vibes.'

It seemed fitting.

He dropped his gaze to the cup, that same stern look across his features he always had. "I told you already—this is a projection, so there is no need to actually make me tea. I can't drink it."

"And I told you that if I ever had anyone over and didn't offer them tea, Gran would find a way to punish me even from the afterworld."

He pressed his lips together with an unhappy look, but one with more affection than I would have expected, as though Gran had been, if not a friend, at least a worthy opponent. "Leave it to her to find a way to torture me even after she is gone."

I chuckled and picked up my own cup, blowing the steam from the top before sipping it. The hot cocoa was divine, and I refused to feel a speck of guilt over drinking it. As it turned out, I hated tea, and I refused to force myself to drink it anymore. "So, the world isn't going to end?"

"It seems not. All signs show the buildup of spirits in purgatory has started to drain slowly without Lilith there to hold them. We have received new residents in hell, along with the other levels of the afterlife reporting the same."

I nodded, glancing to the side to see the spirit of an overly friendly multi-level-marketing candle saleswoman waving at me and smiling. She'd been around for about a week, but damn, it was nice to have her there instead of missing.

I'd never thought I'd be happy about seeing spirits, but here we were. "Yeah, it seems like they aren't getting stuck anymore, either. Freshly minted spirits are bothering me as always. Might have to open some sort of ghost daycare system to give me a break." Even as I said that, I knew it wasn't entirely true. I'd started to actually listen to the spirits, to help those that needed it.

I mean, I still wasn't murdering people for them, but a shoulder for ghost tears now and then was in the realm of possibilities. I'd even started to slip back to purgatory during my sleeping hours to help free some of the trapped spirits, to offer those who needed it a kick to get moving.

I took out the item that I'd held on to, the item which was the real reason I'd called him. After a moment, I dropped it on the table between us.

Lucifer stared down at Lilith's ring. "Your favor was this. It is yours." Even as he spoke, a hesitation in his tone told me the truth. He wanted it, but rules were rules.

"I needed it to find her, but I don't need to keep it."

He blew out a breath, then shook his head. "It would be inappropriate, like going back on a favor. I have a reputation to uphold."

I refused to take the ring back. "Look, I want you to have it, and if you don't take it, I'll just keep bothering you. If this is a weird rules thing, how about you just give me another favor? I know you want it, and you *should* have it. It was Lilith's, so it should go to you."

He swallowed hard, the action strangely charming, as if his uncertainty made him more…human?

"That is acceptable," he said, and the ring turned into smoke as it disappeared. "Did she suffer?" he asked quietly.

"I did what I could so she wouldn't, and I'm pretty sure she's in a better place now," I answered as honestly as I could. The reality was that purgatory *was* suffering. Still, I hadn't added to it, had tried to end it. "You knew all along that she wasn't alive anymore, didn't you?"

"Yes. When she returned to me, after the fallout with Adam, I knew as soon as I saw her."

"Is that a trick of the devil?"

"It is the trick of a father," he answered.

My comment felt unkind, from the censure of his tone.

Sometimes it was easy to see Lilith as the villain, to see Lucifer as the enemy. It was more difficult to remember that Lilith was a victim in her own right, and Lucifer a grieving father.

"If you knew, why didn't you do anything about it?"

"What was I to do? If I'd confronted her, she may have become unstuck."

"Wouldn't that be good?"

"She would be gone then, outside my ability to even see her. Perhaps it was selfish, but..." He let out a slow sigh. "I couldn't lose my only access to her."

As much as I wanted to fault him, I got it. I'd made my father yank Gran from her afterlife just because I missed her only hours after her death. Could I have let her go if she'd been stuck? Could I have worked toward losing her?

"But you never thought the spirits were her doing?"

"Why would I? I thought she was a form of poltergeist. She was angry, but I never thought anger could turn her so cold, could twist her that way. I certainly never knew she could bend purgatory like that."

"Anger does that to a person," I admitted. "It eats away at us, traps us where we are, keeps us from seeing we can move forward."

He stared at me as if my words were unexpected. "You know, when I first met you, I never would have thought you to be wise."

"Well, you did meet me when a hellhound was ready to eat me and after a rough couple days in hell. I wasn't at my best."

"Indeed." I chose to ignore the way he didn't deny the whole *not at my best* thing. "You now have time before you, Ms. Harlin. I wonder what you will do with it."

I stared down at the hot cocoa, smiling as I finally had an answer. After spending my whole life trying to be something else, trying to twist and deny myself until I fit a mold I never would, I now knew my direction. "I have no fucking idea."

He tilted his head, a line appearing between his eyes. "That sounds like a horrible answer."

I shook my head. "It really isn't. Maybe I'll travel or maybe I won't. Maybe I'll go back to insurance or train otters to rob banks or make oversized dildos to sell by the roadside, but no matter what it is I pick? I won't do it because it's safe or because I think I'm supposed to or because it's normal and will make me fit in. Whatever I decide to do, no matter how stupid or crazy or weird, it'll finally be exactly what *I* want, because I want to, and that's something I never really thought I'd get."

* * * *

Maybe we should take a break.

I reread my text message for the fiftieth time that day, hating it a little more each time I saw it.

I shouldn't have pressed Send. I should have relegated it to the same place that drunk texts go—a pit in hell so deep that no amount of spelunking could reach it.

Instead, I'd sent it. To *all* of them.

And no one had answered.

I missed Gran all the more in that moment. I wanted someone to talk to, someone who could grab me by the shoulders and shake some sense into me. I had four amazing, handsome, brave and absolutely frustrating men that I had no doubt I loved.

Not to mention the best sex I'd ever experienced in my life by a long shot.

Still, when we'd returned, when life had ground forward as if it hadn't ever been different, my nerves had gotten the best of me.

They *all* had lives of their own. They had paths they'd been on before I'd gotten on their radar and messed it all up.

Kase had a coven to deal with. Troy had a pack who were all the more interested in him now. Grant had a pissed-off guild, and Hunter...well he wasn't even really *from* the living realm. They all had their own messes to clean up without me causing more trouble.

It wasn't that I wanted to stop whatever we had. In fact, there was nothing I wanted more than to see them.

I just needed to give them that choice.

It was what I'd found from Lilith, what I'd really learned at the end of this whole mess. I had choices. I'd grown up believing I was trapped on some path that I couldn't escape, that I was helpless against the whims of fate.

Instead, what I discovered was that I decided where I would go, *who* I would be. Those things were mine and mine alone to shape.

And no matter how much I hated it, I had to give the men I loved the same choices.

They needed time to acclimate, to decide if being with me was what they really wanted. I was asking a lot from them, really. I'd shown that trouble followed me, and through this mess that I'd dragged them into, they'd all risked everything. It wasn't the future any of them had planned on, so was it really the one they wanted?

I spent the day away from home. The house had been too quiet, too still. It felt like a mocking reminder of my life after that text, like the universe was giving me a lovely preview of my loneliness to come.

I wonder if that Elder One who collected cats can give me one to start my collection.

Eventually, I found myself back at the place I often went to think—across the street from the fire station where my mother had left me. I still recalled the last time I'd come, when Gran had shown up and sat beside me.

The place lacked the sadness from before. Maybe I really had learned something. I didn't sit there angry at my mother, wondering what I'd done wrong that made me so unlovable.

Instead, I accepted that I was different, that I was unique, and she simply wasn't equipped to handle it. She'd done what she could for me—the scars from the tattoos were the proof—but hating her did nothing. Wondering who she was and what had been the last straw didn't change where I was, didn't alter my life or who I was at all.

I refused to stay trapped in the past, to let the anger from how things had happened consume me and my future. I had seen where that led a person.

Not just with Lilith.

Troy had let fear of his wolf nearly kill him. Kase's belief that he would end up like his maker had left him with control held so tight that he couldn't really live. Grant thought himself a monster, and his self-loathing had torn him apart. And Hunter? He'd let go of most of his past, of who he had been, but the worry that others couldn't look beyond it had plagued him.

Everyone was trapped and shaped by the things they experienced. Just because something was over didn't mean we would let it go. Funny that it wasn't the event but our holding on to it that really fucked us living creatures over.

Something shifted beside me, a familiar presence I no longer startled from. In the living realm, I couldn't see it, not fully, just the hint of a shadow, but the way the hair on my arms stood up told me what it was.

A reaper.

My father.

Maybe I should have been more weirded out by his visits — we didn't speak — couldn't, I assumed. When I returned to purgatory in my sleep, I spoke to him, but for now? It was just these check-ins. They felt oddly gratifying. When I thought back, I recalled so many times I'd gotten that feeling when I couldn't identify it, and suddenly all those times I'd thought I was alone, I realized I wasn't.

That was what life really was, though. It wasn't about perfection, about fitting in or being right all the time. It was about a lot of fucked-up people doing their best, even when some of those bests really sucked.

I took a deep breath, realizing there was no way I could sit there anymore. Staring at a fire station probably looked weird, and I didn't need to get put on any lists.

The walk home was long, and by the time I arrived, my feet hurt. Still, it helped clear my head. There was something cathartic about tucking my hands into my pockets and just walking, letting the thoughts drip from me and leaving them behind until my mind was blissfully empty.

When I opened my front door, the lights hit me. I was sure I hadn't left them on…

The low male voices from inside drew me forward, frowning. *What the hell?*

As I walked into the living room, the sight stopped me.

Kase and Troy stood near one of the windows, nearly chest to chest, neither looking all that willing to back down from whatever it was that had set them off.

"Locks are foolproof," Troy said as he pointed at the small piece of metal affixed to the window frame. "They work."

"Yes, they work for others—*not* for Ava," Kase responded, the condescension in his tone loud and clear. "She needs a proper security system with both technology, such as security cameras, and magic."

"Magic is useless, and technology? What's next? Are you going to put in turrets?"

"Perhaps." The dry way Kase spoke made me wonder if he was serious.

They didn't look my way, as if they hadn't noticed me at all while arguing about *my* home.

"This is the best thing ever." Hunter's voice made me shift to find him leaning forward on my couch, his elbows on his knees, eyes glued to my television.

Well, *a* television, since the one I'd owned had been far smaller than this one. Exactly when had someone replaced it?

And evidently bought a console gaming system, since Hunter had a controller in his hand as he hit the buttons and the character on the screen hacked apart zombies.

"If you like this, just *wait* until I introduce you to Demon Sucker. You play a demon who has to possess humans and cause mayhem until you rack up enough bad karma to draw angels down to earth," Grant told him, sitting beside him with a controller of his own.

Hunter turned to face the mage, eyes wide as if he'd heard nothing more exciting than that in his entire life.

"What are you doing here?" I asked finally, when the situation couldn't get any weirder.

No, don't say that. You'll just tempt the universe into proving you wrong.

All four men turned their gazes my way, sharing a look that said the same thing—*What do you mean, you idiot?*

I grabbed my phone from my pocket and held it up like a visual aid. "I set you a text message."

"Yes, you did," Kase said impassively. "And I ignored it."

"I deleted it," Troy added.

"I promptly fed my phone and the message to a gorgon," Grant said without a speck of regret.

I turned toward Hunter, waiting for his excuse.

He looked around, as if trying to figure out what everyone was talking about. "Wait, we have phones?"

I rubbed my fingers against my temples, reminded that it was far easier to deal with them individually. Together, their difficulty fed off each other and made it worse.

"She said we should take a break," Grant said.

"Well, I'm glad I never saw it then," Hunter answered. "I might have had my feelings hurt. If I had any, at least."

I tucked my phone into my pocket again. "I'm right about this." When no one answered, I pressed. "Everything was moving so fast. We were thrown into this all. None of you *asked* for this."

Still nothing. No one spoke, as if I were some child talking gibberish and they were just humoring me.

I threw my arms out. "I'm giving you an out here!"

At that, Kase lifted his eyebrow. "I don't think I hear anyone asking for an out."

Finally it felt like I had a target singled from the herd, so I focused in on Kase. "You hired me for a simple job, and I ended up getting you dragged to hell and back, but then also to purgatory. You really don't think you want a minute or two to run a pros-and-cons list here?"

"I told you already, Ava, that I have been waiting for you. I waited for centuries on only Gran's promise that it would be worth it. Do you really believe that after that, I would need even a *minute* to decide something I have had decided for hundreds of years?"

It was hard to fight with that. I turned toward Troy, wanting him to at least see reason.

He didn't even let me talk before he broke in. "You're my mate." He said it with a shrug, as if that answered everything.

To him, it did. I recalled the way he'd drawn me back from Lilith's influence, though, and realized…maybe it answered it to me as well.

"But you hate vampires, and you never wanted to share a mate. You want a simple life, and I'm not simple."

"I also wanted to be human for a long time after I was turned, and I wanted to shave my head for a while, and I thought socks with sandals were a good idea. People change, we grow, we realize what we thought we wanted wasn't what we really needed. I need you." He paused, glancing side to side as if he'd really rather *not* say the next part with an audience but needed to say it more than he needed secrecy. "And you were right—I needed a pack. Never figured it'd be one like *this*, but I'm not sorry about it."

I wanted so badly to argue with him, to explain how wrong he was, but the pack thing got me. For a man who needed that sense of belonging so much, him admitting he'd found it here of all places mattered.

So instead I tried to reason with Grant. "You have a pissed-off guild because of me."

"To be fair, they've been pissed off since I offed the last council. Really, what we did was almost a slap-on-the-wrist offense in comparison. Besides, with you by my side, I have a feeling they'll think twice about coming after me."

"Just think about it," I said.

That was when his smile slid away. "I have. I've spent a long time thinking there was something wrong with me, that I was broken in a way that could never be fixed. The thing is, I don't feel broken, not here, not with you, not even with the boring twins over there." He hiked a thumb at Troy and Kase. "For the first time, I can go to sleep somewhere and not worry I'm going to have my throat slit. I can fight and *know* none of you will stab me in the back as soon as I turn away. I've never had that before, and I'll be damned if I lose it, even for a minute."

I dropped my head back as I sighed. As much as they were the words I desperately wanted to hear, I couldn't shake the feeling that we were rushing, that this was all a big mistake, and they'd realize it.

At least if they realized it now, it wouldn't be as bad as if they did years from now, after I'd gotten so used to them that I couldn't live without them.

Hunter set down his controller, the smirk he wore so often in place. "You know damn well I'm going nowhere, shadow-girl. I've been chasing you since I first caught a glimpse of you, and I plan to keep on doing that. So, you want to run? You want to act unsure? I've got no problem chasing you again. Besides, I rather like to play with my prey after I catch it."

And boy, did his confidence just melt my resolve...

Then again, I'd given them the out because I'd wanted them to have a choice, to get the time to think about it, to figure out what they wanted.

And they were being pretty clear, weren't they?

They wanted *me*.

Who am I to deny them?

As if Hunter knew what I was thinking, he snatched my wrist and pulled me over the back of the couch, drawing a gasp from me until before I knew it, I was in his lap as he returned to his game with Grant. Troy and Kase went back to their argument, this time with Troy agreeing to the cameras but claiming the one in my bedroom was too far—at least until a lifted eyebrow from Kase reminded Troy of the fun that could be.

They were better when they *weren't* working together.

And that was when it really hit me.

All my years searching for a place to belong, trying to fit in, to alter myself enough that others could care about me, and here it was.

Here were four men who had stood with me as we'd saved everything, who hadn't shied away from my weirdness, from my sharp tongue or stubbornness, who had risked everything for me.

It wasn't the family I'd expected, wasn't the life I'd planned for.

No, it was *so* much better.

And to think it had all started with a little grave-robbing....

Epilogue

One year later

By the third time I paced through my living room, I was ready to crawl out of my skin. How could a person be *this* nervous? Especially after everything I'd been through!

Still, when had logical thinking ever gotten me out of a panic attack?

The wood floor creaked beneath my feet, the sound disjointed since at the end of each pass, I'd let my physical body drift away and do the next round in my reaper form. It didn't make things better, exactly, but it was something.

Something more than sitting around and waiting.

Fuck, I hate waiting.

The rhythm kept up as I made myself fall into the familiarity of it, letting my mind relax, trying to make the thoughts and worries go.

Think about rainbows and cheesecake and men who can find a clitoris.

Except, no matter how hard I pushed myself to relax, the stress just wouldn't leave, which was annoying as hell. I hadn't felt fear in so long, yet there it was, soaking into me.

"Boy, do you look all wound up, shadow-girl."

I paused to find Hunter standing in my doorway, his face so familiar it drew a smile from me without me having to think about it. Even annoyed as I was, he never failed to make my heart race when he showed up.

"You smiling at me? Hard to tell when you're all shadows."

That made me look down, realizing I hadn't shifted back into my body. I guessed reaper smiles were harder to identify.

I took my regular form again, rewarded by Hunter's smirk.

"Better," he said. "Now, how long have you been pacing?"

"I'm not pacing."

"What you're not is a good liar. Now, come on and tell Daddy what's wrong."

"*Daddy*?" I made sure to gag a bit at the name.

"What? Not into that?"

"Not even a little."

"Well, I'm old enough to be your Daddy."

"You're old enough to be my great-great-great—" A surprised squeak left me, cutting off my list of 'great's when I found myself hauled up and over Hunter's shoulder, as though I were a misbehaving kid rather than a feared and lethal supernatural being.

And *damn*, it felt nice…

Not that I'd let him know that. "You should seriously put me down." I tried to inject all the threat into my voice that I could.

"And why's that?"

"Maybe because I'm an exceedingly powerful and vengeful creature who could destroy you with a flick of my wrist," I pointed out.

He let out a rough chuckle before dropping me on the bed. "Unfortunately for you, that just makes me want you more."

The way he stared at me, his whiskey-colored eyes heated and so familiar, made me take my bottom lip between my teeth. It took me back to when I'd first met him, when he'd walked into my office and had thrown my world into chaos. I couldn't imagine not having him, not seeing that smirk of his, not tasting the brimstone from his skin.

Except, when I reached for him, something stopped me. A ring of smoke circled my wrist, the feeling of it against my skin odd as ever. It smelled of flames, of Hunter, and more of that smoke joined it.

In seconds I found my wrists held above me as if suspended from the ceiling, and my thighs were spread. The smoke held me still, didn't give me an inch of space to move or resist.

And the more I tried, the wetter my cunt grew. Hunter rarely used his smoke, but when he did? It never failed to get me off. Something about the power, about him using a part of himself he'd feared I'd never accept, made my body purr in response.

I opened my mouth, ready to give him hell, because whether or not I enjoyed it, I wasn't about to just let him manhandle me without me saying anything.

Except, when I did, that smoke pressed past my lips, something he'd never done before. It was solid against my tongue, as if it had form, and surprisingly hot. In fact, while I wouldn't call myself an expert at identifying things with my mouth, I would have guessed it was his cock if I couldn't see him.

And seeing him made it all so much better.

He stood at the foot of the bed, his hand grasping the bulge in his jeans, his lips tipped into a panty-melting smirk. He rubbed himself, his gaze locked on where his smoke pressed into my mouth and pulled back, a mimic of fucking my face. "We both know you'll just dig yourself deeper if you talk," he said. "Course, if you did that, I'd get to have even *more* fun with you." He paused, as if considering that, then shrugged. "No point. I'll just have all the fun I want anyway."

I tried to glare, but it was a little hard to make the action mean anything when my lips were stretched around what was essentially a smoke-cock. And, despite my best efforts, I was getting into it. I tightened my lips and swirled my tongue around it.

A deep groan from Hunter made me wonder if he could feel that, if the smoke wasn't just a form of magic like Grant but rather a part of the hellhound. A devilish idea caught me, and I raked my teeth over the smoke. I didn't do it hard—the last thing I wanted was for him to need the night off to heal—but I did it roughly enough to ensure a reaction.

And sure enough, Hunter winced, an unhappy whine on his lips before flames sparked in his eyes. "You're trouble," he said, lust saturating his voice, before he smiled wider. "Just the way I love you."

I thought I'd won for a moment, that he'd let me go and I'd continue my pacing. Or maybe he'd come over and give me the real thing…

I should have known better, though. Winning with Hunter was always a tricky proposition. The fabric of my leggings pulled off me, the smoke so dexterous I couldn't help but be impressed. At least, I was until I found myself naked and no closer to getting free.

A chill ran over my exposed body, made even better with the way Hunter stared, as if savoring a meal placed in front of him before taking the first bite.

Then, a creeping sensation on my thigh had me looking down. Smoke moved up my leg, drawing a shiver, as if it were pressing kisses up the bare skin, toward my cunt.

Which was a whole lot more than we'd ever done. It was slow, as if judging my reaction, as if asking for permission.

I met Hunter's wild gaze, the question there. Did I trust not just him, but this side of him? I nodded, the answer taking me no thought or time at all.

I trusted every part of Hunter with everything I was.

Those flames in his eyes, the want, exploded. The smoke in my mouth withdrew, and Hunter leaned forward, claiming my lips in an actual kiss. In the meantime, that smoke skirted over the last bit of space, then pressed against my pussy. The sensation was odd.

It was warm, solid, but *not* skin. It slid against my clit in a torturous and focused motion, but at the same time plunged into my waiting cunt. It didn't need to go slow, to warm me up, because I was already melting.

The smoke was thin at first, more like a finger, but spread out quickly. The feeling was different, less of a thrusting and more of a vibration as it grew in length and width, filling me completely.

"You're more than I ever deserved," Hunter whispered against my lips, that smoke of his drawing me so close to an orgasm that I struggled to stay present, to hear him at all. "Mine," he added, biting down on my bottom lip hard enough to make me gasp.

I struggled, squirming against the onslaught of feelings, but he didn't give me any space. I pulled, arching my back, needing more and less and everything. It was all a blur, and all I knew for sure was that I *needed*.

He pressed a hand to my chest and pushed, the smoke moving my hands, pulling me flat so I stretched out across the large bed, still spread out and on the edge and entirely helpless.

Each time that orgasm got closer, Hunter made a soft sound, one full of mock pity, and the smoke would slow, then stop. He edged me until I couldn't even remember what had consumed me so much. There simply wasn't room for it anymore.

I closed my eyes, focused on the frustration growing inside me, the need for that release that teased me, the one just at the edge of my reach, the one I couldn't get, not without his help.

And the asshole seemed to be enjoying this *far* too much.

When something pressed past my lips, into the heat of my mouth, I opened my eyes.

Kase stood above me, his dark eyes smoldering with want. He'd pressed his finger past my lips, and I sucked obediently. He offered me a ghost of a smile, the sort that said I'd pleased him, before he turned his gaze to Hunter. "What exactly was it that she did to warrant this?"

"Found her wearing a path in the hardwoods."

Kase glanced down at me, smile vanishing. "Are you worried, love?" The use of that term of endearment sent a wave of pleasure through me, the sweetness of it always surprising me, especially from a man who was not in the least bit sweet.

I didn't need to answer, though, even if I could have. Between the denied orgasm and Hunter's smoke still fucking me, words were far beyond what I was currently capable of. Still, Kase must have seen it in my face.

He used his free hand to undo the belt and button of his slacks, then pulled down the zipper. Watching him disrobe from this angle was an entire form of mind-fuckery in itself. He loomed over me, seeming larger than life, more terrifying than ever before, and yet fear was the last thing on my mind.

And when he pulled his cock from his pants and wrapped his hand around it, I let out a pathetic and needy moan.

His smile reappeared. "Open your mouth, love," he ordered.

When I did, he leaned over me, sliding his hard dick past my lips. Restrained as I was, I couldn't do anything but accept his length and enjoy the way I felt pinned beneath him as he enjoyed my mouth.

He made the best sounds, the sort a man as carefully controlled as him rarely made. They were mindless, as if I'd stripped away all his rules, all the layers he'd built to keep the real him hidden. It was why I savored them so much, when I tightened my lips around his cock and sucked, to draw more of them from him. I wanted what I knew he'd given no one else.

Not sex. We'd *all* had sex many times before. Hell, from what I'd heard from time to time, it seemed that all the men had had their share of crazy, wild hook-ups with every type of being imaginable.

Instead, it was this closeness, this ability to just feel and do and need without restraint or worry. It was how Hunter used his smoke to fuck me because it pleased him, because it was a part of him, and how Kase let himself groan in that wonderfully delicious tenor because he *could* let his guard down to do it.

Even so, I couldn't get off. Hunter continued his relentless edging, paying close enough attention that no matter how near to that precipice I approached, he pulled it back just in time. Each ruined orgasm grew the desperation inside me, made the stroke of Kase's cock against my tongue and the force of the smoke light up every nerve inside me.

Or so I thought, until hands set on my hips. I couldn't see, not with Kase leaning over me, but an electrical pulse over my skin told me who it was.

"Already occupied," Hunter said with a chuckle.

"Make room," Grant answered, voice strained, as if he was already far too turned on to deal with Hunter's humor. "I'm guessing our little reaper here needed a distraction?"

"She seems rather stressed about tomorrow," Kase answered.

Grant clicked his tongue in disapproval just as the smoke inside my cunt pulled out. I didn't have time to complain, though, before something even better stretched me.

Grant's cock plunged into me with a hard thrust, filling me all at once. I arched up, the action forcing Kase deeper, making me swallow to accommodate him.

Kase growled, a low and hungry sound. "Your throat is *heaven*," he said. "I never expected to make it there, but leave it to you to prove me wrong."

Grant tightened his hands on my hips, pulling me forward slightly, almost into his lap, then set a punishing pace. He fucked me hard, the way he often did, as if he couldn't quite get over the idea that I was there, that he could have me.

Then again, that was often the case with all the men. It was as if they had to reassure themselves that it was all real, that it wouldn't drift away. There were sweet times, of course—nights when sex was slow and lingering and full of whispered promises. As good as those were, though, *this* type of night was my favorite. It fulfilled us all, drew us all closer as if binding us in some monumental way.

It left no room for worries or questions or the past. It was too wild to allow for any of that, too primal for it.

A strange sensation made me tense, something that pressed against my ass. I'd spent a *lot* of time with the men by this point, and I was quite certain Grant only had one penis. If he'd had a second, I would have found it by now…

And yes, despite the fact he took up all the space between my spread thighs and he was fucking deep into my cunt, that pressure against my ass remained.

Hunter's smoke. The reality hit me like a wave, along with my reaction to it.

Sure, I'd never done that before, but Hunter had never steered me wrong. Relaxing wasn't exactly an easy thing to do, not when I was strung as tight as I was, but that didn't stop me from trying.

"Good girl," Hunter said a moment before his real fingers brushed over my woefully ignored nipples, telling me he had enough feeling in his smoke to know I'd at least tried to stop tensing.

And sure enough, the pressure increased there until he slid past the tight ring of muscles, until he pressed into me in a way *no one* had done before, in a way I'd trusted no one to do before.

The sensation was beyond overwhelming. It teased areas of me that hadn't been touched before, set up fireworks behind my eyes and coursed pleasure through my entire body. It made the stroke of Grant's cock and the way Kase fucked deep into my mouth all the better, as if turning up the dial on all my nerves.

If Hunter was trying to edge me, he failed at that point. The orgasm ran through me with the speed and force of a car crash. It battered down any resistance, making me cry out around Kase's cock, making me twist when it was more sensation than could fit inside my body.

I squeezed down on Grant's cock, around the thin smoke still fucking my ass, my hands grasping the smoke that pinned me and kept me stretched out.

Kase let out a curse word that was lost in the haze of feeling, his cock jerking as he pressed impossibly deeper, seating himself fully inside my mouth and throat. I would have panicked before, with anyone else, but even in those moments where I couldn't breathe — I probably couldn't anyway due to the orgasm — I trusted him fully. In fact, it only added to the pleasure, to the surrender.

He pulled back and I sucked in a deep breath. His lips came down on mine, passionate and still hungry, as if even after coming, he wasn't nearly done with me. I returned the kiss, licking into his mouth, wanting to taste him, to lose myself in him.

Except Grant wasn't done. His cock remained hard, and with another thrust, he reminded me that Hunter's smoke was likewise still inside me.

I broke the kiss with a cry at the way it was too much.

Kase pulled away, letting me see Grant for the first time. The myriad tattoos stood out on his body, and, after a year together, I knew each one. I'd traced each with my lips, had lavished affection on each. He stared at me, his green eyes serious in a way he rarely was.

With others he joked, smiled, gave them the carefree version of himself he'd cultivated. With me, however, he let that down. He let me stroke over the wounded areas on him, the ones he hid from everyone else.

It was why it mattered so much to me, why his lack of a smile was often far more important than a smirk.

He pulled back and slammed into me again, deeper. That electricity pulsed over his skin, teasing anywhere we touched, a sign that he lacked the control to hide it. "You won't be worried about anything by the time we're done," he promised me.

Even as he spoke, I struggled to remember what I'd worried about in the first place. It all seemed so insignificant in comparison to this.

I guess their plan is working, then.

He set a brutal pace, Hunter taking my ass in an opposite motion, so I was never actually empty. My body was strung so tight from the last orgasm, never having had the chance to settle down, for my nerves to ease, that each time Grant bumped my clit with his pelvic bone, it felt as if the world exploded all over again.

Grant leaned in, taking my lips in an aggressive kiss, the spark of his powers like tiny shocks anywhere we touched. He swallowed my moan, my gasp, before pulling back to take me harder.

He bottomed out, sweat running down his chest, over the colorful images there, his eyes closed and head thrown back. The way he looked lost to the pleasure was something I'd never forget, never get over. When in his life had he *ever* given in before? When had he been in a place safe enough to do so?

Grant shuddered as he came, and Hunter stilled the smoke inside me, giving me a reprieve from the relentless sensations. For a moment I thought we were done.

Grant proved me wrong by reaching forward and grinding his thumb against my clit, the touch bordering on painful, especially with the power that coursed through him. It shoved me headfirst into another crashing orgasm, into the pleasure pulling me under, and this time, without Kase's cock to muffle the sound, I let out a gasping moan.

Everything was sore, tired, overworked. My body seemed as if it would never move again, and even Grant pulling out was far too much. I cried out weakly.

"We set up a dinner time because *that's* the time we're supposed to eat," came Troy's voice as he walked into the bedroom, his voice carrying from the living room. "Why do we even have a dinner time if it doesn't mean…" He trailed off when he reached the room and his gaze skirted over the scene.

Hunter sat on the bed, near the top, a still hungry smirk on his face. Grant was poised between my thighs, as if reluctant to fully move away, and Kase stood near the door, watching. Then there was me, still bound by the smoke and spread out, the wetness on my cunt telling me Grant's cum leaked from me like some claim.

Oh, and we were all blissfully naked.

A growl was Troy's answer, and there was no doubt that dinner had been all but forgotten. In fact, the way his eyes flashed brighter said he had a far different meal in mind.

He came toward me, all purpose. He hadn't asked why we were doing this — I doubted he cared. Having me was more important than any reason the other men might have.

Hunter rose and shoved Troy as Grant moved out of the way. "I don't think so, wolf-boy."

Troy lifted his lips and snarled. Getting between a wolf and his mate was a *very* dangerous thing to do.

Not that Hunter looked worried. "Shadow-girl is worried about tomorrow, and we're taking her mind off it. You and your fancy penis there tends to slow things down with the whole getting-stuck thing, so you can take her mouth." Hunter dropped his gaze to my cunt, licking his lips in a slow movement that made me whimper. "Besides, I've wanted a taste of her since we started and I am sure as shit not missing out on that."

I could have told him that maybe oral sex right after Grant had come wasn't a good idea, but leave it to Hunter to not give a damn about such social niceties. He moved his hands over my thighs, his smoke spreading me wide, holding me down, before he ran his tongue up my slit.

If he had a problem with Grant's cum, his deep groan didn't show it. After the first lick, he really dove in.

Worse? The smoke I'd come to ignore, the piece of him he'd teased my ass with, started up again. Having my pussy empty while he fucked my ass and tormented my clit was a whole different level of sensation, and I gasped, trying to sort it out in my head.

Troy didn't give me a chance. He stripped out of his clothing, and the tearing of a few seams said his wolf was in control. Troy wouldn't ever ruin his clothing, but his beast never seemed to care. He towered over me, and I opened my mouth without him asking.

When he fed me his cock, when he pushed it into my mouth, I gave in. To him, to them all, to this, to myself. It was the moment that happened when I surrendered it all, when they reminded me what I had fought so hard to protect.

It hadn't ever been the rest of the world. *Fuck the rest of the world.* It had always been this.

It had been my home, the men I cared about more than anything else, who had shown me love I couldn't have imagined before.

Hunter latched his lips around my clit and sucked hard, the pull enough to draw another rush of pleasure through me. I trembled, overwhelmed, at their mercy and loving every second of it.

Hunter grasped my hips and turned me, Troy pulling free only just long enough to allow it. A roar, feral and hungry, had me lifting my gaze.

Kase stood behind Troy, his fangs buried in the werewolf's neck. The familiar lust danced in Troy's eyes, as the venom in Kase's bite worked through him. If Troy had any control before, this would remove it.

Hunter set a large, strong hand on my hip before filling me with his cock in one hard thrust, forcing my body to accept his.

I cried out, and Troy took that moment to shove himself into my open, waiting mouth. Hunter took me as deep as possible, his smoke moving again, making me entirely full, taking every part of me.

Grant slid onto the bed beside me, reaching beneath me to tease my breasts as they hung free, as if he needed his own claim on me, needed to touch me as well.

Troy slid his fingers into my hair, the tips of his nails having turned to sharp claws, and he used them to hold me still as he fucked my mouth. Troy gave in, not fighting his wolf or me or the other men. He had me the way he wanted me, at the same time as the other men took me, as if it were the most natural thing in the world.

And it *was*, at least for us. It wasn't easy, not all the time, but it was right. It was a pack, a family, a safe home that none of us had ever found before, that none of us had believed was even possible.

No matter how much the thought of the next day scared me, no matter what would end up happening, no matter what the world threw at us, the men took my fear away. They held it for me, reminded me that the world could do its worst, because I wasn't ever alone.

I had a place, and they didn't mind showing me it was right between their strong, sexy and sometimes frustratingly annoying bodies.

While I hadn't expected to find happiness pinned between four immortal men, I wasn't sorry about it in the least.

* * * *

"You're late." Hunter leaned against the doorway of Gran's shop when I showed up, sure enough a good hour and a half after I was supposed to arrive.

"Hellhounds don't have watches, so how would you even know?"

He huffed a soft laugh at the stupid joke. "You're lucky you're cute. Come on, let's get in there before Grant decides to try to summon you on his own."

"We both know portals don't work right on me. If he tried it, I'd end up god only knows where."

"Yeah, but he's annoyed enough that he might just try it. If you ended up in Antarctica, it wouldn't be any worse for him."

A kid rushed up, his short red hair cut haphazardly around his head with the tips singed black, no doubt from a spell he hadn't quite managed. The truth was that most of his spells still went wrong. "Ms. Ava!" He crashed into me, hard enough that it took a hand from Hunter to keep me upright.

I patted his back, then crouched down when he disentangled enough for me to do so. "Hey, Nick. How're you?"

As he went into a warp-speed monologue about everything that had happened in the past two weeks since I'd been by—including the time he saw a bug on the sidewalk—I couldn't help but smile. He'd been so skinny when I'd first met him, and unwilling to even look me in the eye, far too much like most of the young mages we took in.

What a far cry from the rambunctious little kid who just about lived in the shop now. We'd found him a foster home, but I was pretty sure he didn't spend much time there. He preferred to be in the know, in the thick of things, and often had his nose pressed into an old book.

"We better get going," Hunter broke into the spiel, and Nick cast his gaze up at Hunter without a speck of wariness.

Then again, the kid had been amazed the first time Hunter had shown him his true form, when he'd gotten to study the way the smoke Hunter used worked. Nick had touched the scales, even measured the sharp white fangs that filled Hunter's mouth.

And Hunter? I didn't think I'd ever seen a man so happy to have someone *not* be afraid of him. It took me back to the story he'd told me about when he'd protected those kids who had never accepted him.

I wouldn't have pegged Hunter as someone who liked kids, yet he'd become a de facto assistant, a guardian as devoted to the protection of the kids as the rest of us. He didn't hold any official title, but he didn't need one. He'd spend hours late into the night working to help the children we'd taken in, the ones who needed homes and help and guidance.

We moved toward the back of the shop, passing the young woman I'd hired to work the counter. It had taken all of five minutes to recognize that I didn't have the skills necessary, but the idea of closing down seemed sacrilegious. Hiring folks to do what I couldn't was an obvious choice. Once we entered the storage closet, Nick held up his wrist, the bracelet there glowing as it passed the doorway and opened the portal.

Grant had ensured we had permanent portals so I could use them, even though it never was much fun. After the rush of sickness, when Hunter put his arm around me for balance and Nick grasped my hand, both knowing I didn't handle traveling that way well, I blinked slowly.

The sky, that odd reddish color, felt homier than it had when I'd first seen it. Then again, I'd fallen asleep there many times, with the heat of the realm relaxing me like a hot tub rather than hell. Maybe it was the lack of humidity that made it not so bad.

The realm where the Jade Room was, where we'd spoken to the council, was the perfect place for us. The council hadn't dared to oppose Grant when he'd claimed it. It wasn't like they were doing anything with it, anyway...

Standing in the hallway were Kase and Troy, drawing a smile from me despite my nerves. Kase still had business with the coven despite having taken a step backward, and Troy's demanding work as a detective meant he often missed events. I hadn't asked either to come, prepared to do this on my own, to face down my fears without the backup.

"You're late," Kase said as I walked up, disapproval coloring his tone. He didn't tend to care for plans changing.

"So I've heard," I answered. "I didn't expect you to come."

He reached out and dragged his thumb over my cheek. "You should have known better."

"No," Troy broke in. "You should have asked us to come."

I tucked my hands into my pockets. "I figured you were busy."

"Yes," Kase acknowledged. "I was."

"So why are you here?"

Troy snorted softly, the sort of sound that said I should have already known. "You were nervous—of course we moved things around to come."

I pressed my lips together, looking between the two men, shaken again by how simple that was. They'd known how afraid I'd been, and without me having to tell them, without me having to beg or even ask them for help, they'd shown up.

It was the reality. They'd *always* show up for me.

Kase twisted, looking over his shoulder. "We will see you inside. You'll do fine."

I wanted to argue, but Troy caught my chin and pulled me closer, offering a sweet kiss. He smiled, his silver eyes enough for me to get lost in. "Stop worrying so much. You've faced down worse than this."

He turned away, following Kase. Hunter went with them, along with Nick, all heading in through a door, leaving me alone for a moment.

I took a deep breath, trying to shake off the fears, to hype myself up, to find any of the confidence they seem to have in me.

A throat cleared behind me, making me turn to find a very unhappy-looking Grant standing there, his arms crossed. He wore his jean jacket, faded, but with a collared shirt beneath it like some compromise between his normal rebellious look and what he thought he should look like as a person in power.

He opened his mouth — no doubt with a lecture ready — but I interrupted him. "I know, I know. I'm late."

"Almost two hours late, now. You know, this isn't the best start for you."

"If you expect me to be on time, this is never going to work."

"No wonder you've been unemployed for a year."

I cut him a sharp look. "I lost my wonderful job with benefits because I had to save the world. *You're welcome.*"

He offered a slight grin, one that said he enjoyed riling me up. "I'm pretty sure you get better *benefits* now."

He isn't wrong…

"Yeah, well, those benefits are exactly why I was late. You can't keep me up all night and expect me to wake up on time."

"I told Kase we needed to leave someone to babysit you," Grant said with a laugh. "He said anyone who stayed would just keep you up later. Might have been worth it." Grant nodded down the hallway. "You've procrastinated long enough — let's get going. And stop worrying — you'll do great."

"Stay out of my head," I said.

"Stop thinking so loudly."

Before I could argue more, he all but pushed me into a room, and in it sat at least thirty kids, some I recognized and some I didn't know yet.

It reminded me of just how fast the place was growing.

Grant stood beside me for a moment. "Please welcome Ms. Ava, and treat her with the same respect you give to any other instructor here."

A murmured, "Yes, Headmaster Grant," came back from the children, including Nick, who took his seat in the front row.

Grant moved away, claiming a spot in the back beside Hunter, who had his feet up on the desk beside him like the most annoying student in the world. Still, their smiles gave me courage. To their left, Kase and Troy sat, the four of them sticking out compared to the children, who ranged from five to sixteen.

Still, all of them there gave me the confidence to pull my shoulders back. We'd faced down the end of the world together, so a room full of kids would be easy, right? I could deal with anything so long as they were there with me.

"Many of you know me, but for those who don't, I'm Ms. Ava," I said with a smile. "I'm a reaper. I've been to purgatory and hell. I can speak to spirits, and I have tea with Lucifer once a week. He's sort of a jerk."

The wide eyes made me laugh, and I had to admit, it felt nice to accept who and what I was, to not need to hide it.

"In this class, we'll go over what I've learned and what you need to know about life, the afterlife and everything in between."

I grinned before picking up the stick that looked like a pencil, the one Grant had taught me to use, and wrote on the wall to leave glowing black letters that spelled out the name of the class Grant had manipulated me into teaching at his school for wayward mages.

When I turned, I pointed at the words. "Welcome to Saving the World and Other Bad Ideas."

Want to see more from this author? Here's a taster for you to enjoy!

Dark Sanctuary: Bound by Fear
Jayce Carter

Coming January 2022

Excerpt

"You don't look like you belong here, little fox." The man who spoke — tall, lean and dressed like a devil — was the epitome of everything Sunny had feared she'd find inside the BDSM sex club called Sanctuary.

Her breath sped, and her chest tightened as the large room shrank to nothing.

This is a horrible mistake. What was I thinking?

"Do you want to come sit with me and talk?" Devil-man asked, his lips curling into a smile below the line of his black mask. It wasn't a vicious smile, at least on the surface, but it sure felt sinister.

The desire to say no perched on her tongue, but she couldn't make it come out. She'd learned that saying no was dangerous, that it never got her what she wanted. The lesson was one that had stuck with her no matter what.

So, instead, she darted her gaze toward the crowd of people and pretended to spot someone she knew, waving in that direction.

The man stayed in his spot, letting her go, and she made a quick path for the bathroom. Once safely inside — the one place where no man would try to talk her into anything — she set her hands on the white porcelain sink and stared into the mirror.

Maybe a fox had been a stupid costume. She'd tried on a few different ones that radiated strength, but they had felt like a lie. Sunny was as soft as they came, so when she'd tried on the little white sundress, along with the fox mask that obscured her eyes, and some drawn-on whiskers, she'd known it was more *her*. Foxes were smaller than other predators, but quick and clever. She connected with that, understood it. At least, it had made sense until she'd walked into a club full of lions and tigers and dragons.

Suddenly, her fox didn't seem so clever.

One night. Prove that you don't want this anymore.

She nodded and straightened herself, pulling her shoulders back. She was here for a reason. She'd go out there, find someone to play with, and by the end of the evening, she'd know that she was done with all this nonsense. She could wake up tomorrow sure of herself, able to put this behind her. The plan helped her move forward.

The door to the bathroom opened as a woman in lingerie and a cat mask walked in, the music from outside deep and rhythmic. Her hair was blonde and beyond stunning, so pale it was nearly white. Even from behind the half-mask, her almost gray eyes shone brightly.

The woman approached, a smile across her pink lips, the color smeared as though she'd been kissing someone just before. "It's so much fun tonight, right?"

Sunny nodded despite not feeling quite so sure. "Yeah."

The woman glanced down at Sunny's wrist, at the cuff the receptionist at the door had placed there with a white ribbon. "Oh, you're new? Is this your first time?"

First? Try only. Instead of saying that, Sunny tried to smile. "Yes."

The woman stuck her hand out. "My name is Kat." She winced as soon as she said it. "I know—it's a masquerade party—it's supposed to be all anonymous. You don't have to give your name. I'm just not good at the whole secrecy thing. And *yes*, I know, Kat—cat costume—cliché, but why not, right?"

Sunny had trouble understanding Kat. She'd figured the sort of people in a place like *this* would terrify her. The men would be scowling brutes, lumbering around just looking for a victim, and the women quiet, frightened little things who cowered at everything. *That's what I was...*

Kat wasn't anything like that.

Sunny shook the offered hand, unsure how to answer, other than the fact that she wouldn't be giving her name. That would negate the entire point of her coming here on *this* night. Sunny needed to do what she'd come to do then leave—no ties threatening to trap her.

Kat chuckled, as if she could read the nerves that poured off Sunny. "Afraid of the big bad Doms? Come on—you can hang out with me. Safety in numbers, you know."

Sunny wanted to say no—it felt too much like putting herself into a life she was trying desperately to get out of. Still, having a partner next to her did feel better.

"That would be nice," Sunny admitted softly.

Kat asked her to wait a moment so she could use the restroom, then washed her hands before tucking her arm through the crook of Sunny's. It was an oddly safe feeling, as though Sunny had found a guide to this absolutely terrifying place. Sure, Kat wasn't all that intimidating, but at least Sunny wasn't alone.

They walked out, with Kat holding securely to Sunny's arm. "I love the last Saturday of the month. Something about dressing up makes everything more fun, plus it's the day we let the new folks come. It gets boring with the same old folk every weekend, and new blood is always good."

It also let Sunny move around the club with a sense of privacy, without feeling everyone was looking at her, could see her.

Sunny's gaze couldn't settle on any one thing. The bodies that moved on the dance floor, the groupings of people, the colors and costumes and activity, all fought for her attention.

And it all overwhelmed her. Sunny's world was quiet, calm. She'd worked hard to create a haven away from the craziness of everyday life.

So what was she doing *here*?

She turned her attention back to Kat, to the cuff around her wrist—identical to Sunny's except for the fact that it had a myriad of ribbons on it. Red, teal, green and yellow striped—they meant nothing to Sunny. She vaguely recalled the receptionist explaining it to her as she'd signed in, but Sunny hadn't heard any of it. Her anxiety had been far louder than rules or color coding.

"What do the ribbons mean?" Sunny asked, trying to find something to fill the silence with.

Kat held up her wrist to show the leather cuff with the colored ties. "For members, we use these to identify what people are looking for and what limits they have.

We still ask of course, just to make sure, but these make it obvious right from the start. If someone hates something you love, you know it may be a bad fit before even trying. Nothing worse than a hardcore masochist falling for a Soft Dom who doesn't like to even raise their voice. Makes everyone unhappy when people don't click."

Sunny frowned when the explanation didn't make any sense to her.

Doms never care what their subs want.

However, she kept that to herself. People saw what they wanted, and Kat seemed the type to let romantic notions blind her to the truth. No doubt she'd say the Doms here were different, that they were somehow exempt from the reality Sunny had experienced before. There wasn't any reason to argue over it, so Sunny let the topic drop.

They went to one of the tables set out with coffee and snacks, and Kat filled a small plate with items for them both. "I love your costume. You sure do fit in with the whole primal and prey thing."

And *that* made the damn panic creep up again. She hadn't thought of the fox as *prey*. It was a predatory creature, just smaller than some of the others. It seemed others saw it differently.

Kat looked past the table and locked eyes with a man across the room, one who wore a black mask with horns and a smirk. He crooked his finger to call her over. She let out a sigh full of want. "I'll be right back…" She pulled away before Sunny could answer, leaving Sunny with the plate of food and no backup.

A pit started in Sunny's stomach at the way Kat had followed the demand, at the memory of how many times Sunny had done the same thing, when she'd dropped everything she'd wanted and done as she'd been told. She remembered a crooked finger, a silent demand that came a split second before anger, before violence.

It sickened her, threatened to drag her under so many worse memories.

"There you are, little fox." The devil-man from earlier came up from behind Sunny, his voice already tattooed on her brain.

She jumped, those overactive nerves of hers taking over, struggling to separate him from her past.

He's just a person. You're fine.

Right, because telling herself that made it reality… Saying it didn't make her safe, didn't do anything.

Still, she turned toward him, her shoulders hunched forward in on herself to make herself smaller. "Hello."

This is why you came. Don't chicken out now. Just one night.

He smiled, but she couldn't shake the way her brain screamed danger at her. Whether he was actually dangerous or not didn't really matter. Her body had decided, and it wasn't listening to her. It went off history, off what she knew to be true — men, especially dominant men, couldn't be trusted.

"Why don't you come on over to the couch there? We can have a talk, get to know each other. I've been watching you since you came in, and you look amazing."

Sunny tried to swallow down her fears, her doubts, but they stuck in her throat. She shifted her weight from foot to foot, unable to shake all the '*hell no*' swirling in her head. No matter how many times she reminded herself that she was here for this, she couldn't get herself to agree, to even want to agree.

He wrapped his fingers around her wrist, the one with the cuff, and tugged gently. "Come on, little sub, I don't bite too hard — at least not unless you beg."

Sickness churned in her stomach, the room becoming stifling, the air thinning.

He didn't yank, didn't tighten his fingers to the point of pain, didn't show any sort of violence or anger, yet she couldn't catch her breath. She couldn't stop herself from seeing him as the devil he had dressed as.

She followed, her body frozen and unable to fight back, to just yank and tell him no. What the hell was wrong with her?

Fear. It was what was always wrong with her, that beast she couldn't kill no matter what she did. Even when she thought she had it under control, it always reared its ugly, unwelcome head and turned her into *this*.

"I saw you the *second* you walked in," devil-man said. "You look like prey, and I am a man who likes to chase."

"I'm a man, Sunshine, and I have needs." The voice that haunted her dreams came back to her. It ran in her head as clear as if the monster from her past stood there right then, and the room blurred.

Just when she was sure she'd pass out, that she'd fall to the floor there in front of everyone, a large hand grasped devil-man's shoulder.

It wasn't violent, but it was a *clear* message of stop. "Hold up there, Jordan."

Devil-man — *Jordan?* — paused and turned toward the man who'd spoken, someone who made Sunny want to pull even farther back. This new man was tall, his body lean but strong. He wore a silver mask that covered his eyes, and his lips were pressed into a tight, unhappy line.

She did *not* want that sort of displeasure directed her way.

In fact, right then, going off with Jordan sounded like one hell of a good idea. His lean build would do far less damage than what this new man could dish out. It was like being faced with two monsters and picking the one with the smaller teeth.

"Yeah?" Jordan asked, his tone confused but not upset.

"Does she look like she wants to go with you?"

Jordan tipped his lips down, then took another slow look at Sunny, his expression lacking anger. "She didn't say no."

"Sure she did, just not with her lips. Come on now, take a better look at her."

Jordan peered down—as if just noticing the way Sunny were as far back as her arm would allow, how she leaned away and not toward him—and released her instantly. "I'm so sorry," he said, his voice softening and losing the sharpness it had before. It seemed he'd slipped from his Dom role. "Without the eyes, I have some trouble reading cues, I guess."

Silver released Jordan. "We'll talk about it later."

"Of course." Jordan looked at Sunny, somehow managing to have shrunk from the devil-man he'd been to a regular person, deflating before her eyes. "I'm really sorry, Miss. Can I get you something? A drink?"

Sunny shook her head, afraid her voice wouldn't work if she said anything. Even though he wasn't the monster he'd been moments before, her body had already thrown itself headfirst into panic.

"Why don't you go grab her something warm and sweet, Jordan, as an apology," the new man said.

Jordan nodded and rushed off, leaving Sunny there with only the man in the mask, the one who made

Jordan look more like a cub. "Hey there, fox. Breathing helps, you know?"

The words struck Sunny as entirely asinine, until she realized…she wasn't breathing. She gasped in a breath, and right away her head cleared some. *Just how long was I holding it?*

"Better," the man said, then gestured toward a couch near the back, but one in view of the rest of the room. "You want to sit down before you fall down?"

I never should have come. She never should have tried to prove she was better, or that she didn't need this. Why couldn't she have stayed in the nice, safe little rut she'd spent years creating?

"I should go," Sunny said, her voice so soft that she doubted he could hear her over the music.

Yet he shook his head, that hard edge Doms wielded refusing to be argued with. Any thought that the man before her wasn't dominant fled. "Not yet. You can barely walk right now, about a mile deep into that panic attack you've got going. If I let you walk out now, you'll collapse in the parking lot if you're lucky. Do you have a friend here? Someone who can take you home?"

Again, she shook her head. There was Kat, but she wasn't really a friend. Just some girl she'd met in the bathroom.

She'd spoken to the owner, Toya, to get her invite to the event, but she wouldn't say she knew her either. Not to mention that the last thing she wanted was to talk to the one person who knew who she actually was.

Nope. She'd walked into the wolf's den all by herself, like an idiot.

"That's fine. Why don't you just take a seat? I'll sit on the other couch, give you space while you calm down. Soon as you get your wits about you, you can go. I'm not trying anything."

Sunny wanted to say no, but when she shifted her weight to her other foot, the leg gave out. It seemed her panic had taken more out of her than she'd realized, had snuck up on her without her knowing.

The man caught her, as if he'd been expecting it. "Yeah, not leaving just yet, are you? Come on." He helped her over to the couch, then pressed a hand to the back of her neck to guide her head down, to lean her forward. As soon as she did, he let her go and sat on the other couch, just as he'd said he would.

Which made her all the more suspicious. Men didn't do things to help for no good reason. They didn't give up what they wanted — *especially* Doms.

Still, she closed her eyes, focusing on the music, on the steady beat, going through the things her therapist had taught her. Focus on the now, on the scent of leather, of vanilla, of cinnamon. Pick five things she could hear — the laughter of a woman, the quiet conversation between two men, the music, the wind striking the sides of the building, the deep tone of a man — *no, not that one!*

She pulled herself together, piece by piece, until her chest eased, and she didn't feel as if she'd pass out.

Though, when she lifted her head, when the world didn't seem quite so scary, she wished she *had* passed out. Then she wouldn't have her savior in the silver mask looking at her so intently — the studying gaze of a man who knew too much already. That was perhaps the worst thing about dealing with Doms — they saw everything and were only too quick to use it to their advantage.

He held a drink, steam escaping the top. "Hot chocolate. Jordan brought it as an apology, but he figured you'd prefer if he was on the other side of the club when you looked up."

As much as she wanted to deny it, he'd been right.

He handed over the drink, and while Sunny should have thought twice about drinking it—it was from a stranger, after all—the warmth called to her. She sipped it, and the moment the sugar hit her tongue, she let out a moan. Then tried to silence it immediately. This was *not* the sort of place to make such noises.

Sure enough, the man's lips curled into a smile that made her warm in other, far less innocent places. And that reaction scared her more than anything else. She'd come here to prove she *didn't* want this, right?

She needed to sit her body down and have a long talk with it about good choices and bad choices, but that would have to wait.

"Feeling better?"

Sunny nodded, the cup in her hands like a leash for her own bravery. "Yes. Thank you."

His smile spread. "That's a pretty voice you have. It's a shame you don't use it more often."

She tried to tuck her hair behind her ear before remembering she'd braided it back.

"There you are," came another voice, one that made Sunny cringe again. A new man walked up—no, wait, two men—in metallic masks identical to the one worn by the Dom she was already with, except for the color.

The original man had a silver mask, the new one who'd spoken was in a black mask, and the third man had a golden one.

Friends? Lovers?

Sunny knew better than to ask, so she stayed quiet to figure it out on her own. Men didn't react well to a suggestion that they weren't straight, in her experience. It was like questioning their masculinity, and the last thing she wanted was to piss off these three.

"Sorry," Silver said. "I found a cornered fox who needed some rescuing."

Black lifted his gaze to Sunny, his lips sliding into a teasing smile. "So I see. Quite the prize you found yourself."

The words made her heart do that skipping-a-beat thing—not in a good way—but Silver was quick to come to her defense.

"She's jumpy, so give her some space. Jordan wasn't reading cues so well, didn't realize this fox isn't good at saying no with her words."

Gold turned his head, revealing long blond hair that had curls in it that reached nearly to his shoulder blades. He twisted as if to go explain things to Jordan, though *explain* probably meant *beat some sense into*.

Silver smacked Gold's arm. "It's fine. I told him we'd educate him later a little better—maybe we need another class on body language. He brought over some hot chocolate to help the fox get her breath back." Silver turned back to Sunny. "This is—"

Sunny shook her head. She didn't *want* to have their names. That had been her biggest rule when coming here, that no matter what happened, she could walk out, and no one would know it was her.

Well, no one except the owner, who'd marked down each person and their costume in case complaints were lodged later, but had assured her that information was confidential.

Sunny knew what happened when a person entangled their life with a Dom, when they welcomed such a person into their world—*nothing good.* Without names, without identities, Sunny could leave at the end of the night without worrying about turning into someone's property, without fear that she'd lose everything.

Again.

Silver huffed a soft laugh. "No names, huh? Well, Fox works well enough, and I suppose you can use mask colors for us. These are my friends." He gestured at the other two.

Black sat next to Silver, and Gold took a seat in the chair to the side of both couches. Strange that Sunny could feel so trapped even when none of them were right beside her.

There was something about the men that took up all the space, as if the rest of the world disappeared with them there. The music, the lights, the bodies of the other guests didn't matter anymore, not with these three surrounding her.

"So, Fox, is this your first time? Pretty sure I'd have remembered you if you were here before," Silver asked.

Sunny nodded, trying to act braver than she felt. She didn't want to look like easy prey, like something they could pick off with little work. "I just wanted to check it out."

"Doesn't seem your style," Black added, his voice not as deep, not as rough, and full of humor. "Sometimes this is all too much. No shame in being vanilla."

The tone felt condescending, as though Sunny were a prude who had never experienced anything in her life. She'd long dealt with her youthful face and sweet disposition making people think she was some naïve fawn, especially when added to her name. "I've done *this* before," she said, waving at the club to explain what she refused to say.

She'd done the whole BDSM thing. She'd experienced it all and knew exactly how badly it always turned out.

"Really?" Silver asked. Even without seeing the top half of his face, she could *feel* his lifted eyebrow.

"Yes." The word was short, but try as she might, she knew it held all the years of terror it brought back. How couldn't it?

None of them spoke for a long moment, until finally Gold answered. "And clearly it was a bad situation. Guess that explains why you're jumpy, don't it?"

Sunny curled forward more, staring into her cup as if the answer were somewhere in the swirling chocolate. Besides, not looking them in the eyes felt safer. "I don't want to talk about that."

Silver nodded. "That's fine. Not our business. A little advice, though? You need to learn to tell people no, to use that voice of yours."

Sunny opened her mouth to tell them that she'd *done* that before, and it hadn't worked. What was the point in fighting if she always lost? In her experience, 'no' only made it all the worse, only angered Doms.

Before the all-too-telling words escaped, though, she shoved them down.

What was it about these men? After her panic had ebbed, when she could think straight, she'd found herself willing to say things she knew she shouldn't. They created a wall around her, one that kept her safe from anything outside the small circle they'd formed.

And that was a dangerous thing to think and feel, especially because she should fear them more than anything else.

Will I never learn?

"You look like you feel better," Silver said. "At least, you don't look like you're about to fall down again."

Low standards.

"You want the front to call a cab? Or did you drive yourself?"

Sunny lifted her gaze toward the door, tempted by the thought of leaving. She could go home, back her little one-bedroom house, back to the quiet, the emptiness and the solitude.

And she could think about *here* more.

She returned to her dreams, the ones where she woke sweating and so close to release, with the memory of faceless men, with her wrists bound, her eyes covered and their rough, commanding voices in her ears, with her craving something she denied herself. What sort of life was that?

She'd come for one reason — to prove that *this* wasn't for her anymore. She'd get a taste, then go back to her real life understanding that the desire was just her own stupid brain playing tricks. It was nothing more than her mind wanting to relive her trauma, as if it could make sense of it if she tried again. She'd thought about it for months, looked at the website for the club and started an email to the owner over and over again. It had taken her so long to get to this point. She needed to be brave enough to face this, to prove to herself that this wasn't the life she wanted so she could finally let it go.

So Sunny shook her head. "I don't want to leave."

"Really? What is it you want then, little speechless Fox?" Silver asked.

Sunny swallowed and set her drink on the table before her trembling hands dropped it. "I want to try."

"Try what?"

"Everything."

Home of Erotic Romance

Sign up for our newsletter and find out about all our romance book releases, eBook sales and promotions, sneak peeks and FREE romance books!

About the Author

Jayce Carter lives in Southern California with her husband and two spawns. She originally wanted to take over the world but realized that would require wearing pants. This led her to choosing writing, a completely pants-free occupation. She has a fear of heights yet rock climbs for fun and enjoys making up excuses for not going out and socializing.

Jayce loves to hear from readers. You can find her contact information, website details and author profile page at https://www.totallybound.com